Women in the Shadows

Women in the Shadows

Ann Bannon

CLEIS
PRESS

Published in the United States by Cleis Press Inc., P.O. Box 14684, San Francisco, California 94114.

Printed in the United States.

Cover design: Scott Idleman

Text design: Frank Wiedemann

Logo art: Juana Alicia

10 9 8 7 6 5 4 3 2 1

Chapter One

JUNE 8: *God help me. God help me to stand it. Today was our second anniversary. If I have to go on living with her I'll go crazy. But if I leave her—? I'm afraid to think what will happen. Sometimes she's not rational. But what can I do? Where can I turn?*

That damn party was awful. Anniversaries are supposed to be happy affairs, but this one was more like a wake. Everybody got drunk and sang songs, but there was always that corpse there in the middle of the room...the corpse of that romance. Jack got terribly drunk, as usual. There's another one. If he doesn't crack up it won't be because he hasn't tried. What's wrong with us all, anyway? What's the use of living when things are like this all the time?

Laura shut her diary with a sudden furtive gesture, her pen still poised, and strained her ears at a sound. She thought she heard the front door open. It would be Beebo coming back. But it was only the dachshund, Nix, scratching himself on a stool in the kitchen. Laura sighed in relief and turned back to the diary. She ordinarily kept it locked in a little steel strongbox on the closet floor, and she wrote in it only when she was alone, in the evenings before Beebo got home from work.

Beebo had never read it—or seen it, in fact. It was Laura's own, Laura's aches and pains verbalized, Laura's heart dissected and wept over, in washable blue ink. If Beebo ever saw it she would tear it up in a frenzy. She would make Laura swallow it, because it did not say very nice things about Beebo. And Beebo always did things in a big way, the good along with the bad.

Laura opened the notebook once more and wrote a last brief

1

entry: *Jack asked me to marry him again…but I could never marry a man, not even him. Never.*

Then she closed it quickly and took it back to the closet and locked it in the strongbox. She sat down from sheer inertia on the closet floor and picked up a shoe. It was one of her pumps, rather long and narrow—too large to be really fashionable. But it had the proper shape and the newest styled heel. Beebo liked to see her smartly dressed. She cared more about that than Laura did herself. Laura had worn these shoes to the unfortunate anniversary party two nights before.

Beebo was still hungover from that long night of dreary festivity. Jack was always hungover, so he didn't count. As for Laura, she had learned from Beebo to drink too much herself, and she was learning at the same time how it feels the next day. *Bad.* Plain bad.

It had been a strange night, with moments of wild hilarity and stretches of gloom when everybody drank as if they made their living at it. Laura remembered Jack arriving ahead of everybody else with a couple of bottles under his arm. "Thought I'd better bring my own," he explained.

"Jack, you're not going to drink two fifths all by yourself!" Laura had exclaimed. She always took things at face value at first, a little too seriously.

"I'm going to try, Mother," he said, laughing, his eyes behind horn-rimmed glasses sparkling cynically at her.

Beebo had been in a sweat of preparation all day, and the apartment ended up looking almost new. A fever seemed to have gotten hold of her. This had to be a big party, a good party, a loud, drunk, and very gay party. Because this party was going to prove that Beebo and Laura had lived together for two whole years, and in Greenwich Village that is a pretty good record.

Friends were invited, to admire and congratulate. Oh, to get drunk and live it up a little too, on Beebo and Laura. But mostly to stand witness to the fact that the girls had been together two whole years. Or rather, Beebo had hung on to Laura for two whole years.

Maybe that's a hard way to say it. Maybe it isn't fair. After all, Laura stuck with Beebo, too. But Laura stuck because she didn't have the courage to let go, because her life was empty and without a purpose, and living with somebody and loving—or pretending to love—seemed to bring some sanity into her world. But for a long time she had begun to squirm and struggle under Beebo's jealous scrutiny.

Laura let Beebo make most of the arrangements for the party. She felt almost no enthusiasm for it. The whole thing had been Beebo's idea in the first place. Laura felt almost as outside of it as a late-arriving guest. She ran a few errands, but it was Beebo who planned and organized, who put up streamers and cleaned the apartment, who called everybody, who picked up the liquor and the ice cubes, and even made hors d'oeuvres.

She treated Laura with unwonted gentleness and attention all day. She wanted her in a good mood for the party. They had quarreled so much and so bitterly lately that they were both a little sick over it. Beebo wanted to have a good day behind them, a day full of good will and even tenderness.

There wasn't much time to foster tenderness, though, with the vacuum going, the kitchen upside down with food in various stages of readiness, the dog barking, and the phone ringing in an endless hysterical serenade. But still, Beebo tried. She touched Laura's hair softly when she passed her or brushed her hands over Laura's face. And once she stopped to kiss her, so carefully that Laura was touched in spite of herself and submitted, though without returning the kiss. Beebo went away flushed with success. Laura had not suffered herself to be kissed for nearly a week.

So when the guests finally started arriving, Beebo greeted them with high color in her cheeks and almost too much heartiness. Everything had started out so well, it had to end well.

It was a weird group that assembled to fete the anniversary. Beebo had wanted a big party. "Jesus, honey," she complained. "How many people down here stick it out this long? We have something to be proud of, for God's sake. Let's advertise it."

"What have we got to be proud of?" Laura said sarcastically. "We're just a couple of suckers for punishment. We just happen to enjoy beating each other's heads in."

Beebo had risen to the occasion with her quick and awful temper and left Laura crying. And she had had her way. They invited just about everybody in the neighborhood: the ones they knew, the ones they knew by sight only, and the ones they didn't know at all, male and female. Beebo did all the calling, so it came as a shock to Laura to see two of Beebo's old flames among the guests. But she said nothing about it. There would be time to shout about it afterwards. And shout they no doubt would.

Jack came early because he liked the chance to talk to Laura by himself now and then. He liked to be with her lately, since his own life had taken a sickening dip into loneliness and frustration. They were old friends; sometimes they thought of one another as each other's *only* friend. They were very close. It could never be a question of physical love between them, only deep affection, a mutual problem, a sort of harmony that sprang from sympathy and long acquaintance.

They were both homosexual. And if Laura could never understand why a man would desire another man, she at least knew, very well, how it was to love another woman. And so she could build a bridge of empathy on that knowledge and comfort Jack when some lovely boy was giving him hell. And he could do the same when Beebo raked her over the coals.

The party went along well enough for the first hour or so. Every time Beebo came near Laura she pinched her or bussed her. It was a part of her advertising campaign—a way to say, "She's still mine. And it's been two years. Hands off, the rest of you!" And she would look around at the guests a little defiantly.

But for Laura it was tedious. It scared her and bored her all at once. The fierce passion for Beebo that had boiled when they first knew each other flared up rarely now. And when there was no love there was nothing but fighting between them. She hated to be put on exhibit like this. And yet she kept her peace and let Beebo kiss her when she felt like it. After all, it was a party. Have a good time. If you can. Forget. If you can. Everybody drink up and laugh. Laugh, damn you all! If you can.

It was when Lili (she *would* spell it that way; she was born plain Louise) was well plastered that the party took a downward curve from which it never recovered. Lili was a former amour of Beebo's; Lili of the ash blonde hair and carefully blackened lashes; Lili of the lush, silk-draped body; Lili with the lack of inhibitions. Laura hated her with a good healthy female jealousy. It had been intolerable at first when she was still in love with Beebo and Lili had tried to manage their lives for them. Now it was just an exasperation to Laura to have her around.

Lili got high in a hurry. She believed in getting things done efficiently, and getting drunk was one of the things. She began to saunter from group to group around the small apartment, flirting, feeding sips from her martini to interested parties, telling tales. She came upon Beebo in the kitchen, getting more sandwiches from the refrigerator. The kitchen was crowded with people waving empty glasses and looking for refills. Jack was pouring them as fast as he could and sampling them all.

"Important to get it just right," he said. "Takes a good concentration of alcohol or you don't get fried till three in the morning. Terrible waste of time."

Lili wriggled through the crowd to Beebo and stood in front of her, weaving slightly, her underlip thrust out.

"I want something from you," she pouted. Beebo offered her a sandwich, but she shook her head murmuring, "No, no, no, no, *no!*"

"Jack's handling the concession," Beebo said a little nervously, jerking her head toward him.

"I don't want liquor," Lili said. "I want you. How come you never come to see me anymore, Beebo? You're enough to drive a girl frantic."

It was typical cocktail party drivel and Beebo was impatient with her. "You know why, Lili," she said. "Now scram."

5

But Lili was pugnacious. "If it's because of that bitchy little Laura out there, everybody knows you're all washed up. It's been obvious for weeks. You do nothing but fight. In fact, I was saying to Irene just five minutes ago that I can't imagine why you wanted to give this party in the first place and—" She stopped. Beebo's face had gone pale and dangerous.

"You say that once more and I'll kick you out of here on your fat can," Beebo snapped.

Lili drew herself up. "Okay, lie to yourself, I don't give a damn," she said. "Only it's perfectly clear—"

"Damn you, Lili, don't you understand English?" She said it loud enough to make heads turn.

Lili smiled. She generally performed better with an audience. "I understand," she cooed. "I understand you prefer a button-breasted bad-tempered little prude to a real woman."

Beebo took her roughly by the arms and pushed her out of the kitchen to the front door, causing a stir of curiosity in her wake. "Now get out of here and stay out!" she said.

"You never *could* handle me right," Lili smiled. Suddenly she took hold of her dress at the neckline and pulled it—soft, unresisting knit—down far enough to disclose that she wore nothing underneath. Two creamy, full breasts were bared. "All right, you fool—suffer!" Lili cried dramatically and burst out laughing. Beebo stared and then slammed the door.

There was some confusion among the guests. It was funny. And yet there was Laura, watching the whole thing. Everybody was uncomfortable. There was uncertain laughter. Jack, who took it all in from the kitchen door, said simply, "Don't worry about it, it's nothing new. She did it to Kitty Jackson last week."

After that there was obvious tension between Laura and Beebo. Beebo didn't kiss her anymore and Laura had nothing to say to Beebo. She eyed her coolly from across the room, and moved away if Beebo drew near. The guests absorbed the mood.

Jack took it with quiet cynicism, the way he took most things.

He saw and he understood but he said very little. It was not his affair. No matter that he had brought Beebo and Laura together once, a couple of years ago. He hadn't forced them to fall in love. That was their idea and he took no credit. And no blame,

Laura came suddenly into the kitchen where he was lounging by the liquor bottles, waiting for customers and watching the company through the door.

"She's impossible!" Laura cried. "God, I can't stand it anymore!" She covered her face with her hands, and her usually ivory skin crimsoned under her own harsh fingers.

"Take it easy, Mother," he said mildly, crossing his arms over his chest. "She may be impossible, but she loves you."

"That doesn't excuse the way she's acting—"

"She loves you a hell of a lot, Laura. She wouldn't hang on to you like this if she didn't."

"I don't want to be hung on to. I hate it! Jack, help me get out of here."

"I can't, honey, it's your mess. I wish to God I could. If I were young and female I'd lure her away from you. But I'm middle-aged and male. And short on allure."

Laura took advantage of the momentary seclusion of the kitchen to speak confidentially. She went to Jack and stood beside him, facing the sink, while he watched the door for intruders.

"She's in there showing off with that damn dog again,"
Laura said.

"Nix is a nice dog."

"Jack, we can't go to bed without that animal." She turned away to blow her nose. "Sure, he's a nice dog. But he eats more than I do, and he isn't housebroken when he's excited—which is right now. I swear Beebo loves that dog more than she loves me." Nix gave a volley of excited barks from the living room and they heard Beebo's throaty laugh. "Do it again," she was saying. "Come on, Nix, do it again."

"He will, too." Laura sighed. "He'll do anything she tells him to. And wet the rug like a happy idiot. Do you know what that rug cost me? Seventy-seven bucks. And I paid for it myself. Beebo didn't even have a rug in this place before I moved in."

"Okay," Jack said slowly. "The dog isn't housebroken and Beebo's old mistresses are a pain in the neck. Still, she loves you, Mother. So much that it astonishes me. I never thought I'd see that girl fall for anybody. Maybe you don't want her love, but you have to respect it. Real love isn't cheap, Laura. When you give it up once you sometimes never find it again."

"If it has to be like this, I don't ever *want* it again."

Jack finished his drink quickly, put it down on the kitchen counter, and turned Laura around to face him. He was the same height as she was but Laura looked up to him with her mind and heart.

"Mother," he said gently. "Don't ever say that. Don't ever throw love away. If it gets so you can't stand it, move out. But don't degrade it and don't disdain it. You can't stop her from loving you, Laura."

"I wish I still loved her. That's an odd way to feel but it would solve everything."

"You do love her, in a way. Only she exasperates you."

"No. It's all over, Jack. The only problem is how to get out without hurting her too much."

"No, the problem is to realize what your own feelings are and then have the courage to live with them."

"What you're trying to say is, you don't believe me. You think I still love her."

"Yes," he said.

"Why?"

"It's true."

"It's not!" she cried, grasping his arms, and then she heard Beebo laugh again and looked up to see her standing in the other room against the far wall. She was strikingly handsome and for a moment Laura felt the old feeling for her, but the love left almost as fast as it had come.

Beebo was a big girl, big-boned and good looking, like a boy in early adolescence. Her black hair was short and wavy and her eyes were an off-blue, wide, well spaced. She had come to New York from

8

a small town near Milwaukee before she was twenty, and she had had a sort of heartiness then, a rosy-cheeked health that had faded too fast in the hothouse atmosphere of Greenwich Village. She took odd jobs where she could, anything that would let her wear pants. And she ended up running an elevator and wearing a blue uniform with gold trim. She had been there for over ten years.

The manager took her for "one of those queers, but perfectly harmless." But he meant a *male* homosexual, to Beebo's endless hilarity. She was fond of remarking, "I'm the world's oldest adolescent. I'm a professional teenager." It was funny enough the first time, but Laura was sick of it.

Now she stood in the living room of their small apartment playing with Nix, and her merriment brought color to her cheeks. She had begun to wear clothes that made her look sportier and healthier than she was: men's jackets and slacks, men's shirts. And even, to Laura's dismay, a sort of riding habit, with modified jodhpurs, a slightly fitted coat, and boots. She had a pair of high black boots in butter-smooth leather with little ankle straps, boots made to fit the finely shaped feet that she was proud of. It made her one of the sights of the village.

"You look like a freak!" Laura had exploded when Beebo first tried them on, and succeeded in offending Beebo royally. But the older girl stuck stubbornly to her outfit.

"I'm no man. Okay. But I'm sure as hell no woman, either. I don't look good in anything. At least these things fit me," she defended herself.

"Your underwear fits you, too, darling," Laura said acidly. "Why don't you parade around in that if you want to cause a sensation?" But though she needled her, Laura couldn't make her change.

Now Beebo stood in the living room, visible to Laura through the kitchen door, dressed in the riding clothes. She did not look mannish like some Lesbians. She simply looked like a boy. But she was thirty-three years old, and there were very faint lines around her eyes and mouth.

Laura's little flash of desire faded almost before it bloomed.

And when she found that Nix had wet the floor, that Beebo had kissed Frankie Koehne and Jean Bettman, and that the police had appeared saying they had two complaints and the party would have to simmer down, Laura gave up.

She stormed into the bathroom and locked the door—the one lockable door in the apartment. The guests took the hint and filed out, leaving the apartment a quiet shambles.

When Laura came out, only Jack and Beebo were still there. They were sitting in the kitchen where they had collected most of the glasses, and were finishing up whatever liquor was left in them.

Beebo looked up when Laura came in. She was quite drunk and through the mists she saw Laura, with her long blond hair and pale face, as a sort of lovely vision. "Hi, sweetie," she murmured. "You sure got rid of the company in a hurry." She grinned.

Laura glanced disapprovingly at the used glasses Beebo was drinking from. "You'll get trench mouth," she predicted.

"Will you make love to me when I've got trench mouth?"

"NO!"

Beebo laughed. "You won't anyway, so it doesn't matter," she said dryly. "Come sit on my lap."

Laura leaned against the kitchen counter near Jack. "No," she said.

"Be nice to me, baby."

"Nix is nice to you. You don't need me. Nix ruins the rug for you. He barks loud enough to wake the dead. He even sleeps with you."

But Beebo felt too much desire for her to be jockeyed so fast into an argument. "Please, baby," she said softly. "I love you so."

And Jack, watching her, felt a pang of sympathy and regret go through him. She sounded too much as he sounded himself a couple of months ago. And Terry had left him anyway and wrecked his life. It was all so sad and wrong; unbearable when you're mismated and desperately in love.

"Go to her, Mother," he said suddenly. "She needs you." Laura was miffed at his interference. But she knew what was bothering him, and to soften it for him, she went. Once she was on Beebo's lap, everything seemed to relax a little. Beebo held her, leaning back against the wall and pulling Laura's head down on her shoulder, and Jack watched them enviously. He knew, as Laura knew, and even Beebo must have known in her secret heart, that the affair was doomed, that the party had celebrated an ending, not a new beginning. And yet for a moment things were serene. Beebo held Laura and whispered to her and stroked her hair, and Jack listened to it as if it were a lullaby, a lullaby he had heard somewhere before and had sung once himself. But it was a mournful lullaby and it turned into the blues—a dirge for love gone wrong.

Beebo nuzzled Laura and Laura lay quietly in her arms and endured it. She relaxed, and that made it better. She didn't want Beebo to excite her; she didn't want to give her that satisfaction. So she shifted suddenly and asked Jack, "Do you think they had a good time?"

"Lili did. She loves to promote her bosom," he said.

"Laura, baby." Beebo turned Laura's face to hers and tickled her cheeks with the tip of her tongue. "You taste so sweet," she whispered. "I want to lick you all over like a new puppy."

Laura couldn't stand it. The once-welcome intimacy sickened her now that she no longer loved Beebo. She got up abruptly and walked over to the stove. "Anybody want some coffee?" she said.

"You and your goddamn coffee," Beebo said irritably.

"You could use a little," Laura said, "both of you."

"I'd be delighted," Jack said, speaking with deliberate care as he always did when he was drunk.

Laura made the instant coffee and passed the cups around. Jack doctored his with a double shot of scotch and took a cautious first sip. "Delicious," he said, looking up to find a storm brewing. Beebo was glowering at Laura.

"I said I didn't want coffee," she said. "Nobody around here understands English tonight."

"If you're referring to Lili, I don't like to be classed with your old whores," Laura said.

"Why not? You're in good company baby. You don't think you're any better than they are, do you?"

"You should have told me you asked Lili! You should have told me, Beebo! And Frankie, too. God, don't you think I have feelings?"

"Good." Beebo grinned. "I didn't think you could get jealous any more."

"Oh, grow up, Beebo!" Laura cried, exasperated. "I can be humiliated. I can be embarrassed and hurt."

Beebo poured her coffee into an empty highball glass, which cracked from the heat with a loud snap. Her eyes looked up slyly at Laura, expecting a reprimand, but Laura ignored it, too angry to do anything. Beebo laughed and poured herself a watery drink from another glass. "Did I hurt you, Laura, baby? Did I really? How did it feel? Tell me how you liked it."

Laura didn't like the way she laughed. "Does that strike you funny?" she said sharply.

Beebo began to chuckle, a low helpless sort of laugh that she couldn't control; the miserable sort of laugh that comes on after too much to drink and too little to be happy about. "Yes," she drawled, still laughing. "Everything strikes me funny. Even you. Even you, my lovely, solemn, angry, gorgeous Laura. Even me. Even Jackson here. Jack, you doll, how come you're so handsome?"

Jack grinned wryly, twisting his ugly intelligent face. "The Good Fairy," he explained. "The Good Fairy is an old buddy of mine. Gives me anything I want. You want to be handsome like me? I'll talk to him. No charge."

Beebo kept laughing while he talked. She sounded a little hysterical. "No, I don't want to be handsome," she said. "I just want Laura. Tell your damn fairy to talk to Laura. Tell him I need help. Laura won't let me kiss her any more." She stopped laughing suddenly. "Will you, baby?"

"Beebo, please don't talk about it. Not now."

"Not now, not ever. Every time I bring it up, same damn thing. 'Not now, Beebo. Please, Beebo. Not now.' You're nothing but a busted record, my love. A beautiful busted record. Kiss me, little Bo-peep." Laura turned away, biting her underlip, embarrassed and defiant. "Please kiss me, Laura. That better? *Please*." She dragged the word out till it ended in a soft growl.

Laura hated Beebo's begging almost more than her swaggering. "If you didn't get so drunk all the time, you'd be a lot more appealing," Laura said.

Beebo got up and lurched across the room in one giant step and took Laura's arms roughly. She turned her around and forced a kiss on her mouth. They were both silent afterwards for a moment, Laura looking hot-faced at the floor and Beebo, her eyes shut, holding the love she was losing with awful stubbornness. Jack watched them in a confusion of pity.

He liked them both, but he loved Laura as well. In his own private way he loved her, and if it ever came to a showdown it was Laura he would side with.

At last Beebo said softly, "Don't shut me out, Laura."

Laura disengaged herself slightly. "If you didn't drink so much I wouldn't shut you out."

"If you didn't shut me out I wouldn't drink so much!" Beebo shouted, suddenly. "I wouldn't have to."

"Beebo, you drink because you like to get drunk. You were drunk the night I met you and you've been more or less drunk ever since. *I* didn't do it to you, you did it to yourself. You like the taste of whiskey, that's all. So don't give me a sob story about my driving you to drink."

"There you go, getting holy on me again. Who says *you* don't like whiskey?"

"I have a drink now and then," Laura flashed at her. "There are so many damn whiskey bottles in this apartment I'd have to be blind to avoid them."

Jack laughed. "I'm blind," he said, "most of the time. But I can always find the booze. In fact, the blinder I am the better I find it." He chuckled at his own nonsense and swirled the spiked coffee in his cup.

"Laura, you lie," Beebo said. "You lie in your teeth. You just like the way it tastes, like me."

Laura had been drinking too much lately. Not as much as Beebo, but still too much. She didn't know exactly why. She blamed it on a multiplicity of bad breaks, but never on herself. "If you wouldn't drag me around to the bars all night," she said. "If you wouldn't continually ask me to drink with you...."

"I *ask* you, Bo-peep. I don't twist your arm." She eyed Laura foggily.

Laura turned to Jack. "Do I drink as much as Beebo?" she demanded. "Am *I* an alcoholic?"

Beebo gave a snort. "Jack," she mimicked, "am *I* an alcoholic?"

"Do you have beer for breakfast?" he asked her.

"No."

"Do you take a bottle to bed?"

"No."

"Do you get soused for weeks at a time?"

"No."

"Do you...have a cocktail now and then?"

"Yes."

"You're an alcoholic."

Beebo threw a wet dishcloth at him.

"I'm going to bed," Laura announced abruptly.

"What's the matter, baby, can't you take it?"

"Enough is too much, that's all."

"Enough of what?"

"Of you!"

Beebo turned a cynical face to Jack "That means I can sleep on the couch tonight," she said. "Too bad. I was just getting used to the bed again...." She hiccuped, and smiled sadly. "Don't you think we make an ideal couple, Laura and me?"

"Inspirational," Jack said. "They should serialize you in all the women's magazines. Give you a free honeymoon in Jersey City."

"Knowing us as well as you do, Doctor," Beebo said, and Laura, her teeth clenched, stood waiting in the doorway to hear what she was going to say, "what would you recommend in our case?"

"Nothing. It's hopeless. Go home and die, you'll feel better," he said

"Don't say that." Suddenly Beebo wasn't kidding.

"All right. I won't say it. I retract my statement."

"Revise it?"

"God, in my condition?" he said doubtfully. "Well...I'll try. Let's see... My friends, the patient is dead of the wrong disease. The operation was a success. There is only one remedy."

"What's that?" Laura asked him.

"Bury the doctor. Oops, I got that one wrong too. Excuse me, ladies. I mean, *marry* the doctor. Laura, will you marry me?"

"No." She smiled at him.

"I'm an alcoholic," he offered, as if that might persuade her.

"You're damn near as irresistible as I am, Jackson," Beebo said. She said it bitterly, and the tone of her voice turned Laura on her heel and sent her out of the room to bed. Beebo went to the open kitchen door and leaned unsteadily on it.

"Laura, you're a bitch!" she called after her. "Laura, baby, I hate you! I hate you! Listen to me!" She waited while Laura slammed the door behind her and then stood with her head bowed. Finally she looked up and whispered, "I love you, baby."

She turned back to Jack, who had finished the coffee and was now drinking out of the whiskey bottle without bothering with a glass. "What do you do with a girl like that?" she asked.

Jack shrugged. "Take the lock off the bedroom door."

"I already did."

"Didn't work?"

"Worked swell. She made me sleep on the couch for five days."

"Why do you put up with it?"

"Why did you? It was your turn not so long ago, friend."

"Because you're crazy blind in love." He looked toward her out of unfocused eyes. Jack's body got very intoxicated when he drank heavily, but his mind did not. It was a curious situation and it produced bitter wisdom, sometimes witty and more often painful.

Beebo slumped in a chair and put her hands tight over her face. Some moments passed in silence before Jack realized she was crying. "I'm a fool," she whispered. "I drink too much, she's right. I always did. And now I've got her doing it."

"Don't be a martyr, Beebo. It's unbecoming."

"I'm no martyr, damn it. I just see how unhappy she is, how she is dying to get away from me, and then I see her brighten up when she's had a couple, and I can only think one thing: I'm doing it to her. That's my contribution to Laura's life. And I love her so. I love her so." And the tears spilled over her cheeks again.

Jack took one last drink and then left the bottle sitting in the sink. He said, "I love her too. I wish I could help."

"You can. Quit proposing to her."

"You think I should?"

"Never mind what I think. It's unprintable. I'm just telling you, quit proposing to her."

"She'll never say yes," he said mournfully. "So I don't see that it matters."

"That's not the point, Jackson. I don't like it."

"I'm sorry, I can't help it."

"Jack, you don't want to get married."

"I know. It's ridiculous, isn't it?"

"What would you do if she did say yes?"

"Marry her."

"Why?"

"I love her."

"Drivel! You love me. Marry me."

"I could live with her, but not with you," he said. "I love her very much. I love her terribly."

"That's not the reason you want to marry her. You can love her unmarried as well as not. So what's the real reason? Come on."

If he had not been so drunk he would probably never have said it.

"I want a child," he admitted suddenly, quietly.

Beebo was too startled to answer him for a moment. Then she began to laugh. "You!" she exclaimed. "*You!* Jack Mann, the homosexual's homosexual. Dandling a fat rosy baby on his knee. Father Jack. Oh, God!" And she doubled up in laughter.

Jack stood in front of her, the faintest sad smile on his face. "It would be a girl," he mused. "She'd have long pale hair, like Laura."

"And horn-rimmed glasses like her old man."

"And she'd be bright and sweet and loving."

"With *dames,* anyway."

"With me."

"Oh, God! All this and incest, too!" And Beebo's laughter, cruel and helpless, silenced him suddenly. He couldn't be angry, she meant no harm. She was writhing in a net of misery and it eased the pain when she could tease. But the lovely child of his dreams went back to hide in the secret places of his heart.

After a while Beebo stopped laughing and asked, "Why a girl?"

"Why not?"

"You're gay. Don't you want a pretty little boy to play with?"

"I'm afraid of boys. I'd ruin him. I'd be afraid to love him. Every time I kissed him or stroked his hair I'd be thinking, 'I can't do this any more, he'll take it wrong. He'll end up as queer as his old man.' "

"That's not how little boys get queer, doll. Or didn't your mama tell you?"

"She never told me anything." He smiled at her. "You know, Beebo, I think I'm going mad," he said pleasantly.

"That makes two of us."

"I'm serious. I'm even bored with liquor. By Jesus, I think I'll go on the wagon."

"When you go on the wagon, boy, I'll believe you're going mad for sure. But not before." She put her own glass down as if it suddenly frightened her. "Why do we all drink so much, Jackson? Is it something in the air down here? Does the Village contaminate us?"

"I wish to God it did. I'd move out tomorrow."

"Are we all bad for each other?"

"Poisonous. But that's not the reason."

"It's contagious, then. One person gets hooked on booze and he hooks everybody else."

"Guess again."

"Because we're queer?"

"No, doll. Come with me." He took her by the hand and led her on a weaving course through the living room to the bathroom. The dachshund, Nix, followed them, bustling with non-alcoholic energy. Jack aimed Beebo at the mirror over the washbowl. "There, sweetheart," he said. "There's your answer."

Beebo looked at herself with distaste. "My face?" she asked. Jack chuckled. "Yourself," he said. "You drink to suit yourself. As Laura said, you drink because you like the taste."

"I hate the taste. Tastes lousy."

"Beebo, I love you but you are the goddamn stubbornest female alive. You don't drink because anybody asks you to, or infects you, or forces you. You're like me. You need to or you wouldn't! Ask that babe in the mirror there."

"I can't live with that, Jack," she whispered.

"Okay, don't. I can't either. I just made up my mind: I'm quitting."

She turned and looked at him. "I don't believe you."

He smiled at her. "You don't have to," he said.

"And what if you do? How does that help me?"

He shook his head. "You have to help yourself, Beebo. That's the hell of it." He turned and walked toward the front door and Beebo followed him, scooping Nix off the floor and carrying him with her. "Don't go, Jack," she said. "I need somebody to talk to."

"Talk to Laura."

"Sure. Like talking to a wall."

"Talk anyway. Talk to Nix."

"I do. All the time." She held the little dog tight and turned a taut face to it. "Why doesn't she love me anymore, Nix? What did I do wrong? Tell me. Tell me..." She glanced up at Jack. "I apologize," she said.

"What for?"

"For laughing about your kid. Your little girl." She stroked Nix. "I know how it feels. To want one. You just have to make do with what you've got," she added, squeezing Nix.

Jack stared a little at her. "You know, it comes to me as a shock now and then that you're a female," he said.

"Yeah. Comes as a shock to me too."

He saw tears starting in her eyes again and put a kind hand on her arm. "Beebo, you're trying too damn hard with Laura. Relax. Ignore her for a couple of days."

"Ignore her! I adore her! I die inside when she slams that door at me." She dropped Nix suddenly and threw her arms around Jack, nearly smothering him. "Jack, you've been through it, you know what to do. Help me. Tell me. Help me!" And her arms loosened and she slumped to the floor and rolled over on her stomach and wept. Nix licked her face and whimpered.

Jack stood looking over her, still smiling sadly. Nothing surprised him now. He had lived with the heartbreaks of the homosexual world too long.

"Sure, I know what to do," he said softly. "Just keep living. Whatever else turns rotten and dies, never mind. Just keep living. Till it's worse than dying. Then it's time to quit."

"Ohhhh," she groaned. "What shall I do?"

"Stop loving her," he said.

Beebo turned over and gaped at him. Jack shrugged and there was sympathy in his face and fate in his voice. "That would straighten things out, wouldn't it?"

Beebo shook her head and whispered, "I can't You know 1 can't."

"I know," Jack repeated. "Goodnight, Beebo."

Chapter Two

THE BEDROOM DOOR opened and Beebo surprised Laura sitting on the closet floor fingering her shoes and dreaming. The party was two days past, the hangovers were still with them, but love was seven days behind them. Beebo didn't know how much longer she could take it. She had tried, since Jack's advice about relaxing, to keep her distance from Laura. It had not worked miracles, but it had helped.

However, Laura resented the love she could no longer return. Perhaps it was anger at her own failing, her own empty heart. Laura felt a sort of shame when Beebo embraced her. She blamed herself secretly for her fading affection. Beebo's love had been the strongest and Beebo's words, when she spoke of it, the truest. And yet Laura had said those same words and felt those same passions and believed, as Beebo had believed, that it would last.

She could not be sure where she had gone wrong or when that lovely flush of desire had begun to wane in her. She only knew one day that she did not want Beebo to touch her. When Beebo had protested, Laura had lost her temper and they had had their first terrible fight. Not a spat or an argument or a disagreement, as before. A fight—a physical struggle as well as a verbal one. An ugly and humiliating thing from which they could not rise and make love and reassure each other. That had been almost a year ago. Others had followed it and the breach became serious, and still they clung to each other.

Only now Laura's need was weakening and it was Beebo who held them together almost by herself. It was Beebo who gave in when a quarrel loomed, who took the lead to make peace afterwards, to try to soothe and spoil Laura. Beebo had the terrible fear that one of these days the quarrel would be too vicious and Laura would leave her. Or that she would go beyond the point of rational suffering and kill Laura.

Once or twice she had dreamed of this, and when she had wakened in sweat and panic she had gone to the living room and turned the light on and spent the time until dawn staring at it, repeating the jingles of popular tunes in her mind as a sort of desperate gesture at sanity.

Now Beebo stood looking down at Laura and at Nix, who was chewing on a pair of slippers, and she felt a wrenching in her heart. It just wasn't possible for her to ignore Laura any longer. She had kept hands off since the party and her talk with Jack. There had been no begging, no shouting, no furious tears. Now she felt she deserved tenderness and she knelt down and took Laura's chin in her hand and kissed her mouth.

"I love you," she said almost shyly.

And Laura, who wanted only to leave her, not to hurt her, lowered her eyes and looked away. She could not say it anymore. *I love you, Beebo.* It wasn't true. And Beebo knew it and the knowledge almost killed her, and yet she didn't insist. "Laura," she said humbly. "Kiss me."

And Laura did. And in a little wave of compassion she said into Beebo's ear, "I don't want to hurt you anymore."

Beebo took it the wrong way, the way that hurt her least. She took it to mean that Laura was apologizing and wanted her love again. But Laura meant only that Beebo had been dear to her once and that it was awful to see her so unhappy. "It's my fault," she said. "Only—"

"Only nothing," Beebo said quickly. "Don't say it. Say sweet things to me."

"Oh, Beebo, I can't. Don't ask me. I've forgotten the sweet things." Suddenly she felt like crying. She had never meant to wound Beebo. She had had the best intentions of loving her faithfully for the rest of her life. And yet now every pretty face she saw

21

on the streets caught her eye, every new set of eyes or curving lips at the lunch counter.

Laura was afraid and ashamed. She had always protested hotly when somebody accused Lesbians of promiscuity. And yet here she was refuting her own argument, at least in her thoughts and desires. It was still true that in the whole time they had lived together, she had never betrayed Beebo with another woman.

Knowing how Beebo felt only made Laura's conscience worse. It made her resentful and gentle by fits. Either way it was nerve-wracking and left her exhausted.

Suddenly Beebo picked her up and put her on the bed. She sat down beside her and slipped her arms around her and began to kiss her with a yearning that gradually brought little darts of desire to Laura. She didn't want it until it happened. And then, inexplicably, she did. It was good, very good. And she heard Beebo whisper, "Oh, if it could always be like this. Laura, Laura, love me. Love me!"

Laura turned her head away and shut her eyes and tried not to hear the words. Gradually the world faded out of her consciousness and there was only the ritual rhythm, the wonderful press of Beebo's body against hers. It hadn't been like this for Laura for months, and she was both grateful and annoyed.

Beebo made wonderful love. She knew how, she did it naturally, as other people eat or walk. Her hands flowed over Laura like fine silk in the wind, her lips bit and teased and murmured, all with a knowing touch that amounted to witchery. In the early days of their love Laura had not been able to resist her, and Beebo had loved her lavishly.

Often Laura had felt an ache for those days, when everything was sure and safe and certain in the fortress of passion. She had taken passion for love itself, and she had been secure in Beebo's warm arms. Now it seemed that Beebo had been just a harbor where she could rest and renew herself at a time when her life was most shattered and unhappy. She didn't need the safe harbor now. She was grateful, but she needed to move on. It was time to face life again and fight again and feel alive again. For Beebo the time of searching was over. It ended when she met Laura.

She had a small ten-watt bulb in a little bedstand lamp that shed a peachy glow around them, and she always had it on when they went to bed. Laura had loved it at first, when just the sight of Beebo's big firm body and marvelous limbs would set her trembling. But later, when she was afraid her slackening interest would show in her face, she asked Beebo to turn it out. It had been one more in a series of harsh arguments, for Beebo had known what prompted her request.

Now they lay beside one another, their hearts slipping back into a normal rhythm, their bodies limp and relaxed. Laura wanted only to sleep; she dreaded long intimate talks with Beebo. But Beebo wanted reassurance. She wanted Laura's soft voice in her ears.

"Talk to me, Bo-peep," Beebo said.

"Too sleepy," Laura murmured, yawning.

"What did you do today?"

"Nothing."

"Shall I tell you what I did?"

"No."

"I got a new shirt at Davis's," Beebo said, ignoring her. "Blue with little checks. And guess who rode in my elevator today?"

Laura didn't answer.

"Ed Sullivan," Beebo said. "He had to see one of the ad agency people on the eighth floor." Still no response. "Looks just like he does on TV," Beebo said.

Laura rolled over on her side and pulled the covers up over her ears. For some moments Beebo remained quiet and then she said softly, "You've been calling me 'Beth' again."

Laura woke up suddenly and completely. Beth...the name, the girl, the love that wound through her life like a theme. The tender first love that was born in her college days and died with them less than a year later. The love she never could forget or forgive or wholly renounce. She had called Beebo "Beth" when they first met, and now and then when passion got the best of her, or whiskey, or nostalgia, Beth's name would come to her lips like an old song. Beebo had grown to hate it. It was the only rival she knew for certain she had and it put her in the unreasonable position of being help-lessly jealous of a girl she didn't know and never would. Whenever she mentioned her, Laura knew there was a storm coming.

"If I could only *see* that goddamn girl sometime and know what I was up against!" she would shout, and Laura would have to pacify her one way or another. She would have to protest that after all, it was all over, Beth was married, and Beth had never even loved her. Not really. But when Laura grew the most unhappy with Beebo, the most restless and frustrated, she would start to call her Beth again when they made love. So Beebo feared the name as much as she disliked it. It was an evil omen in her life, as it was a love theme in Laura's.

Laura turned back to face Beebo now, nervous and tensed for a fight. "Beebo, darling—I'm sorry. I didn't mean to."

"Sure, I know. *Darling.*" She lampooned Laura's soothing love word sarcastically. "You just pick that name out of a hat. For some screwy reason it just happens to be the same name all the time."

"If you're going to be like that I won't apologize next time."

"*Next* time! Are you planning on next time already? God!"

"Beebo, you know that's all over—"

"I swear, Laura, sometimes I think you must have a girl some-where." Laura gasped indignantly, but Beebo went on, "I do! You talk about Beth, Beth, Beth so much I'm beginning to think she's real. She's my demon. She lives around the corner on Seventh Avenue somewhere and you sneak off and see her in the evenings when I work late and her husband is out." Her voice was sharp and probing, like a needle in the hands of a nervous nurse.

"Beebo, I've never betrayed you! Never!"

Beebo didn't really believe she had. But Laura had hurt her enough without betraying her and Beebo, who was not blind, could see that Laura would not go on forever in beautiful blamelessness.

"You will," Beebo said briefly. They were the words of near despair.

Laura was suddenly full of pity. "Beebo, don't *make* me hurt you," she begged. She got on her knees and bent over Beebo. "I swear I've never touched another girl while we've lived together, and I never will."

"You mean when you stumble on a tempting female one of these days you'll just move out. You can always say, 'I never cheated on Beebo while we lived together. I just got the hell out when I had a chance.'"

"Beebo, damn you, you're impossible! *You're* the one who's saying all this! I don't want to cheat, I don't want to hurt you, I *hate* these ugly scenes!" She began to weep while she talked. "God, if you're going to accuse me of something, accuse me of something real. Sometimes I think you're getting a little crazy."

Beebo clasped her around the waist then, her strong fingers digging painfully into Laura's smooth flesh, and sobbed. They were hard sobs, painful as if each one were twisting her throat.

"Forgive me, forgive me," she groaned. "Why do I do it? *Why?* Laura, my darling, my only love, tell me just once—you aren't in love with anybody else, are you?"

No!" said Laura with the force of truth, resenting Beebo's arms around her. She wanted to comfort her, yet she feared that Beebo would pounce on the gesture as a proof of love and force her into more lovemaking. Her hands rested awkwardly on Beebo's shoulders.

"If you ever fall for anybody, Bo-peep, tell me. Tell me first, don't spare me. Don't wait till the breach is too wide to heal. Give me a chance. Let me know who it is, let me know how it happened. Don't keep me wondering and agonizing over it. Anything would be better than lies and wondering. Promise you'll tell me. *Promise,* love."

She looked up at Laura now, shaking her so hard that Laura gasped. "Promise!" she said fiercely.

"All right," Laura whispered, afraid of her.

"Say it."

"I promise—to tell you—if I—oh, Beebo, please—"

"Go on, damn you!"

"If I ever fall—for somebody else." Her voice was almost too weak to hear.

Beebo released her then and they both fell back on the bed, worn out. For a long time they lay awake, but neither would make a move toward the other or utter a word.

The next day Beebo awoke feeling that they had come closer to the edge of breaking up than ever before, and she could feel herself trembling all over. She got up before Laura was awake and, taking Nix with her into the kitchen, she poured herself a shot. She was ashamed of this new little habit she was acquiring. She hadn't told anybody about it, not even Jack. Just one drink in the morning. Just one. Never more. It made her hands steady. It made the day look brighter and not quite so endless. It made her situation with Laura look hopeful.

She took the hot and satisfying amber liquid straight, letting it burn her tight throat and ease her. Then she washed out the shot glass and returned it to the shelf with the bottle.

"Nix," she said softly to the little dog, "I'm a bad girl. Your Beebo is a wicked bitch, Nix. Do you think anybody cares? Do you think it matters? What the hell good is it to be a bad little girl if nobody notices you? What fun is it then? Shall I have another shot, Nix? Nobody's looking."

He whimpered a little, watching her with puddle-bright eyes, and made her laugh. "You care, don't you, little dog?" She leaned down and picked him up. "You care, anyway. You're telling me not to be an ass and let myself in for a lot of trouble. And you're right. Absolutely."

She sat down on a kitchen chair and sighed. "You know, if she loved me, Nix, I wouldn't have to do it. You know that, don't you? Sure you do. You're the only one who does. Everybody else thinks I'm just turning into an old souse. But it's not true. It's because of Laura, you know that as well as I do. She makes me so miserable. She has my life in her hands, Nix." She laughed a little. "You know, that's kind of frightening. I wish I knew if she was on my side or not."

There was a moment when she thought she would cry and she dumped Nix off her lap and quickly poured herself one more shot. It went down easier than number one, but she washed the shot glass out as before and put it and the bottle back on the shelf as if to tell herself: *That's all, that's enough.*

Beebo turned and smiled at Nix. "Now look at me," she said. "I'm more sober than when I'm really sober. My hands have quit shaking. And I'm not going to quarrel with her when she gets up. I'm going to say something nice. Come here, dog. Help me think of something....

"I'd sell my soul to be an honest-to-God male. I could marry Laura! I could marry her. Give her my name. Give her kids...oh, wouldn't that be lovely? So lovely...." Jack's desire for a child didn't seem grotesque to her at all anymore.

"But Nix," she went on, and her face fell, "she wouldn't have me. My baby is gay, like me. She wants a woman. Would God she wanted me. But a woman, all the same, She'd never take a man for a mate."

She felt the vile tears sneaking up on her again and shook her head hard. "She couldn't take that, Nix. It'd be even worse than— than living with me." And she gave a hard laugh.

Beebo heard the bedroom door open and she dropped Nix and went to the icebox. Within moments Laura entered the kitchen.

"'Morning," she said.

"Good morning, Madam Queen. What'll it be?"

"Soft boiled egg, please. Have to hurry, I'll be late to work." She had a job in a tourist trap over on Greenwich Avenue, where they sold sandals and earrings and trinkets.

Beebo busied herself with the eggs and Laura poured orange juice and opened the paper. She buried herself in it, moving just a little to let Beebo put her plate down in front of her.

Beebo sat down opposite her and ate in silence for a minute, eating very little. She lighted a cigarette after a few minutes and sipped cautiously at her hot coffee.

"Laura?" she said.

"Hm?"

"Even in the morning, with your hair up and your nose in the paper and your eyes looking everywhere but at me...I love you, Laura." She said it slowly, composing it as she went and smiling a little at the effect. The liquor had loosened her up.

"What?" said Laura, her eyes following a story and her ears deaf.

"I have a surprise for you, Bo-peep," Beebo tried again.

"Oh. Says here it's going up to ninety today...A surprise?" She lowered the paper a bit to look at Beebo.

"Um-hm. I didn't get you an anniversary present. I thought we might get you a new dress tonight. Stores are open."

Laura was embarrassed. It still upset her to have to accept gifts from Beebo. She felt as if each one was a bid for her love, a sort of investment Beebo was making in Laura's good will. It made her resent the gifts and resist them. And still Beebo came home with things she couldn't afford and forced them on Laura and made her almost frantic between the need to be grateful, the pity she felt, and the exasperation that was the result of it all.

"I don't need a dress, honey," Laura said.

"I want you to have one."

"God, Beebo, if I bought all the clothes you want me to have we wouldn't have money to eat on. We'd be broke. We'd be in hock for everything we own."

"Please, baby. All I want to do is buy you an anniversary present."

"Beebo, I—" What could she say? *I don't want the damn dress?*

"I know," Beebo said abruptly. "I embarrass you. You don't like to be seen in the nice stores with me. I look so damn queer. Don't argue, Bo-peep, I know it," she said, waving Laura's protests to silence. "I'll wear a skirt tonight. Okay? I look pretty good in a skirt."

It was true that Laura was ashamed to go anywhere out of Greenwich Village with her...Beebo, nearly six feet of her, with her hair cropped short and her strange clothes and her gruff voice. And when she flirted with the clerks!

Laura had been afraid more than once that they would call the police and drag Beebo off to jail. But it had never happened. Still, there was always a first time. And if she had a couple of drinks before they went, Laura wasn't at all sure she could handle her.

"Why don't you let me find something for myself?" Laura asked, pleading. "I know you hate to put a skirt on. You don't have to come. I'll pick out something pretty." But she knew, and so did Beebo, that unless Beebo went along Laura would buy nothing. She would come home and say, "They just didn't have a thing." And Beebo would have to face the fact that Laura resented her little tributes.

So she said, "No, I don't trust your taste. Besides, I like to see you try on all the different things."

So it was that Laura met her at Lord and Taylor's on Fifth Avenue after work. It had to be a really good store, and Beebo had to pay more than they could afford, or she wasn't satisfied. Laura anticipated it with dread, but at least it was better than another awful quarrel. If Beebo would just be quiet. If she would just keep her eyes—and her hands—off the cute little clerks in the dress departments. Laura always tried to find a stolid middle-aged clerk, but the shops seemed to abound in sleek young ones.

Still, Beebo, subdued perhaps by her plain black dress and by Laura's nervous concern, kept quiet. Laura noticed a little whiskey on her breath when they met outside the store, but nothing in her behavior betrayed it.

"Do I stink?" she had asked, and when Laura wrinkled her nose Beebo took a mint out and sucked on it. "I won't disgrace you," she said. She was making a real effort.

They zigzagged around the Avenue, finding nothing that both looked right and could be had for less than a fortune. At Peck and Peck, near nine o'clock, Laura said, "Beebo, I've had it. This is positively the last place. I don't want you to dress me like a damn princess. I'd much rather have one of those big enamelware pots—"

"Oh, goddamn the pots! Don't talk to me of pots!" Beebo

exclaimed and Laura answered, "All right, all right, all right!" in a quick irritated whisper.

She went up to the first girl she saw, determined to waste as little time as possible. "Excuse me," she said. "Could you show me something in a twelve?"

The girl turned around and looked at her out of jade green eyes. Laura stared at her. She was black-haired and her skin was the color of three parts cream and one part coffee. In such a setting her green eyes were amazing. There was a tiny red dot between them on her brow, Indian fashion, but she was dressed in Occidental clothes. She gazed at Laura with exquisite contempt.

"Something in a twelve?" she repeated, and her voice had a careful, educated sort of pronunciation. Laura was enchanted with her, pleased just to look at her marvelous smooth face. Her skin was incredibly pure and her color luminous.

"Yes, please," Laura said.

With a light monosyllable, unintelligible to Laura, the girl shrugged at a row of dresses. "Help yourself," she said in clipped English. "I cannot help you."

Laura was surprised at her effrontery. "Well, I—I would like a little help, if you don't mind," she said pointedly.

"Not from me. Go look at the dresses. If you see one you like, buy it."

Laura stared at her, her dander up. "You just don't care if I buy a dress or not, do you?" she prodded. The girl, who had begun to turn away, looked back at her in annoyance.

"Can you think of one good reason why I should?" she asked.

"You're a clerk and I'm a customer," Laura shot back.

"Thank you for the compliment," she said icily. "But I am no clerk. And if I were, I wouldn't wait on you."

It was so royal, so precise, that Laura blushed crimson. "Oh," she said in confusion. "Please forgive me. I—I just saw you standing there and I—"

"And you took it for granted that I must be a clerk? How flattering."

She stared at Laura for a minute and then she smiled slightly and turned away.

Laura was too interested in her just to let her fade away like that. She started after her with no idea of what to say, feeling idiotic and yet fascinated with the girl. She touched her sleeve and that lovely beige face swiveled toward her, this time plainly irritated. But before either of them could speak Beebo came toward them. She had a couple of dresses over one arm and she sauntered up with typical long strides, a cigarette drooping from one corner of her mouth. Laura saw her coming with a sinking feeling.

"I found these, Laura. Try them on," she said, looking at the Indian girl. There was a small awkward silence. "Well?" Beebo said suddenly, smiling at the strange girl. "Friend of yours, Bo-peep?"

Laura could have slapped her. She hated that pet name. It was bad enough in private, but in public it was intolerable.

"No, I—I mistook her for a clerk," Laura said. Her cheeks were still glowing and the girl looked from her to Beebo and back as if they were both dangerous. Laura's hand fell from her arm and she stepped backwards, still watching them, as if she half-feared they would follow her.

"Don't mind her," Beebo told her, thumbing at Laura. "She thinks her best friends are clerks. She's just being friendly." Laura heard the edge in her voice and became uneasy.

But the Indian girl, if she was an Indian girl, unexpectedly relented a little and smiled. "It's all right," she said. She looked at Laura. "I'm not a clerk," she said. "I'm a dancer."

"Oh!" Suddenly an unwelcome little thrill flew through Laura. She couldn't have explained it logically. The girl was very demure and distant. But she was also very lovely, and Laura had a brief vision of all that creamy tan skin unveiled and undulating to the rhythm of muffled gongs and bells and wailing reeds.

She must have looked incredulous for the girl said suddenly, "I can prove it."

"Oh, no! No, that's all right," Laura protested, but the girl handed her a little card with a name printed on it, and Laura took it eagerly. "I did not mean I would demonstrate," the girl said carefully.

Beebo laughed. "Go ahead," she said. "We're dance lovers. I don't think Laura'd mind a bit, would you, baby?" She was mad at Laura for flirting and Laura knew it.

The little card read, *Tris Robischon* and underneath, *Dance Studio* and an address in the Village. "I just didn't want you to think I was lying," the girl said, somewhat haughtily. And before Laura or Beebo could answer her she turned and left them standing, staring after her.

Beebo turned to frown at Laura. "You made a hit, it seems," she said acidly. "Let's see her card." She snatched it from Laura's reluctant fingers.

"Take it. I don't want it!" Laura said angrily, for she did want it very much. She turned away sharply, giving her attention to a row of dresses, but she knew Beebo wouldn't let her off the hook so easily. There would be more nastiness and soon.

"You got her name out of her, at least. Pretty smooth." Beebo's voice was hard and hurt. "Tris Robischon. Doesn't sound very Indian to me."

"How would you know, swami?" Laura snapped. "If you throw a jealous scene in here I'll leave you tonight and I'll never come back, I'm warning you!" she added in a furious hiss, and Beebo glared at her. But she didn't answer.

Finally Laura dragged some dresses off the rack and turned to her. "I'll try these," she said. Beebo followed her to the dressing room and watched her change into one and then another in angry silence.

At last Laura burst out, "I didn't ask her for the damn card. I don't know why she gave it to me."

"It's obvious. You're irresistible."

Laura took two handfuls of Beebo's hair and shook her head till Beebo stopped her roughly and forced her to her knees. Fury paralyzed them both for a moment and they stared at each other helplessly, trembling.

Laura wanted that card. She wanted it enough to soften suddenly and play games for it. "Beebo, be gentle with me," she pleaded, her tense body relaxing. "Don't hurt me," she whispered. "I don't know who the girl is and I don't care."

Beebo stared at her suspiciously till Laura reminded her, "We came to get a dress, remember? Let's not spoil it. Please, Beebo."

Beebo released her and sat staring at the floor. Laura tried on dresses for her, but Beebo wouldn't look at them. No tender words, no coaxing, no teasing that would have been so welcome any other time worked with her tonight. When Beebo got jealous she was a bitch—irrational, unreasonable, unkind.

"I'm going to take this one," Laura said finally, a little desperate. "Whether you like it or not."

Beebo looked up slowly. "I like it," she said flatly, but she would have said, "I hate it," in the same voice.

Laura went over to her and took her face in both hands, stooped down, and kissed her petulant mouth. "Beebo," she murmured. "You love me. Act like it." It was so foolishly selfish, so unexpected, and so almost affectionate that it was funny, and Beebo smiled wryly at her. She took Laura's shoulders and pulled her down for another kiss just as a clerk—a genuine clerk—stuck her face in and said, "Need any help in here?"

"No thanks!" Laura blurted, looking up in alarm. Beebo put her head back and laughed and the clerk stared, pop-eyed. Then she shut the door and sped away. Beebo stood up and swept Laura into her arms and kissed her over and over, all over her face and shoulders and ears and throat until Laura had to beg her to stop. "Let's get out of here before that clerk makes trouble!" she implored.

When they left the dressing room Laura noticed that Beebo had put Tris Robischon's card in the sand pail for cigarettes. It stuck out like a little white flag. Laura risked her purse—with $15.87, all they had for the next week—to get the card back. She left the purse on the chair as she followed Beebo out. And so it was that she was able to make an excuse to go back and retrieve them both, purse and card, while Beebo paid for the dress.

Chapter Three

IT'S AN AWFUL THING ABOUT JACK, Laura wrote in her diary, sitting on the floor by the closet door. *Such a nice guy, so bright and so—this will sound corny—so fine. But ever since Terry left him he's been a little crazy. I was really afraid of how much he was drinking until tonight when we had a beer at Julian's. Or rather, I had a beer. Jack's on the wagon. Maybe that will straighten him out. If he can stick with it. If he'd been straight I think he would have done something wonderful with his life. But is it fair to blame the failures on homosexuality? Is it, really? I'm selling junk here in the Village because Beebo wants me near her. She runs an elevator so she can wear pants all day. And Jack's a draughtsman so he can be in an office full of virile engineers. What's the matter with us? We don't have to spend our lives doing it. So why do we?*

She had asked Jack the same question at Julian's little bar just off Seventh Avenue, earlier that evening. "Why do we do it, Jack? Throw our lives away?" she said.

"We like to," he shrugged. "We all have martyr complexes."

"We give away the best part of ourselves—our youth and our health are all just given away. Free."

"What sort of profit did you expect to make on them?" he said. "You want to get paid for being young and healthy?"

Laura glared at him. "That's not what I mean—"

"If you're not giving, you're not living, doll," he said. "I quote the sob columns. Give yourself away, what the hell. What's youth for? And health? And beauty, and the rest of it. Keep it and it turns putrid like everything else. Give it away and at least somebody enjoys it."

"Jack, you know damn well I mean *wasting* it. Wasting it all day

34

long on costume jewelry or a push-button elevator or a slide rule. God, when I think of what you—"

"Don't think of all the fine things I could have done with my life, Mother," he pleaded. "You give me the shudders. I'm not happy, but I'd be worse off trying to live straight. I like men. My office is full of them."

"You hate your work."

"I never have to think about it. Purely mechanical. I just sit there and flip that little slip stick and I say, 'Evens, Johnson is straight. Odds, he's queer. If Johnson is queer on Tuesday—according to the slide rule—I make it a point to give him a kind word."

"Johnson is straight and you know it. Every man in your office is straight Why do you torture yourself?"

"No torture, Mother. When the whole world is black, pretend it's rosy. Somewhere, in some little corner. If everybody's straight, pretend somebody's gay."

"That's a short cut to the bug house."

"I wouldn't mind the bug house. If they'd let me keep my slip stick." He laughed to himself and leaned over the bar to order. "One whiskey and water," he said.

"How about you, Mann?" Julian asked.

"Nothing."

"Are you on the wagon?" Laura was stunned. When he nodded she said, "Just a beer for me. I'm drinking too much anyway." Then she smiled. "You'll never last, Jack. You know what you need?"

"Do I know? Are you serious?" He grinned at her, but it was a pained smile.

"You need a real man," Laura said softly. "Not a bunch of daydreams at the office. That's enough to drive anybody nuts. You worry me, Jack."

"Good." He smiled and squeezed her arm. "Now I'll tell you what I really need." He looked at her through his sharp eyes set in that plain face Laura had come to love and find attractive. "I don't need a man, Laura," he said. "I'm too damn old to run after pretty

35

boys anymore. I look like a middle-aged fool, which is exactly what I am. When Terry left me, I was through."

"Do you still love him? Even after what he did?"

"I won't talk about him," he said simply. "I can't. But he was the last one. The end. I want a woman now. I want you, Laura." He turned away abruptly, embarrassed, but his hand remained on her arm.

Laura was touched. "Jack," she said very gently. "I'm a Lesbian. Even if you renounce men, I can't renounce women. I won't even try."

"There was a time when you were willing to try."

"That was a million years ago. I wasn't the same Laura I am now. I said that before I even met Beebo—when another girl was giving me hell, and I was new to the game and to New York and so afraid of everything."

"So now you know the ropes and you're absolutely sure you'd rather give your life away to the goddamn tourists and a woman you don't love than come and live with a man you do love."

"Jack, darling, I love you, but I don't love you with my body. I love you with my heart and soul but I could never let you make love to me."

"I could never do it, either," he said quietly. "You're no gayer than I am, Laura. If we married it would never be a physical union, you know that." Somewhere far back in his mind the sweet shadow of that little dream child hovered, but he suppressed it, lighting a cigarette quickly. His fingers shook.

"If it wasn't a physical union, what would it be?" Laura asked. "Just small talk and community property and family-plan fares?"

He smiled. "Sounds a little empty, doesn't it?"

"Jack," Laura said, speaking with care so as not to hurt him, "you're forty-five and life looks a little different to you now. I'm only twenty-three and I can't give up my body so casually. I could never make you promises I couldn't keep."

"I wouldn't ask that promise of you, Laura," he said.

"You mean I could bring girls home? To our home, yours and mine? Any girls, any time? And it would be all right?"

"Let's put it this way," he said. "If you fell in love with somebody, I'd be understanding. I'd welcome her to the house, and I'd get the hell out when you wanted a little privacy. I'd keep strict hands off and just one shoulder for you to cry on. As long as you really loved her and it wasn't cheap or loud or dirty, I'd respect it."

He knocked the ashes off the tip of his cigarette thoughtfully. "...Only," he said, "you'd be my wife. And you'd come home at night and tuck me in and you'd be there in the morning to see me off." He sounded so peculiarly gentle and yearning that she was convinced that he meant it. But she was not ready to give in.

Laura smiled at him. "What would there be in all this for you, Jack?" she said. "Just getting tucked in at night? Is that enough compensation?"

"Nobody ever tucked me in before." He said it with a grin but she sensed that it was true.

"And breakfast in the morning?"

"Wonderful! You don't know what a difference it would make."

"That's nothing, Jack, compared to what you'd be giving me."

"You'd be my wife, Laura, my honest-to-God lawful legal wife. You'd give me a home. You don't know what that would mean to me. I've been living in rented rooms since I was out of diapers. You'd give me a place to rest in and be proud of, and a purpose in life. What the hell good am I to myself? What use is an aging fag with a letch for hopelessly bored, hopelessly handsome boys? Christ, I give myself the creeps. I give the boys the creeps. And you know something? They're beginning to give *me* the creeps. I'm so low I can't go any place but up. If you'll say yes."

"What if I did? What about Beebo?" Laura said softly, as if the name might suddenly conjure up her lover, jealous and vengeful.

"It would solve everything," he said positively. "She could still see you, but you wouldn't be her property anymore. It's bad for her to have the idea she owns you, but that's the way she treats you. If you were my wife she'd have to respect the situation. It would be a kind way to break with her," he added slyly. He was feeling too selfish to waste sympathy on Beebo now.

Laura thought it over. There was no one she respected more than Jack, and her love for him, born of gratitude and affection, was real. But it was not the love of a normal woman for a normal man she felt for him, and the idea of marrying him frightened her.

"Do you think, if we married, we could keep our love for each other intact, Jack?" she asked.

"Yes," he said.

"Even if I were having an affair?" She was thinking at that moment of Tris Robischon, the lovely, lithe Indian girl.

"Yes. I told you 'yes.'"

Laura finished her beer in silence, gazing into the mirror over the bar and pondering. She knew she would say no. But she didn't quite know how. "I can't, Jack," she said at last, in a small voice.

"Not now, maybe?" He wouldn't give up.

"Never."

"Never say never, Mother. Say 'not now' or something."

She did, obediently. But she added, "We'd quarrel and we'd end up destroying our love for each other."

"We'd quarrel, hell yes. I wouldn't feel properly married if we didn't."

"And there's always the chance that *you'd* fall in love. And regret that you married me."

He turned to her with a little smile and shook his head. "Never," he said. "And this once it's the right word." He took her hands. "Say yes."

"No."

"Say maybe."

"No."

"Say you'll think about it, Laura. Say it, honey."

And out of love and reluctance to hurt him, she whispered, "I'll think about it."

Laura was walking up Greenwich Avenue, searching for number 251. She had a small white card in her hand to which she referred occasionally, although she had memorized the address. It was a hot day, late in the afternoon, and she had just come from work, wilted and worn and bored. The idea of going home right away depressed her and she had decided to walk a little.

She hadn't gone two blocks before she was daydreaming of Tris Robischon and suddenly shivering with the thought of seeing her again.

Beebo wouldn't be home until nine o'clock that evening, and Tris's studio address was only a short distance from the shop where Laura worked. All at once she was walking fast.

She found the address with no trouble at all. In fact it was almost too easy, and before she knew it she was standing in the first floor hallway of the modest building reading the names on the mailboxes. TRIS ROBISCHON. There it was. Third floor, Apartment C. Laura climbed the stairs.

What will I say to her! she asked herself. *How in God's name will I explain this visit? Ask her for a dance lesson? Me?* She had to smile at herself. Her long slim legs would never yield to the fluid grace and discipline of dancing.

Laura stood uncertainly before the door of Apartment C, a little afraid to knock. She could hear the sounds of music inside— rather sharp, tormented music. Laura glanced at the card once again. It had been almost three weeks since the Indian girl had given it to her. Perhaps she wouldn't even remember Laura. It might be embarrassing for them both. But then Laura envisioned that remarkable face, and she didn't care how embarrassed she had to be to see it once again. She knocked.

There was no response. She knocked again, hard. This time there was a scampering of feet and the music was abruptly shut off. Laura heard voices and realized with a sinking feeling that Tris wasn't alone.

Suddenly the door swung open. Laura was confronted with a young girl of twelve or so in a blue leotard. "Yes?" said the little girl. There were three or four others in the room in attitudes of relaxation, and then Tris appeared around a corner, wiping her wonderful face on a towel and coming quickly and smoothly toward the door. It was almost a self-conscious walk, as if she expected any caller to be a prospective pupil and had to demonstrate her talent even before she opened her mouth to speak.

She stopped behind the young girl and looked up. Laura waited, speechless and awkward, until Tris smiled at her, without having said a word. "Come in," she said.

"I hope I'm not interrupting a class," Laura said, hesitating.

"It does not matter. You are welcome. Please come in." Laura followed her into the room and Tris waved her to a seat. It was only a bench, set in a far corner of the room, but Laura went to it gratefully and sat there while Tris collected her charges and put them through a five-minute routine. It looked very pretty to Laura, although the Indian girl seemed dissatisfied.

"You can do much better than that for our visitor, girls," she said in her dainty English that Laura had nearly forgotten. It was a strange accent, like none Laura had ever heard, very precise and softly spoken, but not noticeably British or anything else. Laura puzzled over it, watching Tris move and demonstrate things to her students. She had on black tights and a small cotton knit bandeau that covered her breasts and shoulders but left her long supple midriff exposed. She was the same luscious tan from waist to bosom, and Laura, sitting there watching her, was helplessly fascinated by it; almost more by what she could see than by what she couldn't.

Tris gave two sharp claps with her hands suddenly. "That is all for today, girls," she said, and they broke up quickly, running into another room to change their clothes. Tris turned to look at Laura. She simply looked at her without saying anything, a stare so frank and unabashed that Laura lowered her eyes in confusion, feeling the red blood come to her cheeks.

"What is your name?" Tris asked her then, and Laura

answered, surprised, "Laura." *Of course, I'd forgotten. She doesn't even know my name!*

Laura looked up to find Tris studying her with a little smile. The girls began to file past saying goodnight to her. She smiled at one or another, touched their heads and shoulders, and spoke to some. In between little girls she watched Laura who felt rather like a specimen on exhibit.

The studio was bare except for the bench, a record player next to it on the floor by Laura's feet, and mirrors. The mirrors were everywhere, long and short, all over the walls. Most gave a full view of you to yourself. The room where the children dressed was furnished as a bedroom. Laura could see parts of it, and there were more mirrors in there. There was a swinging door, shut now, which apparently led to a kitchen. Laura gazed around her, trying to appear interested in it, so she wouldn't have to look at Tris.

The front door shut finally, rather conspicuously, and a small silence fell. They were alone.

"You like my little studio, then?" said Tris.

Laura dared to look at her then and found that the last child was certainly gone and the studio was empty. Awfully empty.

"Yes, I like it," she said. She felt the need to excuse her presence and she began hurriedly, "I hope you won't think I—"

But Tris never let her finish. "Shall I dance for you?" she said suddenly with such a luminous smile that Laura felt her whole body go warm with appreciation. She returned the smile. "Yes, please. If you would."

Tris walked to the record changer beside Laura, knelt, and slipped a record into place. Then she looked up at Laura, her eyes larger and greener than Laura remembered, and infinitely lovelier seen so close. She waited there, looking at her visitor, until the music began to flow. It was not harsh like the music Laura had heard through the door, but languid and rhythmical, perhaps even sentimental.

Tris began to move so slowly at first that Laura was hardly

41

aware that she was dancing. Her arms, long and tender and graceful, began to ripple subtly toward Laura, and then her head and body began to sway, and finally her strong legs, deceptively slim, moved under her and brought her, whirling slowly, to her feet.

It was a strange dance that flowed and undulated. This marvelous body seemed to float and then to sink like mist, and at one point Laura had to shut her eyes for a minute, too thrilled to bear it. She wanted terribly to reach out, put her hands on Tris's hips and feel the rhythm move through her own body.

The music stopped. Tris stood poised over Laura, looking down at her, and for a moment she remained there, balanced delicately and smiling. Laura felt a familiar surge of desire and she watched Tris like a cat watching a twitching string, ready to pounce if Tris made a sudden move. And yet afraid Tris might touch her and startle her passion into the open.

But Tris relaxed as the needle began its monotonous scratch, and she turned off the machine. She sat on the floor then, grasping her black-sheathed knees in her arms, one hand holding the wrist of the other.

"Did you like it?" she said, glancing up, and she seemed for a moment to be unsure and distant, as she had been in the dress shop.

"I thought it was wonderful," Laura said, herself a little shy. "I didn't know dancing could be like that."

"Like what?" Tris demanded suspiciously.

"Well—like–I don't know. It was like nothing I've ever seen…as if you were floating. It was beautiful."

Tris softened a little. "Thank you, Laura," she said. And Laura felt a wild confusion of delight at the sound of her own name. "I dance very well," Tris went on oddly. "There is no point in false modesty. I hate that sort of thing, don't you? It's so hypocritical. If you dance well, or do anything else well, say so. Be frank. I think men like a girl who is frank. Don t you?"

Laura was taken aback. "Oh, yes," she affirmed quickly. But

she stared. *She can't be straight!* she thought to herself, in a sudden agony of doubt. From the first she had taken it for granted that the lovely Indian girl was a Lesbian. It seemed so right, perhaps only because Laura wanted it that way. And too, Laura always prided herself on being able to tell if a girl were homosexual or not. She was sick at the thought that Tris might love men.

Tris watched her, interested. "What are you thinking of?" she said.

"Nothing," Laura protested uneasily.

"All right. I will not pry." Tris smiled. "Will you have some tea with me?'

"Thank you." Laura was glad to ease the tension a little. Tris got up and she followed her through the swinging door into the kitchen.

Tris made the tea while Laura watched her in a rapture of pleasure. "You moved so beautifully," she blurted, and then blushed. "I—I mean, it shows in all your movements. Dancing, or walking, or just getting down the teacups." She laughed. "I feel like a clumsy ox, watching you."

"You are wrong," Tris said. "I have been watching you, too. You move well, Laura. You could learn to dance. Would you like to learn?"

Laura looked away, confused and delighted but scared. "I'd be your worst pupil," she said.

"I find that hard to believe."

"It's—probably very expensive."

"For you...," Tris shrugged and smiled, "nothing," she said.

Laura turned to look at her, surprised. "Nothing?" she repeated.

"Or perhaps your friend...the big one," Tris added softly. "Perhaps she would be interested?"

"Beebo?" Laura exclaimed. "Oh God no!"

Tris handed her a cup quickly, as if to make her forget the suggestion. "Do you like me, Laura?" she said, her green eyes too close and her sweet skin redolent of jasmine.

"Yes, Tris," Laura said, saying her name for the first time and feeling the fine shivering return to her limbs.

"Good." Tris grinned at her. "That is payment enough." Laura felt suddenly like she had better sit down or she would fall down. "You say my name now, that means you feel closer to me, hm?" Tris asked.

"Yes. A little." Laura gazed at her, completely confused, afraid to move, until Tris gave a little laugh.

"Come, we'll sit in the other room," she said, and Laura once again followed her across the bare studio into the bedroom.

The room was fitted up Indian fashion with rich red silk drapes on the bed. The bed itself was actually more of a low couch, very capacious, and covered with tumbled silk cushions. There were books and records scattered around, a couple of pillows on the floor to take the place of chairs, and a number of ashtrays.

"This is my bedroom, my living room, my den, my playroom— whatever you want," Tris said smiling, and sat down on the bed. "Come, don't stand there looking afraid of me," she said, "sit down." And she patted the bed beside her.

Laura came and sat there and as she did Tris lay back on the cushions and watched her. She put her tea on the floor while Laura held hers carefully, anxious about spilling it on the lush red silk.

"Are you—are you Indian, Tris?" she asked awkwardly, turning to look at her.

Tris crossed her black-sheathed legs. "Yes," she said. "Half Indian, at least. My mother was Indian but my father was French."

"Did you grow up in India?"

"Yes. In New Delhi. Have you been there?" Her clear eyes looked sharply at Laura.

"No. I've never been anywhere," Laura said. "Except New York and Chicago. I was born in Chicago."

"Is your family there?"

"Just my father. He's all the family I have."

"Do you see him often?"

"I never see him." She looked away, suddenly overwhelmed with the thought of her father. She had not seen him for two years. Not since she had gone to live with Beebo and admitted to him that she was a Lesbian. There had been a terrible scene. And then Laura had fled and Merrill Landon, for all she knew, had gone back to Chicago.

"Is that where your roommate is from? Chicago?" Tris asked slowly.

"No. Milwaukee." Laura turned to frown at her and Tris, sensing her reticence, changed the subject. "Would you like to see my scrapbook?" she said. Before Laura could answer she was off the bed and searching for it among some books and papers across the room. She came back and sat next to Laura, spreading the green leather book open over their knees and putting an arm around Laura's waist.

"These were all taken six months ago," she said. "This boy is German. Isn't he handsome? I love blond hair. He's wonderful looking."

He was indeed. Jack would have appreciated the view more than Laura, for he was young and muscular and nearly naked. His body had been oiled so that every smooth ripple on arms and back and tight hips and long legs was highlighted. He had a shock of rich blond hair and particularly handsome features, and he was shown in a number of poses: some that looked like Muscle Beach shots and others that seemed like dance positions.

"He does dance," Tris said, anticipating Laura's question. "With me. He's named Paul Cate. We have a lot of routines together. We are a sort of—*team*."

"Are you engaged?" Laura asked. It sounded ridiculous once it was said, but she found herself unreasonably jealous of the boy.

Tris threw her head back and laughed. "Engaged!" she exclaimed. "He is a homosexual, Laura."

"A homosexual?" It sounded like fake innocence, even to Laura.

But Tris was too amused to notice. "Yes, of course," she said, still laughing. "Can you imagine two homosexuals getting married? Could anything be sillier? What would they do with each other?" And her laughter was too hard.

Laura was shocked at her crude dismissal of the possibility of a homosexual marriage, which made her feel instantly protective and tender about Jack. But she had said, "Two homosexuals," and

Laura's heart rose. "Are you gay, Tris?" she asked, almost in a whisper, afraid to look at her.

"Not really." Tris flipped the words at her casually, turning pages in the scrapbook and concentrating on them. Laura sensed embarrassment in her concentration.

"Either you are or you aren't," Laura said, more boldly.

"Then I'm not," said Tris and startled her visitor. "If you force me to choose between black and white, I'm white," she explained, and Laura thought she heard a double emphasis on the word "white." "I like men. More than women." Laura was cowed into bewildered silence.

There were many enticing photographs of Tris. "The photographer is a friend of mine," she told Laura with a smile. "He always makes me look good." There was a series of her with the German boy, in dance poses. Tris was so lovely that Laura felt the gooseflesh rise up on her with Tris's breathing in her ear and her warmth touching Laura's arms.

"You would think we were madly in love," Tris said with a little laugh. "Oh, look at this one. This is my former husband."

Laura did look, hard. "You were married?" she said, unwilling to believe it.

"Yes. To him. He is handsome, no?"

"Yes." He was pictured lying on his side, very much of a young athlete, with curly hair and an honest sort of face, a little like Jack's long-lost Terry. He looked Irish. "Was he gay, Tris?"

"Yes," she said and the annoyance was plain in her voice. "It was an ugly mistake. We hated each other after we got married. Before that, we were the best of friends. So you see, I know what I am saying when I tell you gay marriages are hell."

Laura considered this in silence while Tris turned pages. "Have some dinner with me," Tris said, piling the pictures on the floor at the foot of the bed.

Laura looked at her watch. It was only seven. Beebo wouldn't be home for another two hours.

"I never cook," Tris said, going across the room to pick up the phone. She began to order sandwiches, glancing at Laura for suggestions. "They bring them up from the corner shop," she said when she hung up. Laura looked up at her from her seat on the bed, and Tris began to move slowly, undulating, as if she were musing on a dance.

"Where did you learn to dance, Tris?" Laura asked her.

"England. Where do you live?"

"Cordelia Street. One-twenty-nine."

"With the big one? What did you say her name is?"

Laura felt uncomfortable at the mention of her lover, and resentful of Tris's curiosity about her. "Her name is Beebo," she said rather sullenly.

"Oh, yes—Beebo!" Tris laughed. "It almost sounds Indian," she said. "Is she nice?"

Laura shrugged. "I guess she is."

"You aren't sure, hm?" Tris seemed amused. "Are you in love with her?"

Laura was reluctant to say no, but determined not to say yes. "I—I was," she admitted finally.

"It is all over, then?"

Laura didn't like her bright-eyed interest. "We still live together," she said defensively.

"Does she still love you?"

"Yes. Yes, she does," Laura said sharply, looking Tris square in the eye.

"I'm sorry," Tris said softly, her gaze dropping. "I shouldn't pry."

"There are better things to talk about than Beebo," Laura said.

The food came and they were both relieved to turn to something else.

When the food was gone a quiet little interlude fell when Tris simply sat on the bed and watched Laura and Laura wandered idly around the room.

There was a terrible growing excitement in Laura. She felt she must run, escape somehow, get out of the studio before she made a fool of herself and an enemy of Tris. She turned at last and looked down at Tris. There was only one lamp lit in the room, and in the pale pink light Tris looked even riper and lovelier than she did in bright daylight.

"Tris, I—I have to go," Laura said. "It's getting late. I had a lovely time…"

"Then why go?"

"I must. I shouldn't have come, really."

"Will Beebo be angry with you?"

"She isn't home yet."

"Then you don't have to go yet. I'll bet she has a fine temper." She waited for an answer, but Laura ignored her remark. She was thinking only of the possibility of staying longer. Her heart fluttered with the temptation. She was afraid of Beebo and yet, in another way, even more afraid of Tris.

"Come sit beside me," Tris urged her, whispering, And Laura, unable to refuse her, came slowly toward the bed, as if she were in a trance, and sat down. Tris leaned back into the pillows, her hand on Laura's arm, and pulled Laura after her.

Laura lay on her back next to Tris for a while, breathing softly, nervously aware of the sound of her breath. She held herself in as if she expected to explode. She was tense and the sweat rolled down her body, and yet she was happy, very happy.

They lay that way for some time, silent, gazing at the ceiling, neither one speaking, yet neither able to relax. At last Tris took Laura's hand in her own warm brown one and said, "You're afraid of me, aren't you, Laura?"

There was a slight pause, almost a panic, while Laura tried to collect herself. "Yes," she mumbled at last.

"Why?"

"You're so beautiful…" Laura fumbled.

"Does beauty frighten you?"

"Yes. I don't know why. Maybe because I never had it."

Tris chuckled, a sweet throaty sound, and said, "Who ever told you that?" And it occurred to Laura, strangely, that Tris spoke without any accent at all. It sounded clear and plain, like Laura's own English. But it was only a quick impression and it passed. She thought Tris was teasing her, imitating her.

"Don't kid me," she said.

"Take your hair down, Laura," Tris said, her fingers playing with the prim bun at the back of Laura's head. Her hair had grown so long—Beebo wouldn't let her cut it—that she was obliged to roll it up one way or another in the back. It hung nearly to her waist when it was loose. She took the pins out of it now, raising herself on one elbow to accomplish the job. Tris helped her and the roll of hair came free suddenly and fell around Laura's shoulders like silk streamers, pale gold and scented. Tris took a handful of it, pressing it to her face.

"How lovely!" she exclaimed. "Lovely blond hair…"

She put her hands on Laura's shoulders and pushed her down into the pillows, bending over her to study her face. "I think you're very pretty," she said, and made Laura smile.

"I don't believe you," she said.

"I'll bet Beebo thinks you're very pretty, too."

"Please, Tris. Let's not talk about Beebo."

Tris leaned down and kissed her forehead very softly. "Now do you believe me?" she asked.

Laura stared at her, her heart suddenly pounding. "No," she said in a whisper.

Tris kissed her cheeks, so lightly that Laura could hardly feel it "Now?" she said.

"No," Laura breathed.

And Tris kissed her lips. Laura lay beneath her, too thrilled to move, only letting the lovely shock flow through her body and closing her eyes to feel it better. At last Tris moved away—only a breath away—and she said, "Now?"

"Tris…" she murmured and all the melody of suppressed passion sang in the name. Her hands went up to Tris's bare arms, over the bandeau and down that silky midriff, and then they went around Tris's waist and pulled her close and kissed her.

It was a long kiss, so leisurely, so lovely, that Laura never wanted it to end. And when it did she followed Tris, laughing, all over the bed, kissing her wherever she could reach her, feeling Tris's fine body move beneath her hands and the fire of her own longing bursting in her bosom.

Suddenly Tris got off the bed and stood looking at Laura and trying to catch her breath. "No," she said. "No! That's enough! It's late."

Laura stared at her, amazed. "What do you mean?" she asked. "Tris, come here. Come to me. Don't do this to me. Tris!"

But Tris pulled her off the bed with sudden strength.

"Tris, it's only nine-thirty," Laura said.

"Nine-thirty? Is it that late? Laura, you must excuse me." She was transformed. All the play and warmth had gone out of her.

"But—" Laura began, but Tris interrupted sharply, "Time for you to go home to Beebo." There was no smile on her face.

Laura looked at her incredulously a minute longer, her cheeks burning, and then she smoothed her clothes out with lowered eyes. She was too proud and too hurt to speak. She walked noiselessly to one of the mirrors, taking her purse with her, and ran a comb through her long hair.

She stared at herself—her flushed face and trembling fingers, her body so ready for love only moments ago and now weak with denial and outraged nerves. Two feet of unpinned hair hung down her back to remind her of Tris's admiration. But it would take five minutes to get it up again properly.

Laura looked into the mirror over her own shoulder at Tris, who was standing on one foot and then the other, bent forward slightly and obviously waiting for Laura to get out of her way. What secret activities would occupy her as soon as she got rid of Laura? Her impatience was audible in her sharp breathing. Laura dared not risk her displeasure by taking the time to wind up her hair. She simply turned and walked out of the bedroom without a backward glance, without a word.

At the front door her heart jumped when Tris called after her. Laura turned to find her running lightly across the bare studio and she waited, holding her feelings in warily.

Tris stopped at the door. "I'm sorry," she said self-consciously. "I didn't know it was so late. I have something to do tonight, it slipped my mind."

Laura looked at her haughtily. "Goodnight, Tris," was all she said. When she turned to walk down the stairs Tris added, "Say hello to your bad-tempered roommate for me."

Incensed, Laura almost ran out the door below.

Chapter Four

LAURA WALKED HOME as full of hope as of frustration and anger. Tris had treated her badly but she had treated her beautifully too. With a little start of alarm, Laura knew she was falling in love. Maybe it was worse than that already.

It was a dark soft night with no moon, only the dozens of quiet yellow streetlights. Her heels rang against the cement sidewalk as she turned down Cordelia Street and she left the world outside with regret when she opened her apartment door.

She knew Beebo would be there by now. *If only she's not drunk,* she thought to herself. "Beebo?" she called aloud. She heard a little groan from the bedroom and went toward it with a sinking feeling. *She couldn't be drunk already. She'd only been home forty-five minutes. Unless she cut work again. God forbid!*

Laura walked across the living room slowly, in no hurry to face the argument that would result if Beebo was full of whiskey and had been sitting there fuming because Laura was late. Beebo would have been phoning all over the neighborhood for her—a practice Laura abhorred but couldn't break her of. She touched her long loose hair nervously, wondering what Beebo would say when she saw it.

Laura pushed open the bedroom door. The first thing she saw was Nix—Nix, lying on the floor with his belly slit open from jaws to tail. Beside him was a crimson chef's knife. Laura recognized it from the kitchen.

She stared at him for a full ten seconds in a paralysis of horror. Then she screamed with a force she had never suspected in herself.

She turned back to the wall with her hands over her face and sobbed with all her strength. And while her face was hidden she heard another groan and knew it was Beebo, and she was too terrified even to open her eyes and look.

"Beebo?" she whispered, and her voice was rough with fear. "Beebo?"

Another sickening groan, and suddenly Beebo's voice saying confusedly, "Laura? Baby, where are you? Laura…" It faded out and Laura brought her hands away from her face quickly and looked around the room, carefully avoiding Nix. Beebo was on the bed.

Her clothes were torn—what few she still had on. Her shirt was in shreds and the jacket appeared to be ripped down the back, though she was lying on most of it and Laura couldn't be sure. She had nothing on from the waist down and there were several ugly bruises on her body. Laura felt nausea well in her. Beebo's face was not so badly hurt. There was a cut over one eye that was beginning to swell but that seemed to be all. Laura clapped her hands over her mouth and stood weaving by the bed, afraid to leave and afraid to stay, feeling the sandwiches she had just shared with Tris like a load of poison in her stomach. Until Beebo opened her eyes and looked at her.

"Laura!" she said, with such passionate relief that Laura went to her instantly and threw her arms around her and wept.

She could feel Beebo's tears on her face and she hugged her tight in a frenzy of sympathy and sorrow and whispered over and over, "Beebo, darling. Beebo, darling."

It was a long time before either of them made sense; a long time before either could speak. Laura finally raised herself on one elbow so she could see Beebo better.

"What's the matter with me?" she said softly. "I should be taking care of you. Crying isn't going to do you any good." She started to get up but Beebo caught her, and Laura was heartened to feel the strength in her arms.

"Stay with me, baby," she said, almost fiercely.

"Let me clean you up, Beebo. Let me make you comfortable. Please, sweetheart."

"Laura, I don't need anything but you. Just let me feel you lying beside me and I'll get over it somehow. I won't lose my mind. If you'll just stay with me. Please."

There were tears in her voice and rather than make her more miserable, Laura obeyed. She put her arms around Beebo and cuddled against her in a way she had almost forgotten.

"Beebo, can you talk about it, darling? Can you tell me what happened?"

"Not now. Not yet,"

"I think you ought to see a doctor. You've got some awful-looking bruises."

"You're my doctor."

"Beebo, I'm scared. I don't even know what happened to you. I want to call a doctor," she said urgently.

"I don't *need* a doctor," Beebo declared.

"Please tell me what happened," Laura pleaded. She lay at the edge of the bed, her face away from the floor and the grisly spectacle of the little dog she had never liked very well and now felt such a horrified pity for.

"It's an old story," Beebo said, her voice tired and bitter, but curiously resigned. "I don't know why it didn't happen to me years sooner. Nearly every butch I know gets it one way or another. Sooner or later they catch up with you."

"Who catches up with you?"

"The goddamn sonofabitch toughs who think it's smart to pick fights with Lesbians. They ask you who the hell do you think you are, going around in pants all the time. They say if you're going to wear pants and act like a man you can damn well fight like a man. And they jump you for laughs…God."

Her hand went up to her face, which was contorted with remembered pain and fury. After a silence of several minutes while she composed herself a little she resumed briefly, "So they jumped me. They followed me home, hollering all the way. I hollered back. I—I was pretty tight and it was pretty noisy. I should have been more careful. I shouldn't have brought them here, but I knew you wouldn't be home so soon...I didn't work today, baby." She said it guiltily, and Laura knew it meant she had spent the day at Julian's or the Cellar or one of the other homosexual bars. But she didn't condemn her or shout, "You'll lose your job!" as she would have another time. She only listened in silence.

"So anyway," Beebo said, after an awkward pause, "I came home early. About four-thirty, I guess. They just followed me in. Oh, I got in the apartment all right and slammed the door and locked it. But one of them came up the fire escape and he let the others in. Gave me this." She pointed to the cut under her eye, and Laura kissed it. "I thought I'd gotten rid of them, baby, but those bastards followed me right up here and tried to prove what men they are." She spat the words out as if they had a bad taste and then she stopped, looking at Laura to see how she was taking it. And Laura, lying next to her and holding her tight, was overwhelmed with helpless anger and pity and even a sort of love for Beebo.

Beebo felt Laura clinging to her and the flow of sympathy warmed and encouraged her. Finally she said, softly, as if the whole thing had been her fault and she was ashamed of it, "I'm not a virgin anymore, Laura. Don't ever let a man touch you." She said it vehemently, her fingers digging into the submissive girl at her side and her hurt face turned to Laura's. Laura let out a little sob and pulled closer to her.

"Beebo, darling," she said in a broken voice, "I can't stand to think of it. I can't stand to think of how it must have hurt. I know I'm a coward, I can't help it." And then, in her anxiety to heal the bitter misery of it, she blurted, "I love you, Beebo."

Beebo pulled her very close and lifted her face and kissed it delicately, almost reverently, for a very long time. At last she whispered, her lips against Laura's lips, "I adore you, Laura. You're my life. Stay with me, stay with me, don't ever leave me. I can stand this, I can stand anything, if you're with me. Swear you'll stay with me, darling."

Laura's voice stuck in her throat. She couldn't refuse. And yet she knew full well she would be swearing to a lie. It made her hide her face in painful indecision for a moment.

"Swear," Beebo demanded imperiously. "Swear, Laura!"

"I swear," Laura sobbed. She felt Beebo relax then with a sigh, running her hands through Laura's hair.

Beebo gave a faint little laugh. "I never thought anything so rotten ugly could have a good side," she murmured. "But if it's brought us back together, I'm glad it happened. It was worth it."

Laura was shocked. Beebo sounded a little unbalanced. "You can't be grateful for anything that horrible, Beebo," she protested. "You *can't,* not if you're in your right mind."

"You can if you're as much in love as I am!" Beebo said, looking at her. Laura was shamed into silence.

After a little while, Laura raised herself on an elbow. "Beebo, I'm going to call a doctor."

"You're going to do no such goddamn silly thing."

Laura lost her patience. "Now you listen to me, you stubborn idiot!" she exclaimed. "You've been badly hurt. It's just madness not to have medical help, Beebo. You know that as well as I do. Don't argue with me!" She cut Beebo off as she was about to protest. "Besides," Laura went on, "you might want to prosecute them. How could you prove anything without medical evidence?"

"*Prosecute?*" Beebo stared at her and then she gave a short, sharp laugh. "Are you kidding? Who's going to mourn for the lost virtue of a Lesbian? What lawyer is going to make a case for a poor queer gone wrong? Everybody will think I got what I deserved."

Laura stared at her, disbelieving. "Beebo," she said finally, as if she were explaining a simple fact to a slow beginner, "you don't go into court and say, 'I am a Lesbian.' You don't go to a lawyer and say it. You don't say it to *anybody,* you nut! You say, 'I'm a poor innocent girl and I was criminally assaulted and hurt and raped and I have medical proof of it and I can identify the man who did it!'"

Beebo turned on her side and laughed, and her laughter made Laura want to weep. "Not man, Bo-peep," she said when she got her breath. "*Men.* Bastards, every last one. There were four of them." Laura moaned, an involuntary sound of revulsion.

"No thanks, baby," Beebo said, her voice suddenly tired. "I've got enough trouble in the world without advertising that I'm gay. I always knew this would happen and I always knew what I'd do about it...just exactly nothing. Because there's nothing I *can* do. It's part of the crazy life I live. A sort of occupational hazard, you might say."

Laura pleaded with her. "I just want to be sure they didn't do you some awful harm you don't know about, darling!" she said. "I'm no doctor, I can't give you anything but Band-Aids and sponge baths and love."

"That's all in the world I want, baby," Beebo smiled. "I'll get well in no time."

But Laura was too genuinely frightened to let it go at that. "What if they come back?" she asked. "Then they'd get us both."

"No, they wouldn't," Beebo said and her face became hard. "Because I'd kill any man who laid a hand on you. Any man. I don't care how. I wouldn't ask any questions. I'd do it with whatever was handy—a knife or my own hands." Laura started, staring, at her. "No man will ever touch you, Laura, and live. I swear."

Laura went pale, wondering how Beebo would react to a marriage between herself and Jack; wondering how much violence she was capable of. "All right, Beebo," she said. "Will you—just tell me one thing? Why won't you see a doctor?"

Beebo turned away from her then, petulant as a child. "I haven't seen a doctor in twenty years, Bo-peep," she said.

"Why?"

Beebo sighed. "Because they might find out I'm a woman," she said quietly.

Laura covered her face with her hands and cried in silence. It was futile. Beebo *was* a woman, no matter how many pairs of pants hung in her closet, no matter how she swaggered or swore. And while she could fool some people into thinking she was a boy, there were a lot more she couldn't fool, and to them she looked foolish and rather pathetic. But Beebo was too sick to argue with. Laura was afraid of the way she talked, of the harsh way she laughed.

"We'll talk about it in the morning," she said.

"We won't talk about it at all," Beebo said, facing the wall, her back to Laura. "Where were you tonight, Laura?"

Laura swallowed convulsively before she could answer. "I was at the movies," she said.

She waited for Beebo to question her further, but there was no questioning.

"I guess I'd better wash," Beebo said. She rolled over and looked at Laura. "Do you really love me, baby?" she asked, and her eyes were deep and clouded.

"Yes," said Laura with a sad little smile, afraid to say anything else.

Beebo gazed at her for a while, returning the smile. "Thank God," she whispered, her hand caressing Laura's shoulder. And then she said, "Where's Nix?" She started to get out of bed but Laura stopped her.

"They hurt him, Beebo," she stammered.

"Hurt him? How?"

"They—darling, I don't know how to tell you—please, Beebo!" she cried in sudden fear as Beebo pushed past her. She stopped at the edge of the bed, staring with huge eyes at her little pet.

"I didn't realize—it was so bad," Beebo blurted inanely.

"He's dead," Laura whispered.

"Oh. Oh, that was too much. Too much..." Beebo stared at him, her face almost stupid with sorrow. She didn't scream as Laura had, or turn away sick. She just gaped at him for a while with Laura clinging to her and murmuring, "It's all right, darling, it's all right," because she didn't know what else to say.

Beebo got off the bed and went to him, kneeling beside the ruined little body, and picked him up in her arms.

Beebo looked at Laura with the blood running all over her and there was grief on her face. "He was just a dog," she moaned. "Such a little dog. There was nothing queer about *him*!…And he could talk, too." She almost shouted it and Laura waited, trembling, for her to move.

"He was so sweet, Laura," she said with tears coursing down her face. "You never liked him much, but he was such a good dog."

"I loved him, Beebo, he was a part of your life," Laura protested anxiously.

But Beebo ignored it. It was half a lie, spoken in affection, but still a lie. "I could always talk to him and it seemed as if he understood," Beebo said. "I know you thought I was crazy. But there were times when I had to talk to somebody and there wasn't anybody. Only Nix. I had him for seven years…since he was six weeks old." And she clutched him to her and wept and Laura looked at her, all bloodied and heartbroken, and thought, *She feels worse about the dog than about herself.*

"Now that he's gone…at least we'll have one less thing to fight about." Beebo looked very pale and odd. "Won't we, baby?" she said.

"I—I guess so," Laura said. *She's cracked!* she thought. She went into the living room then, leaving Beebo alone for a few minutes, and called Jack. He was alone.

"Jack, I don't know how to tell you. I—they raped Beebo." Her voice was low and shaky.

Jack wasn't sure whether she was kidding or not. He wasn't even sure he heard her right. "Lucky bitch," he said. "I wish they'd rape me instead. I'm never in the right place at the right time."

"I'm serious, Jack."

And when he heard the catch in her throat he believed her. "*Who* raped her, sweetheart?" he said, and the levity was dead gone from him.

"She doesn't know. Some hoods. God knows who they were."

"Did you call a doctor?"

"She won't let me!" Laura's voice rose with indignation. "Of all the nonsense I ever heard in my life! She's afraid the doctor will find out she's a female. I think we're all going crazy—" But she felt Beebo's hand then taking the phone from her, and she surrendered it without arguing and went to the couch and collapsed.

"Jack?" Beebo said. "I'm all right. It looks worse than it really is. I'll live." The front of her was sticky with Nix's blood.

"You talk like it happens all the time," Jack said with scolding sympathy. "Like getting you teeth drilled, or something."

Beebo smiled wryly. "How is it you always know just what to say to a girl, Jackson? Make her feel real swell?"

"How is it that you're such a goddamn prude you won't let a doctor examine you? The doctor doesn't give a damn what sex you are."

"They killed Nix." She threw it at him unexpectedly, silencing him about the doctor. And she described him with such detail that Laura didn't want to listen. She got up and went into the bedroom to escape the conversation.

Beebo joined Laura on the bed ten minutes later, wearing her men's cotton pajamas. Laura was too tired and weak to move. Beebo undressed her where she lay on the bed and dragged her under the covers naked.

"I don't know what to do with Nix," she said. 'I'll have to figure something out in the morning."

They lay in each other's arms, absorbed in their own thoughts. Laura's mind was a potpourri of vivid impressions. She would never forget the bloody little dog, nor the fragrant skin of the Indian dancer, nor Beebo's misery, nor those sinfully sweet kisses she stole from Tris....

"Jack's coming over tomorrow," Beebo said in her ear.

"Good."

"Why 'good'?"

"He'll help us. He'll make you see a doctor and he'll do something about Nix. I don't know, I just feel better with him around."

"If I didn't know for goddamn sure how gay you are, baby, I'd hate that guy."

Laura had to laugh. "Beebo, if you get jealous of Jack I'll send you to a head shrinker."

"Okay, okay, I know it's nuts. But you talk about him all the time."

"I'm very fond of Jack. You know that. He brought us together, darling." And she said it so gently that Beebo clasped her tighter and was reassured.

Laura slept, finally. But Beebo could not. She spent the night with her arms around Laura, taking her only comfort in Laura's nearness and the sudden apparent return of her affection.

Jack came at eight-thirty. It was a Saturday morning and he had the day to spend. With his usual detachment he wrapped Nix up while Beebo was dressing. He carted him down the stairs in a garbage pail and left him for the morning pickup in a trash bin, well hidden in a shroud of papers. When Beebo came into the kitchen a few minutes later he just said, "He's gone. Don't ask me about it, Beebo. It's all over." He found it almost as hard to talk about as she did.

"Damn you, Jack," Beebo said feebly. But she was glad he had done it for her. She felt lousy. All the excitement and anger that had sustained her the night before were gone, leaving a lassitude and nausea that swept over her in waves.

Laura made her go back to bed and fed her breakfast from a tray.

"Don't leave me, baby," Beebo begged and Laura promised to stay near by. But as soon as Beebo had swallowed a little food and kept it down, she fell asleep, and Jack pulled Laura to her feet and dragged her, whispering protests, into the kitchen.

"How can I talk to you in there?" he demanded and fixed them both some coffee.

Laura drank in silence, listening to his rambling talk with one ear, gratefully. She thought of Tris and wondered whether to confess to Jack about the dancer or keep it a secret. She knew he wouldn't like it.

"Beebo acted kind of crazy last night," Laura said. "I think she felt worse about Nix than about herself."

"No doubt she did. But pretty soon she'll feel her own aches and pains. Maybe I can find her another hound somewhere. I just hope to God she doesn't use this thing to make a prisoner of you, Mother."

"A prisoner?"

"She was getting pretty desperate about you, you know. I think that has a lot to do with all the drinking."

Laura realized then that he didn't put a shot of booze in his coffee. "You're still on the wagon!" she said.

He swirled his coffee reflectively. "I remember," he said, "when Terry was giving me the works a few months back. I nearly drank myself to extinction. Beebo's not above trying it herself."

"Oh, God, that was awful!" Laura said, remembering Terry.

Terry had been enough to drive a strong man mad. If he had been nasty about it Jack could have stood it better. He could have preserved his self-respect and he might have had the strength to kick Terry out sooner than he did. But Terry was nice. He was delightful and cooperative. He was unfaithful, he was taking every cent Jack made as Jack made it, and he was hardly ever home.

But Jack was in love with him; angrily in love with the wrong person, sticking to a doomed attachment as if every new shock and every unexpected pain only strengthened his need for the boy.

Jack knew it was hopeless. He knew it was draining his strength and making a coward of him. In his mind the whole sad farce of the thing was perfectly clear. But he acted on his emotions in spite of himself, and as long as Terry loved him he couldn't let him go.

Curiously enough, Terry did love him. Jack was home base to him; Jack was security. Jack paid the bills and bolstered him when he was low, and no matter how rough and rotten the rest of the world might get, good old Jack was always there, always the same.

But the end had to come. There was never enough money, there was never enough understanding, there was never enough of the right kind of love. It took just one sharp explosion of acid resentment one night, when Jack caught Terry cheating after two years of bitter suspicions, to blow them apart. It was almost too painful to think about afterwards.

It was over now, of course. Terry was gone. But the ache for him and the loneliness, even the desire to be tormented remained.

"You never heard from Terry, did you?" Laura asked.

"No. He took his things and left and I haven't heard from him since. Makes me think he must have left New York."

"Do you still want him?" She asked it not to hurt him but because she knew he had to say it now and then or die of it.

"Of course I want him," he said briefly. "Drink your coffee. Your patient is howling for attention."

Chapter Five

THREE WEEKS, Laura wrote in her diary, sitting in the living room while Beebo slept. *Three weeks of this, and if it goes on much longer I'll end up hating her. I felt so sorry for her at first. It was such a cruel thing and it hurt her terribly. But she's well now—I know she is. She's lying around getting fat and drinking like a fish and not working. If she doesn't get back to work soon I'll lose my mind. And she'll lose her job for sure. They've been calling all week.*

Laura hadn't minded being a nurse at first. She tended Beebo gently and made her rest and, being unsure herself and hounded by her patient to forget it, she never did call a doctor. But Beebo seemed to come out of it fast. Physically the scars healed quickly. At the end of a week she was up and around. She hadn't had a drink since the day it happened, and she talked about going back to work the next Monday.

But then Laura came home late one evening and she found Beebo drunk.

"Where the hell have you been?" Beebo shouted at her when Laura came in and found her in the kitchen. "I'm sick and miserable, I've just been through hell, and you can't even come home from work to make my dinner for me."

Confronted with such a bombardment of nonsense, Laura wouldn't even answer her. She undressed and took a shower, but Beebo followed her into the bathroom and went right on yelling. Laura had pulled the shower curtain but Beebo opened it and watched her bathe.

"Laura," she said, "where were you?" No answer. "Tell me. Tell me, damn it!" It was an order.

"Ask me like a civilized human being, then," Laura said, turning around to rinse her soapy back.

"I'll ask you any way I goddamn please. I have a right to know."

Laura turned the water off and eyed her coldly. "I had dinner with Jack," she said. "He dropped in after work."

"I don't believe you."

"Call him." She stepped out of her bath, cool and dripping and haughty as a princess, and Beebo burned for her.

"I don't believe a word he says. He always lies for you. No matter what I ask him he's always got an answer. I used to like the guy, but Jesus, it's gotten so I can't trust him anymore. He's always on your side."

Laura wrapped herself in a towel and began to rub herself, but Beebo suddenly put her whiskey down and clasped her in a bear hug.

"Laura, darling, I felt so rotten today. And I looked forward so much to having you home. It's so quiet and lonesome around here all day without Nix. I nearly go mad. Baby, I know I've taken up a lot of your time, but I couldn't help it. I didn't *ask* those bastards to rape me."

Laura relaxed slightly in the embrace, since she couldn't squirm out of it. "You felt better today, not worse, Beebo. You told me so this morning."

"That was this morning. I got worse this afternoon," she said petulantly.

"You got worse at exactly five-thirty when I was fifteen minutes late."

"Where *were* you?"

"With Jack. Beebo, you've been drinking. You promised me you wouldn't."

"If you'd been home I wouldn't have to!" Beebo released her abruptly, picked up the whiskey glass with a swoop of her hand, and defiantly finished what was in it.

Laura cinched the towel around herself and approached Beebo. "Do you know what you're saying, you nut?" she said. "You big fool? Beebo, answer me!" But Beebo turned her back and watched Laura with glittering eyes in the mirror on the medicine chest.

"You're saying that you can't stay sober without me, Beebo. Do you realize that?"

"I can't stay sober if you don't love me, Laura."

"Oh, damn you, Beebo!" Laura almost wept with frustration. "You're only saying that to make me feel guilty. To put the blame on *me* instead of on yourself where it belongs! I didn't give you your first drink, God knows. I don't ply you with liquor. You've fixed it with your conscience so no matter when you get drunk it's my fault No matter how much you drink, you're only drinking because Laura is such a bitch. Well, I won't buy it! It's a damn plot to make a prisoner of me!"

"A prisoner! Now where did little Bo-peep get that fancy idea?" Beebo's eyes were narrow and sharp in spite of the whiskey. Her anger brought clarity with it. "That sounds like the kind of propaganda Jack would spout."

"No—" Laura began, but Beebo silenced her with a menacing wave of her hand. Laura found herself trapped against the bathroom door.

Beebo put a hand up on the door on either side of Laura and looked down at her. "Now, suppose you just tell me what Jack said," she said.

"What makes you think Jack said it? I can think for myself and you know it, And I *am* a prisoner here!"

"You can't think for yourself when Jack's around. That bastard is the Pied Piper of Greenwich Village. He opens his yap and all the little fairies listen popeyed to whatever he has to say. Including you."

Laura looked at her and found herself caught by Beebo's spell again. Beebo was born to lose her temper. She looked wonderful when she did. It exasperated Laura to feel a bare animal desire for her at times like this.

"Jack said it. Come on. Jack said it, didn't he?" Beebo insisted.

"All right!" Laura almost screamed. "Jack said it!"

She looked up at Beebo with embarrassed desire and to make her shame complete, Beebo saw it. And she knew she was in command again, even if only for an hour or so. Beebo was learning to live for those hours. The rest of the time nothing much mattered.

Beebo shifted support of her leaning body from her arms to Laura, lifted up Laura's angry helpless face and kissed it. "Why aren't you like this all the time?" she asked. And Laura startled her when she echoed, "Why aren't *you* like this all the time?"

"Like what, baby? Drunk?"

"No…," Laura hesitated. She didn't quite understand what she meant herself.

"Mad?" Beebo asked.

"I don't know."

Beebo laughed. "If it'll help I'll get mad and stay mad, Bo-peep. I'll get drunk and stay drunk. Would you like that?" She interspersed her words with kisses.

"No. I just—I hate it when you act like a spoiled brat, Beebo."

"I never act like a spoiled brat." Her voice was little more than a whisper now.

They sank to the floor where they were and made love then.

And even after Laura had finally fallen asleep, in her arms, Beebo felt a tide of renewed passion. She caressed Laura's hair and back with her hands and thought, *If it can be this good it's not over.*

Laura had left work meaning to go straight home. But as before she hadn't gone far when she knew she was headed for Tris's little studio.

Tris opened the door herself. She had evidently been practicing for she was dressed in tights and breathing hard. Her black hair was smoothed over her head, caught in back with a clasp and braided. The braid, heavy and shining, hung halfway down her back and swung like a whip when she whirled.

Tris paused for a moment when she saw Laura on her threshold and for an awful second Laura thought she might turn her away. But Tris smiled suddenly and said, "Laura. How nice. Please come in."

"I just dropped by to say hello," Laura apologized.

"That is not all, I hope?" Tris said, looking at her.

Laura felt an odd little twist of excitement. "Well...I shouldn't stay. I don't want to interrupt your work."

"Of course you do. That's why you came," Tris said, spinning reflectively in place, her weight shifting delicately to pull her around and around.

Laura didn't know if she was being scolded or teased, if she should leave or stay. Tris stopped twirling and said, "I'm glad you came. I didn't want to work any more anyway."

Laura hesitated, wondering whether to believe her. But when Tris walked across the room to her and kissed her cheek she melted suddenly with pleasure. She stood quietly and let herself be kissed, afraid to return the compliment. She was very unsure of herself with Tris. Even the gentlest gesture seemed to irritate the dancer sometimes. Laura could only let her take the lead.

Tris turned away abruptly, her mood shifting. "Well, now you are here," she said in her careful English. "What would you like to do?" It was a sort of challenge.

"I—I'd like to see you dance, Tris. Would you dance for me?"

"No." She was pouting. "You are my excuse for not dancing any more today, Laura."

"Maybe we could just talk for a little while, then."

"We could...but we won't."

Laura was at a loss for words. She stammered a little and finally she blurted, "I think you'd rather have me go home."

"I think Beebo would like you home more than I would. She doesn't let you out very often, does she?"

Laura colored. "She's not my jailkeeper," she said.

"I don't like this—this interference you force me to make in your love affair, Laura," Tris said and surprised her guest. "I don't know your Beebo, but I have nothing against her. Still, I do not imagine she will like *me* very well if she finds out you are my guest now and then."

"What do you care whether Beebo likes you or not?" Laura demanded, startled.

Tris broke into a charming smile then, as if to placate her visitor. "I want everybody to like me," she said. "I suppose it is a compulsion left from my childhood." And, as if she had made a guilty admission, she turned away abruptly saying, "Let's go into the kitchen. If I stand in here I will feel obliged to dance."

Laura followed her and sat down self-consciously. Tris fixed a plate of cookies and gave her a glass of milk. She smiled.

"I am hard to know, Laura. I am not very gracious. But I like your company." Her smile was as warm and luscious as ripe fruit in the sun.

They finished the food over small talk about men. Laura was lost, silent. She just nodded agreement and listened with dismay. *She's trying to tell me she doesn't like girls,* she thought. *But it's a lie!*

Tris rinsed the plates, watching herself all the while in one mirror or another. It was as if she felt herself on exhibition all the time, as if all those mirrors were scattered around to remind her of her own beauty.

Tris dried her hands and turned to face Laura. There was an awkward pause and Laura realized suddenly that she was supposed to get up and leave. They had had their small talk. She had been served food. That was all she could reasonably expect from her hostess, especially since she was an uninvited guest. She felt her heart contract a little in disappointment, and she thought with a flash of yearning of the intimacies of her last visit.

But she was too proud to overstay her welcome, especially after the way Tris had shown her the door last time. So she got up and said, "Thanks Tris. I have to go."

"Oh?" It was merely polite.

"Beebo's expecting me."

"I see." No protest. Tris followed her toward the front door. "Ask me over to your apartment sometime, Laura. You would make a much nicer hostess than I. Besides, I should like to see how your big roommate looks in pants. She does wear pants?"

"Yes, she does." Laura turned to look at her curiously. "But she's a jealous hellion."

Tris leaned on the wall by the door, crossing her feet at the ankles.

"Does she know you have been here to visit me?" Her smile was sly, interested.

"No. I don't think she even remembers you," Laura said shortly.

"Ah! Flattering. Do you think it's wise to make a secret of our friendship, Laura?"

"It's either that or get my neck broken," Laura said.

Tris laughed a little, as if the idea of such hard play amused her. "Laura...would you like to stay a little longer?" she said. Her voice made it sound very inviting.

"I can't." Laura was upset by all the talk of Beebo.

"As long as you leave by eight it would be all right," Tris said. "I have a date at eight."

"With a man?"

"Certainly with a man. I have no secrets, Laura. I do not like to cheat, like you. You cheat with your Beebo by seeing me. But still—" she hunched her shoulders and smiled—"I like you. You like me. Perhaps it is worth the risk. You are the one who will get your neck broken, not me. I have no right to deny you your pain."

Laura frowned at her. It was an odd thing to say. Tris put her hands on Laura's arms and they stood that way, silent, for a moment.

At last Tris said, "Dance with me."

"I don't know how," Laura said shyly.

"I am a teacher. I teach you. Come on."

"I'm so clumsy, Tris."

But Tris pulled her to the middle of the studio and put a record on. She stood for a minute in front of Laura as if trying to make up her mind where to grasp her, how to start. Laura felt impossibly awkward. But Tris made up her mind quickly and slipped her arms around Laura's neck. Laura was two inches taller than she and Tris was obliged to look up at her when she spoke. "We will just do it like the teenagers!" she said. "There is nothing to it really. Stand in one place and shift your weight from one foot to the other, with the beat. That's it. You've got it. That's a good beginning."

Laura couldn't help laughing. "Even *I* can do that much," she said.

"Ah. Then there is hope. Next year at this time you will do the *tour jeté*."

Laura had her arms around Tris at the waist and they swayed gently to the music, and suddenly all her suspicion and embarrassment faded. She became conscious of the tantalizing jasmine that emanated from Tris—from her throat and her hair and her breasts, barely covered by the bandeau. The black braid moved softly against Laura's bare arms in back and Tris put her cheek against Laura's, tilting her face up. Her lips were near Laura's ear and she whispered, "You know, Laura, I must tell you something. You are a homosexual. Yes?"

Laura swallowed. "Yes," she said.

"You should know then...I am not. Not like you. I like the company of girls, yes. My dance pupils. Friends. But I love men. I love them. Do you understand?"

"No." Laura shut her eyes and pulled Tris a little tighter. "Well, then, I will explain. Men excite me. All men, I mean. The idea of men...It is hard to say. But I would rather be with a man than with a woman. But now and then I meet a woman who interests me. And sometimes the interest goes beyond just talk. You see?"

"No."

"Sometimes I want to kiss her. Or be close to her. But that is all. Now do you see?"

"No."

Tris gave an impatient little sigh. "I am telling you I am not queer like you!" she said sharply and Laura winced with sudden pain. Tris felt it and she amended quickly, "That is an unkind word. You people call it gay. All right. I am not gay. I like you, I like to talk to you and watch you move and sometimes I am moved myself to kiss you or be close to you, like this. Our bodies like this, all up and down. You see? But I don't like to go any farther. Not with a girl. You are only the third girl I have felt this for. It will not happen again for a long time. Perhaps I will marry soon, and then it will never happen again."

"Marry! Who? An Indian?"

"No!" she exclaimed almost contemptuously. "Another. He is *white.*"

"You're full of contradictions, Tris," Laura said, looking down at her in bewilderment. "You said you were gay and you married a gay boy."

"Oh, yes. I did, didn't I?" She looked trapped. "Well, I thought I was then. But I know now—positively—I am not."

"But you said—"

"Such wonderful blond hair you have, Laura. I would give anything for such hair. Why do you always wear it wound up like that?" And she began to slip pins out of the bun, letting them drop to the polished floor, until the coil of gold came loose and Tris gave a delighted, "Ah!"

Laura felt the thrill go through her hard. She forgot her protests about Tris's sex drive and pulled the dancer very close to kiss her full on the mouth. Tris yielded. With one accord they stopped dancing and just clung and kissed, swaying slightly. It lasted for long minutes—just kisses, soft and exploratory, but careful. Laura wondered vaguely, through the fog of lovely sensations, what miserable devil prompted this delectable girl to deny her Lesbian impulses. For Laura could tell that Tris enjoyed this love play as much as she. She encouraged it, even when Laura tried to stop, and pulled her back for more.

By eight o'clock they were lying on the big red silk couch in the bedroom, murmuring inanities to each other, discovering one another's bodies and emotions through twin shields of clothes and caution.

"Will you come and see me again?" Tris asked.

"Are you inviting me?"

"Of course."

"When would it be convenient?" She said it in clipped English, like the English Tris spoke, to tease her.

"It is never convenient. But come anyway."

Laura laughed. "When?"

"Tomorrow."

"No date tomorrow?"

"Yes. Every night."

"Save a night for me, Tris."

Tris gazed at her for a moment before she answered, "No."

"Why not?"

"We do too much in these few short hours. What would we do with a whole night? I do not like to think."

"I think of it all the time. I can't think of anything else."

"Ah, that is a very bad sign. I am sorry to hear you say that. You must not fall in love with me, Laura."

"I'll try to remember," she said sarcastically.

"I am serious," Tris said.

Laura didn't answer her. She lay on her back and looked up at the small skylight directly over the bed. It was a square of violet— the last shade of fading day.

"I do not want you to fall in love with me, Laura," Tris persisted.

"I hear you," Laura said quietly.

"Well, why don't you answer?"

"I don't know how to answer, Tris," she said, turning to look at her in the semi-gloom of the bedroom.

"What are your feelings for me?"

"Do you want a blueprint?" Laura said, hurt. "I can't spell them out for you. I don't understand them myself." But she understood them all too well. She had felt these pangs before for other girls— only two or three, including Beebo, but enough to make them familiar and unwelcome. But still exciting and irresistible.

Tris lay beside her, quiet for a while, and finally she said, "Do you know why I was not very glad to see you at first today?"

"No." Laura reached across the bed to put a hand on Tris's breasts, to feel what she could not see in the gathering darkness.

"I was afraid," Tris whispered. "Of my own feelings. I do not like to become involved with women. It has always been unpleasant for me."

"Do you still want me to come back and see you?"

"Yes." She paused and Laura sensed a smile. "As long as I ask you to come back, Laura, you will know you are safe with me."

"Safe?"

"I will put it another way. If a day comes when I do *not* want to see you, it will be because I am in love with you. And that will be the end. From that day on we will never meet again, until I am cured."

Laura had to smile. Who could take such a charming speech seriously? "All right," she murmured and embraced the lovely dancer.

"Now you must go," Tris told her. "My date will be here soon. He is always prompt."

Laura got up without protest. But it was sweet to take the time to wind up her hair and know she was welcome. "Did you kick me out for the same boy last time?" she asked.

Tris had turned a light on and they watched each other in the mirror before which Laura was combing her hair.

"No. Another."

"I hate him," Laura said with a little smile. "And the rest of them."

Tris gazed at her coolly. "How very foolish," she said. And made Laura laugh.

They parted with a chaste kiss, and for the first time since they had met Laura felt as if she had a slim chance with this odd and irresistible girl who was still so much a stranger to her. She went home to her angry Beebo, her body tense with need. And later, when Beebo demanded her body, Laura surrendered promptly and helplessly.

Beebo, since the night of her attack, had become unbearably suspicious. Everything Laura did, everywhere she went, had to be reported in detail. She called Tris once or twice from work and Tris had bawled her out for not showing up. Laura was more pleased than sorry when Tris sounded jealous—while she bridled angrily at Beebo's jealousy, she was thrilled with Tris's.

Laura had strong doubts about Beebo's illness now. She could have gone to work weeks ago. The bruises were nearly invisible; only a pale yellow shadow stained the spot where the worst had been. Beebo was using it as an excuse to sit around another week and take it easy and drink and bitch over the phone to Lili about her problems.

"I always hated that damn elevator," she declared with her feet up on the coffee table in the living room and a drink in her hand.

"You make me sick!" Laura told her. "You're *well.* Get up and go to work."

Beebo looked at her watch. "At six-thirty in the evening?" she said, and laughed.

"I'm not going to support us both, Beebo," Laura said. "And I'm sick and tired of playing nursemaid."

To her diary Laura confided, *I am in love. I'm sure of it. The more I'm with Beebo the more I want Tris. Oh, God, how much I want her!*

Laura was desperate after two more weeks of Beebo. Beebo drove her frantic when they were cooped up together in the small apartment, as they were every night. And Beebo was wild for the love Laura denied her. The attack she had endured seemed to have touched off a burning core of violence in her that never went out.

When Beebo found the small steel strongbox on the closet floor with Laura's diary inside, she pounded it with a stone to get it open but the lock didn't break. When Laura got home from work and found the battered box on the coffee table in the living room she went pale with alarm, and Beebo, who was lying in wait for her reaction, exclaimed, "Damn it, I knew it. You sure as hell look guilty, Laura. What's in it?" She kicked the box.

"Nothing." Laura walked across the room but her legs felt weak.

"Open it, then."

"No."

"Where's the key?"

"I don't know."

"It's your box, goddamn it. You know where the key is! Why did you hide it from me? What are you ashamed of?"

"I'm under no obligation to show you everything I own!" Laura said frostily. "I'll hide what I please."

"You tell me what's in it," Beebo threatened, "or I'll choke you. I swear I'll choke you, you bitch." She slammed Laura against the wall with one hand to her throat.

Laura gasped in panic. There was only one thing to do with Beebo in these moods and that was go along with her, stall, anything but resist her. That was too painful and Laura even feared that one of these days, with Beebo as crazy as she was, it might be fatal.

"All right," Laura said through a tight throat. "Let me go." She rummaged for the key for ten minutes, knowing all the while that it was in the wallet in her purse.

"Don't tell me you can't find it," Beebo said, watching her through narrowed eyes.

"I almost never use the thing," Laura said as calmly as she could.

"You find it," Beebo said. And something in the tone of her voice made Laura very frightened. *I'm getting out of here,* she thought to herself suddenly. *If I can just get out of this somehow I'll leave her tonight and I won't come back. I'll go to Jack's.*

She turned and faced Beebo, desperate. "Beebo, it's just some personal papers. It's nothing you'd be interested in."

"It's exactly what I'd be interested in. I'd be even more interested in why you went white as a sheet when you saw I had it. Explain *that* to me, Bo-peep."

Laura pressed her teeth together in a small grimace of

exasperation. "It's my birth certificate and my baptism certificate and two insurance policies and some old love letters," she said.

"Love letters from who?" Beebo demanded.

"Beth."

Beebo put her head back and laughed. "Oh!" she said. "Beth! Good old Beth. Your college flame. I'm getting so I *know* that goddamn girl."

"She was a lot more—" Laura began, her cheeks hot. She couldn't bear to hear Beth laughed at, to hear that perfect love ridiculed.

"I know what she was," Beebo said acidly. "She was beautiful. She was bright. She was a queen on the campus and a devil in bed. She was a success. She even liked men, the traitorous bitch. She was so gorgeous and so intelligent and so everything that she could do whatever she damn well pleased—even dump you like a sack of bricks. She loved you so much she got you kicked out of school and got married. To a *man.*" Beebo grinned at her, waiting for Laura to explode. But Laura only glared, too proud to spoil that memory with an ugly spat

"Queen Beth was everything Beebo is not," Beebo said. "You'll never learn, will you? Love isn't pure roses and romance, Laura. You can't live with a girl, however much you love her, and still faint with joy every time she looks your way. It's a shame you never lived with Beth like you have with me. You'd find out fast enough she is a human being, not a goddess…Now, show me the letters."

"Why do you want to read a bunch of miserable old letters?" Laura said, angry that she had to beg. "That's all over, Beebo. It can't do anything but hurt you."

"I'm used to that, Laura. Anybody who lives with you has to be."

"You lie!" Laura flared suddenly. They gazed at each other in electric silence for a minute. Then Laura said quietly, in a move to restore her safety, "Let me fill your glass." She came to take it from her but Beebo held it away. "What are you trying to do, baby, get me drunk? Let's see the letters."

Laura sat down on the bed beside her. Maybe she could

sweet-talk her out of the box. "Beebo," she said. "There's nothing in there you could possibly want to see or be interested in. Will you believe me?"

Beebo looked at her coldly and didn't move. "The letters," she said and held out a hand.

Laura sighed. "After dinner," she begged. "Let's at least eat in peace." And before Beebo could answer she leaned over and kissed her lips. "I love you, Beebo," she said, very softly and hopefully. And there were still times when she wondered if she might not speak the truth. But this wasn't one of them. She spoke out of the need to save her skin.

Beebo swallowed the last of the drink. "Yeah," she said. "The letters."

Laura kissed her again. Beebo submitted to it without returning the kiss. "You're not very subtle, Bo-peep," she said.

"I just want a stay of execution," Laura said with a wry smile. "If we have to yell at each other, let's save it till after dinner. Please, darling. The box won't walk away." And Beebo, in spite of the obviousness of it, in spite of her own better sense and Laura's flagrant flattery, weakened.

"Are they that bad?" she asked. "The goddamn letters from Beth the Beautiful?"

"They're just love letters. They're old and stale and the affair is old and stale. It's over and done with."

"Like our affair?" And Beebo said it so simply, without the histrionics and the swearing and the noisy misery she usually showered on Laura, that Laura was touched. She put her forehead down on Beebo's shoulder and whispered, "I don't know, Beebo. You scare me so sometimes I swear I'll move out of here and run like hell and never come back. Sometimes I really think you mean to kill me."

"Sometimes I really do," Beebo said and her voice was rough. "If I did, I'd kill myself right afterwards, darling."

"A lot of good that would do me!" Laura exploded. But she

softened when Beebo's face went dark. "You don't mean that, Beebo. You'd never really do it...would you?"

"I don't know," Beebo said, staring at her. "I've come close to it, baby. I've come close..."

"If you really love me, you couldn't."

"I really love you. But there are times when I don't think I could stop myself." Her eyes filled suddenly with tears and she looked away, at the wall. "Things that would hurt too much."

"Like what?"

"Like finding out you were cheating on me."

Laura shut her eyes and felt the sweat break out on her face. *But I haven't really cheated with Tris,* she told herself. *We never went all the way. I don't think we ever will.* "Don't be silly," she told Beebo. "Who is there for me to cheat on you with? *Nobody.*"

"Jack."

"Jack?" Laura straightened up, astonished. "He's a man!"

"Sure he's a man. I know what he is."

Laura took Beebo's face in her hands and said, "I promise you I have never cheated with Jack or anybody else. I *swear,* Beebo. You think I have but I haven't. You just make it up."

"Do I just make it up that I love you more than you love me?"

Laura hung her head. "Let's shout about it after dinner," she said.

"Okay." Unexpectedly Beebo surrendered and Laura escaped to the kitchen with an audible sigh of relief.

They ate in near-silence, Laura concentrating on her plate and Beebo concentrating on Laura. They were almost finished with the gloomy little meal when there came a ring of the doorbell and Laura, without knowing why, felt a sudden start of fear.

"Who's that?" Beebo demanded.

"I don't know." Laura didn't even want to look at her. "Probably Jack. Or your darling Lili."

"Oh, Christ, I couldn't stand to see either of them right now. Lili would love to hear us quarrel."

"Let's disappoint her, then," Laura said and they smiled a little at each other. Laura was surprised at the strength of her relief. But when Beebo got up to ring the buzzer that opened the door below, the strange fear returned.

Far away downstairs she heard the front door open. Laura sat in uneasy silence in the kitchen, listening to the steps coming up the stairs out in the hall. She could picture Beebo leaning against the doorjamb, waiting for the knock. More than once she had begged Beebo to be cautious opening that door. She had nightmares about the hoodlums that raped Beebo coming back to try it again—and getting Laura too this time. But Beebo shrugged it off.

"They won't be back," she had said.

"How do *you* know?"

"I know," was the cryptic answer, and that was all Laura could get out of her.

Laura found herself staring into her milk glass and whispering a prayer: *Let it be Jack. Please, dear God. I need him.*

The knock came. Beebo opened the door. There was a moment of silence and then the sound of a sweet feminine voice using a very dainty English. It was Tris!

Laura froze in a panic. For one frightened second she thought of climbing down the fire escape. And then she put her glass down with trembling hands and poised herself, tense with the near-hysterical force piling up inside her.

Suddenly Beebo said, "Well, I'll be goddamned. Hey, Laura! It's our little Indian buddy. From Peck and Peck. Come on in, sweetheart."

"Thank you," Tris said.

Laura held her breath. Beebo's friendliness would last just as long as it took her to start wondering what Tris was doing there and how she found the place. Laura could have slapped Tris. She hardly dared go in the living room and face them both.

Beebo called her. "Get in here, baby. Make like a hostess, for God's sake. How'd you find us?' she said, her voice lowering as she turned to Tris.

"I ran into Laura at the Hobby Shop," Tris said. "I was looking for a gift."

"Find one?" Beebo settled down on the couch, appraising Tris's slim smooth body with a cool and practiced eye. Laura saw the glance as she stood in the kitchen doorway. She disliked the way Tris let herself be admired.

"Hello, Laura," Tris said, almost shyly.

"Hello, Tris." Laura wanted Beebo to stop looking at that warm brown body, lightly sheathed in silk. Her eyes snapped angrily at Tris, and Tris saw it. "Sit down," Laura said.

"So...," Beebo mused, her eyes half-closed and calculating. "You discovered Laura in the Hobby Shop and got chummy, hm?"

"She told me where you live," Tris said, turning to her with an ingratiating smile. "It's not far from me. She said to come over sometime, so here I am. Perhaps I come at a bad time?" She looked from one to the other.

"Any time is a bad time in this little love nest," Beebo said. She thumbed at Laura. "We hate each other," she explained. "We only live together so we can fight."

"Oh." Tris looked uncomfortable.

Beebo grinned at the two girls, pleased to have embarrassed them both, her mind simmering with suspicions. Laura, stony-faced, refused to say anything to Tris to put her at ease. She was furious with her for coming in the first place.

"What's your name, honey?" Beebo said to Tris. "I've forgotten."

"Tris Robischon."

"Didn't you say you were Indian or something?"

"Yes."

Beebo laughed and shook her head. "Yeah...," she said. "Indian."

Tris began to squirm under her gaze. She was no longer so pleased to be looked at as she had been when she entered. Beebo stared so hard, in fact, that Tris finally said coldly, "Perhaps you object to dark skins."

"So what if I do?" Beebo said casually, grinning.

Tris gasped. "Some people," she said sharply, "think all non-whites are inferior. Perhaps you are one of those?"

"Now what gives you a dumb idea like that?" Beebo said. "Do I look unfriendly?"

"You stare at me as if I were not welcome."

"I stare at you as if you were a damn pretty girl. Which you are. You're also too sensitive, but you're welcome. I like that color." She waved at Tris's shapely legs, crossed at the knees and poised on high-heeled shoes. "On you it looks good." And she grinned. There was an awkward pause and Laura saw, with great irritation, that Tris was simply returning Beebo's gaze now, bashfully but rather eagerly.

"Have some coffee, Tris?" Laura said.

"Yes, please." Tris looked at her swiftly, as if she knew Laura didn't like her interest in Beebo.

"What do you do with yourself all day, Tris?" Beebo said. Laura was afraid of the way her voice sounded now.

"I dance."

"Where?"

"My studio. I teach."

"That all?"

"I—I have done professional work."

They talked for a few minutes until Laura brought the coffee in. She gave Tris a cup and placed one in front of Beebo. But Beebo reached out and collared her with one long arm and pulled her down on the couch beside her.

"Let go!" Laura snapped, but Beebo only held her harder.

"So you...just ran into Laura in the Hobby Shop," Beebo said to Tris. "Fancy that." She smiled a dangerous smile.

"Yes. It's not so surprising. I mean I—I live so close by." Laura felt her fear rising in her throat and sweat bursting from her and she was desperately impatient to get rid of Tris.

"You know something, little Indian girl?" Beebo said.

"What?"

"I don't believe you."

The atmosphere became tense and ominous. "I apologize for her, Tris," Laura said with a show of casualness. "She doesn't believe anything."

"Now tell me, Tris," Beebo said, ignoring her, "how did you and Laura really meet?"

Tris looked squarely at her and said, "You know how. I have told the truth." She lied very gracefully. Laura wondered how many lies she had been fed herself. "But I see I am not welcome here," Tris went on. She stood up and replaced her coffee cup carefully in the saucer on the table. "Thank you for the coffee," she said regally and headed for the front door.

Beebo sprang up from the couch suddenly and Laura, frightened, followed her with almost the same movement. Beebo caught Tris at the door and turned her around and without even a pause for breath kissed her harshly on the mouth. It was a long and physically painful kiss, and Laura's furious exclamations did nothing to help. She pounded ineffectually on Beebo's back. "Beebo, stop it!" she cried.

But Beebo stopped in her own good time, and that was not until she had bruised Tris's mouth enough to make her cry.

She cried softly, without a sound, her eyes shut and her head back against the door, still lifted toward Beebo.

Laura was shaken. "Tris—Tris—" she said, trying to get near her, but Beebo shouldered her out of the way.

"That's for being such a good friend of Laura's," Beebo said. "And that's all you get, too, my little Indian. Now get the hell out and don't come back."

"Beebo, please!" Laura felt her own angry tears start up, and it was unbearable to have Tris turn and leave so quickly, so quietly, without giving her a gesture of comfort or apology. "Tris, I'm so sorry!" she called after her, but it sounded trite and insincere.

Beebo shut the door and stood for a moment with her back to Laura. Laura, shaking, moved away from her.

"Where did you meet her?" Beebo asked, still not looking at her. "Tell the truth, Laura."

"At work."

Beebo whirled around. "How long are you going to lie to me!" she said.

"This is the last time!" Laura exploded, throwing her caution out with her patience. "I'm leaving you, Beebo. I've had it. You make me sick. You're ruining my life. I'm so damn scared and so damn miserable that nothing is any fun, nothing helps. Life isn't worth living, not like this!"

"Where did you meet her?" Beebo said, with single-minded jealous fury.

"I went to her apartment!" Laura blazed at her. "I went back for her card and I went to her apartment."

"And made love to her."

"No!" She shouted it angrily at first, but then she repeated it, frightened, "No, Beebo! I swear!"

But Beebo came across the room in one sudden leap of rage and threw her down hard on the floor, her big hands on Laura's slim shoulders, holding her cruelly and banging her head down again and again until Laura screamed with pan and terror. And then Beebo dropped her and slapped her and all the time she kept repeating like a mad woman, "You made love to her, love to her. Where's that key? The *key,* damn it!"

"I'll give it to you," Laura sobbed at last. "Oh, God, Beebo, don't kill me! I'll give it to you."

Beebo let her up then, or rather, dragged her to her feet. Laura stood beside her, swaying and dizzy, her eyes blurred by tears and her head aching. She went into the bedroom, shoving Beebo's hands away from her with sharp gestures of hatred, her teeth clenched. And she opened her purse and pulled out her wallet and gave Beebo the key.

Beebo snatched it from her and picked up the box like a miser going after a cache of gold. And Laura, seeing her chance, grabbed the purse and a sweater that hung on the back of a chair and backed silently out of the bedroom. She fled, on feet made feather-light with fear, to the front door. She ran down the stairs with all the speed her fear could muster and ran all the way—two blocks—to Seventh Avenue.

After a few frantic moments of scanning the street and looking back over her shoulder she hailed a cab and climbed in, crying audibly. "Drive uptown," she told the man. "Just drive uptown for a few minutes."

"Okay," he said, giving her a quick, cynical once over.

Laura looked up and saw Beebo rush into Fourth Street as the cab turned around and headed north, and she sank down in the back seat, her hands over her face. She let him drive her almost to Times Square before she could control her sobs and give him Jack's address.

What if Beebo's already there? she wondered suddenly. *Oh, God!* She would be, of course. But Jack would save her somehow. Better to be with him, even if it meant facing Beebo again.

Chapter Six

LAURA WAS RIGHT. Beebo went straight to Jack's apartment. She stormed in and beat noisily on his door until he opened it.

"Christ in the foothills!" he exclaimed, pulling on the door and looking into her wild furious face. She entered and slammed it behind her.

"She'll be over here in a few minutes," Beebo said wildly, waving the diary at him. "I haven't read much of this but I've read enough to know what a bitch she is. And you—you—" For once in her life Beebo was at a loss for words; "You lousy crawling scum sonofabitch, you've been egging her on! You've been putting ideas into her head—about leaving me."

She ranted hysterically at him, and Jack, although Laura had never described her diary to him, began to get the idea in a hurry.

"Where is she now?" he said quietly when he could get a word in edgewise.

"I don't know, but she'll be here before long. Whenever we have a quarrel she drags her can over here as fast as she can move. You're her father confessor, her lover by proxy. She tells you everything. She only lives with me." She spat it at him enviously. "I'm her lover for good and real but I'm not good enough to know what she thinks or what she does. She saves that for you. I'll kill her! By God, I will."

"Scram, Beebo," Jack said. His low voice was in sharp contrast to her own, loud and hard with wrath.

"What's the matter, isn't my company good enough for you?" She turned on him suddenly. He would have to take her threats till Laura got there; she couldn't hold them back.

"It's just that I don't like prospective murderers," Jack said. "They make me nervous."

"You bastard! You holier-than-thou bastard! You think you're so damn superior because you're still on the wagon. You *are* on the wagon, I can tell. You look so goddamn sober it's repulsive. Repulsive!"

"That's the word for it, all right," Jack agreed. His compliant attitude only goaded her further.

"You hate me because Laura only comes to see you when she feels bad. She *lives* with me. But she doesn't give a damn about you until she feels bad. Then she comes running to good old Jack!"

"Beebo," he said and did not raise his voice. "When I lost Terry I did a hell of a lot of drinking and hollering. I came and drank your whiskey and told you my troubles and you listened to me. And it helped. Now you're welcome to my whiskey—there's still a little in the kitchen—and you're welcome to cry on my shoulder. But you're not going to murder anybody, here or anywhere else."

"Only Laura," Beebo said, and her voice was low now, too.

"Nobody," Jack said. "Now scram, or I'll throw you out."

Beebo grabbed the lapels of his sport jacket. "She cheated on me, Jack. You gave her the idea so don't try to squirm out of it."

"Cheated on you with who?"

"An Indian!" Her eyes were so big and her face so contorted that Jack came very near laughter.

"What tribe?" he asked carefully.

"Not an *American* Indian, you owl-eyed idiot! An *Indian* Indian. A dancer! Jesus!" And she lifted her eyes to the ceiling. "A *dancer!*"

"Classical or belly?"

"Oh, shut up! You think it's funny!" She gave him a hard shove, but Jack didn't shove easily. He just stood his ground and surprised her. "It doesn't matter who she is, anyway," she said and ran a distraught hand through her close-cropped dark hair that waved and rolled around her head and used to delight Laura. "What matters is, they've been sleeping together and that cheeky little bitch—"

"Which one?"

"Jack, goddamn you, quit interrupting me!" She paused to glare at him and then said, "Tris. The dancer. She had the nerve to come over to the apartment. Tried to tell me they met at the Hobby Shop. Oh, God!" And she gave a despairing laugh.

"Maybe they did." He offered it unobtrusively.

"Who're you kidding?" Beebo snapped. "Laura *admitted* she went to the girl's apartment."

"After you pounded it out of her."

Beebo held the diary out to him. "Read this, Jack. It's all in here," she said.

"Does it say they slept together?"

"Damn right!"

"Did you read it?"

"No, but it's in here," she said positively, in the grip of the spiraling violence that possessed her. "Jack Mann, college graduate, engineer, former gay boy, former whiskey drinker, former human being. Current know-it-all and champion bastard of Greenwich Village. *Read* it!"

He shook his head without even glancing at it.

"Are you too proper? Too moral? Don't tell me you've suddenly developed a conscience! After all these years," she said.

He shrugged. "Why read it? You've told me what's in it."

"Maybe you'd like to know what she says about me." He saw her face color up again and a shivering clearly visible in her hands and he said, "No." But Beebo opened the diary, leafing through it for the worst slander she could find.

Jack took the book from her hands so suddenly that she let it slip before she knew what he was up to, and then he socked her when she reached for it, catching her on the chin. She reeled backwards and sank to the floor. Jack leaned down and picked her up, hoisting her over his shoulder. He carried her that way, head dangling in back and feet in front, down the hall and out the door to the apartment building.

There he set her dizzily on her feet. She hardly knew where

she was and let him hold her up. He found a taxi for her on the corner of Fourth and Seventh Avenue and told the driver, "She's drunk. It's only a couple of blocks, but I can't take her home," and handed him five dollars. "Take her upstairs," he said, giving him the address. "Apartment 2B."

He was headed up the steps to his apartment again when he heard Laura's voice calling him, and he turned around to see her running up the sidewalk, hair awry and face like chalk.

"Laura!" he exclaimed and caught her. She began to sob the moment she felt his arms around her, as if she had only been waiting to feel him for the tears to start.

"Is she here?" she asked, and he could feel her quivering. "She left," he said. "I just put her in a cab. Your timing is faultless, Mother."

Laura looked at him out of big amazed eyes. "She's gone? How did you do it?" she asked. "What happened?"

"Come on inside," he said. He led her down the hall and in his kitchen at last, with the front door locked and no Beebo anywhere around and a comforting drink to brace her, she heaved a long sigh of relief.

"Now," said Jack, making himself some coffee. "Who is Tris?"

Laura clasped her glass in both hands and looked into the whiskey for an answer. "She's a dancer—"

"I know that part. I mean, are you sleeping with her?"

"No!" Laura flashed.

"Do you want to?"

And after a pause she whispered honestly, "Yes."

"So Beebo's not imagining things."

"She doesn't have to," Laura cried bitterly. "She's got my diary."

"I saw it."

"Did you read it?"

"No, but Beebo did."

"What did she say?" Laura's throat had gone dry all of a sudden at the idea of Beebo perusing those private pages, and she took a sip of her whiskey.

"She wants to solve the whole thing by murdering you."

"I think she would, too," Laura said, unsurprised. "Oh, Jack, help me. I'm scared to death."

"All right." He came over, pulling his chair, and sat down beside her. "Marry me."

Laura covered her face with her hands and gave a little moan. "Is that all you can think of? Is that all you can say?" she said, and she sounded a little desperate. "I'm in love with Tris, and Beebo wants to *murder* me and you want to *marry* me. What good will that do? I might as well be dead as married!" And she said it so emphatically that Jack was stung.

But he never let personal hurts show.

"Mother, you're in a mess," he said. "Nobody has a perfect solution for you. And you have none at all for yourself. So listen to one from an old friend who loves you and don't stomp on it out of sheer spite."

"I'm sorry," she murmured, sipping the drink again. She let the tears flow unchecked, without really crying. Her face was motionless, but still the tears rolled down her cheeks, as if they had business of their own unrelated to her emotion.

"Tell me something," Jack said gently, putting an arm over the back of her chair and leaning close to her. And as always with him, she didn't mind. She liked his nearness and the fact that he was male and strong and full off affection for her.

Perhaps it was because she knew he would never demand of her what a normal man would; because she felt so safe with him and so able to trust him. "Tell me why you went to live with Beebo two years ago," he said.

"I thought I loved her."

"Why did you think you loved her?" he asked.

"Because she—well, she was so—I don't know, Jack. She excited me."

He lighted a cigarette with a sigh. "And that's love," he said. "Excitement. As long as you're excited you're in love. When it turns flat you're not in love. Lord, what a way to live."

Laura was taken aback by the selfishness she betrayed. "I didn't mean it that way," she said. It had never seemed so cheap to her before.

"Are you in love with Tris?" he asked.

"I—I—" She was afraid to answer now.

"Sure you are," he said. "Just like Beebo. Fascinating girl. More excitement. Beebo's worn out now, let's try Tris. And when we wear Tris out, let's find another—"

"Stop it!" Laura begged.

"Where's your life going, Laura?" he asked her. "What have you done with it so far? Does it matter a damn, really? To anybody but you...and me?"

"And Beebo."

"Beebo's more worried about where her next drink is coming from than she is about you." He knew it wasn't true. He knew if it ever came to a choice, Beebo loved Laura desperately enough to give up drinking. But Jack was fighting for Laura now.

Laura began to cry now, her face concealed behind her hands. "Please, Jack," she whispered, but he knew what he was doing. He had to make her see it his way so clearly, feel the hurt so hard, that she would turn away from the whole discouraging mess of homosexual life and come to live with him far from it all.

"Look at me, Laura," he said and lifted her face. "We can't think straight because we always think gay," he said. "We don't know anything about a love that lasts or a life that means something. We spend all our time on our knees singing hosannas to the queers. Trying to make ourselves look good. Trying to forget we aren't wholesome and healthy like other people."

"Some of the other people aren't so damn wholesome either," Laura said.

Jack put his arms around her suddenly and pulled her tight against him and said, "Let's get out of it, Laura. Let's run like hell while we have a chance. We could get away, just the two of us. But we can't do it alone; we need each other. We could move uptown and get a nice apartment and you wouldn't have to work. We could get married, honey."

"But—"

"Please, Laura, please," he begged her. "Maybe we could even...adopt a child. Would you like that? Would you?" He sounded a little breathless and he leaned back to see her face.

Laura was startled. "I don't know anything about kids. They scare me to death."

"You'd get over it in a hurry," he said. "You're female. You have instinct on your side."

"Do *you* like kids?"

"I love them."

"*I* don't. You're more female than I am," she said.

He laughed. "Flattery will get you nowhere," he said. "Seriously, Laura—would you like a child? A daughter?"

"Why not a son?" she asked him, sharp-eyed.

"Okay." He shrugged warily. "A son."

Laura slid back in her chair and looked at the ceiling. "I never even thought about it before," she said. "I just never dreamed I'd ever have anything to do with a child of my own...with *any* child."

"Do you want one?" He seemed so eager that she was reluctant to hurt him. But she couldn't lie to him.

"No," she said. And when his face hardened, she added, "Because I'd be a terrible mother, Jack. I'd be afraid of it. And jealous, I think. I'd be all thumbs. I'd stick it full of pins and never be sure if I did it on purpose or by mistake."

"You won't always feel that way," he said, and she knew from the tone of his voice that there was no arguing with him.

"Maybe not," she said. "But if I marry you, Jack—" And they were both startled to hear the words, as if neither had really expected Laura to consider it seriously. "If I marry you, I wouldn't dare adopt a child for years. Not till I was sure we were safe together and the marriage would last."

"It would. It will. Say yes."

"I can't," she said and drove him to his feet in a fit of temper. "Goddamn it, Laura, do you want to grow *old* here in the Village?" he said. "Have you seen the pitiful old women in their men's oxfords and chopped-off hair, stumping around like lost souls, wandering from bar to bar and staring at the pretty kids and weeping because they can't have them any more? Or living together, two of them, ugly and fat and wrinkled, with nothing to do and nothing to care about but the good old days that are no more? Is that what you want? Because if you stay here, that's what you'll get.

"Pretty soon you won't know any other way of life. You won't know how to live in the big world. You don't care a goddamn about that world now when you're young. So when you're old you won't *know* a goddamn about it. You'll be afraid of it and of normal people and you'll hide in a cheap walk-up with a dowdy old friend or a stinking cat and you'll yammer about lost loves. Tempting, huh?" And he leaned on the kitchen table, his eyes so bright with urgency that she couldn't look at them and only watched his mouth.

"Horrible," she said.

He straightened up and shoved his hands in his pockets, and when he started to speak again he was gazing out the window. "I want to get so far away from here," he said, "that—"

"That Terry will never find you again," she guessed.

He dropped his head a little. "Yes," he said. "That, too. Terry and Joe and Archie and John and God knows who. We'd go way uptown and leave no forwarding address...nothing. Just fade out of the Village forever. No Beebo, no Terry..."

"No Tris," Laura whispered.

"I told you, Mother...I'm no bluebeard. If you want affairs, have them. You're young, you need a few. Only keep them out of the Village and keep them very quiet."

"Do you think Terry would really come looking for you again?" she asked. "After the way you threw him out?"

"There aren't many men stupid enough to put up with his

antics as I did," he said. "I think he might try to put the touch on me between affairs."

"Damn him!" Laura cried indignantly.

"Yes, he might try to find me. And Beebo would pace the city looking for you. But let them. We'd be through with them forever."

And Laura felt a very queer unwelcome pang for Beebo, for all that wealth of misdirected love. Jack was standing behind her now, his hands on her shoulders. "Well?" he said quietly. "Will you marry me?"

"Could I—answer you in the morning?" she asked.

"What the hell will you do tonight?"

"See Tris."

"Oh. And if she's nice, it's no to old Jack. If she's bitchy, it's yes. Right?" He said it lightly but she knew he was hurt.

"Not quite," she said. "I want to test myself, I guess. Jack, for the first time I feel almost—almost like saying yes. But I want to see her first. Please let me."

"You don't need my permission, Mother."

"Maybe Beebo's found her already."

"Beebo's in bad shape. I lay odds she sleeps it off for a while. Even if she's found Tris she won't be in condition to do either of you much harm. Just call a cop and say she's molesting you."

Laura got up and turned to face him and they gazed at each other for some minutes in silence. "Okay, Mother," he said: "Go. And come back *mine.*"

She smiled and then she walked past him to the door.

Tris was at home giving lessons when Laura got there. She had evening classes twice a week, for adults. She didn't slam the door in Laura's face, but she gave her a black look and directed her curtly to sit down and be quiet. Her delicate mouth was ever so slightly swollen.

Tris went back to work and danced with her pupils for another forty minutes without a word or a glance at Laura. It was lovely to watch. There were only two students—a man and a girl—and they were learning an intricate duet at Tris's direction. They would execute what looked to Laura like a perfect step and suddenly Tris would swoop down on them, shouting temperamental criticisms. She finally made the man dance with her, to give the girl the idea.

Laura watched her fascinated as she leaped into his arms, straight and smooth and beautifully sure of herself. And Laura realized slowly that only when she danced with the man did Tris look over at her to see her expression.

She's trying to make me jealous, Laura thought, and she was suddenly weary; weary of all the envy and ill feeling and violence. She wanted nothing more than to lie down quietly by Tris's side, when the couple had gone, and gently, without explanations or apologies, make love till they both fell asleep. She knew if it happened like that—naturally and easily and without pain—that she would stay with Tris. But she was afraid that even if it were bitter and unhappy, she would stay anyway.

And still, an angry core of resentment smoldered in her, resentment at Tris for having the effrontery to walk in on Laura and Beebo and cause the bitter outburst that had separated them. She was brooding about this when Tris suddenly dismissed her dancers.

The two went into her bedroom to change and Laura waited for Tris to speak to her. But Tris only glared, performing a few indolent turns until her students returned. Then she unexpectedly introduced them all. She was curt, almost unpleasant about it.

The young man smiled at Laura and said, "Never mind her, she's bad company tonight. Thanks, Tris." And he gave her a strange look and left, following the girl.

Tris shut the door after them and turned to Laura. "The girl is insufferable," she said. "She can't dance, and she is a vixen besides."

"The boy can dance," Laura said, not without a jealous twitch.

"Yes, he can. He can make love too. And he does—when I don't have company."

She said it pointedly and Laura felt her whole face go a hot red.

She stood up without speaking and made for the door, her head swimming, but Tris stopped her there by embracing her. Laura was in no mood for Tris's sudden turnabouts.

"Goddamn you, let me go," she exclaimed.

"Tonight, I am grateful for the company," Tris said. "He bores me."

"I've had all I can take from you, Tris. You split me and Beebo up tonight—"

"Ah, then I did you a favor, no?" and she smiled.

"You damn near got me killed!"

"She is not gentle, is she?" Tris said, releasing Laura to touch her bruised mouth, but she was still smiling a little.

"Gentle?" Laura exploded. "Beebo? Gentle like a tornado. Why did you do it, Tris? *Why?*"

Tris shrugged, walking away from her. "I felt like it. I don't know why. I wanted to see you. I wanted to see—well, I wondered what she was like...Beebo."

"You're incredible," Laura breathed, furious, watching her saunter suggestively toward her bedroom.

"Are you coming with me?" Tris asked.

And Laura felt her legs weaken and her heart jump, and she hated herself for it. "No," she said.

"Of course you are. That is why you are here. Come."

And Laura, helpless, went to her. Tris took her hands and led her, walking backwards herself, into the room and onto the low couch. She began to kiss her and Laura felt her fury rise and change into passion. Tris had never been so close to her, so tantalizing.

Somehow her anger made her passion sharper and wilder. She wanted to hurt Tris with it. Beebo believed they had made love, did she? Well, Laura would give truth to her fantasies.

Laura could feel Tris's body begin to respond. A surging feeling of triumph flashed through her. She felt the familiar, wonderful insanity come over her and she relinquished herself wholly to feeling. It took her a few moments to understand that Tris was fighting her. And suddenly she came to herself with a shock and felt Tris slip away from her and saw her standing a few feet from the bed. Tris gave her a look—almost of pity—and then turned and raced from the room. By the time Laura reached the door, it was locked. At first she was stunned, motionless. And then she began to throw her weight against it "Tris! Tris, let me out!" she cried in a panic.

"Stay where you are till you cool off," Tris said. Her voice was very near, just on the other side of the door, and Laura was wild to join her.

"Please, Tris!" she implored and her voice was low with coming tears. "Tris, don't do this to me!" Her whole body ached and after a moment more of futile beating on the door she slumped to the floor, moaning.

A long time later she dragged herself off the floor and back to the bed and lay there, sleepless, until early dawn. She was sick with the need to hurt and the need for love all scrambled inside her; she was imprisoned in her homosexuality and thinking...thinking hard of Jack.

The first daylight was coming in the window when Laura heard the door open and saw Tris glide across the floor toward her. Laura smothered a first harsh impulse to jump at her. Tris came on tiptoe, thinking Laura would be asleep, and when she saw Laura's blue eyes staring at her, she was startled.

Then she came and sat in silence on the edge of the bed and looked at Laura for a while, until Laura, who was restraining herself tightly, saw that Tris was crying. And the crying became suddenly audible and made Tris cover her face with her hands. Laura lay beside her, refusing to touch her, feeling her spite and misery soften a little, feeling even a shade of pity. She wanted to beat the girl and at the same time stroke her shaking shoulders.

Tris turned her back to Laura and finally spoke with considerable effort. "I'm going out on the Island tomorrow," she said. "For two weeks, a vacation. Come with me."

Laura stared at her back, frowning in disbelief. "What?" she said.

"I want you to come with me," Tris whispered. Her voice

sounded, as once before, quite American.

"You must enjoy torturing me," Laura said.

There was a long pause while Tris snatched a piece of face tissue from a box by the bed and blew her nose. Finally she said, "It was torture for me, too. But still, it was inexcusable, what I did to you. I was a beast. I—I can't talk about it," and she gave a quick sob. "But I promise it will never happen again—if you promise never to mention it.. Promise?" And she turned and looked at Laura.

"Why did you do it?" Laura asked.

"I had to! I *had* to! I wanted to hurt you—last night—you made me feel—" and her speech was clipped again and careful—"you made me want you so much, Laura. And I hate it! I *hate* it!" She was almost shrieking.

"Why?" Laura asked.

"Because I'm not really a Lesbian. Not like you. It's men I love, Laura. Really," she added desperately.

And Laura felt compassion for her. "You're sick, Tris," she said, but she said it kindly.

"Sick?" And Tris went a strange ashy color that scared Laura. "How do you mean?"

Laura realized then that she couldn't destroy Tris's illusion without destroying Tris. She raised herself to one elbow and brushed away the tears on Tris's cheek. "Let's put it this way," she said. "If you feel like this about me, we shouldn't be together anymore. In two weeks we'd drive each other wild. I know you feel terrible about last night, Tris, I can see it. I know I can't forget you, or forgive what you did. If we were living together, I'd want you and you'd hate me for it. And pretty soon I'd hate you too, for denying me."

"I won't deny you, Laura," Tris whispered, without looking at her. "I promise you. If you'd just let me do it my way. Don't let it be like last night. When I feel as if I'm losing control, it's as if I were drowning, as if I were losing my sanity along with my will. It's as if—if I let it happen—I—I'll lose my mind." She spoke so painfully, with such evident anxiety, that Laura was touched.

"Poor Tris," she murmured, and smoothed her hair. "I thought I'd be pulling your hair out this morning, not playing with it," she said, running her long fingers over the sleek black braid.

"Come with me," Tris pleaded. "Let me make it up to you."

"Where are you going? Fire Island?"

"God, no!" Tris flared. "*That* place! It's crawling with queers. I wouldn't go near it."

"Tris...," Laura said, a little hesitantly. Her ear did not betray her. Tris's accent fluctuated strangely and roused her curiosity. She asked cautiously, "What part of India do you come from?"

"Why do you ask?" And Tris's eyes narrowed.

Laura lifted her shoulders casually. "You never told me."

"I said New Delhi."

"Oh, yes."

"Besides, it has nothing to do with the vacation. I'm going to a place on Long Island. Stone Harbor. It's not far from Montauk, on the north side. I have a cottage there for two weeks. It's very secluded. No one will bother us. I was there last year and it's really lovely. You'd like it, Laura, I know you would. You can swim every day—we're only two blocks from the beach and—"

"Tris?" Laura stopped the almost compulsive flow of speech and startled the dancer.

"Yes?"

"Why won't you tell me about India?"

"You wouldn't be interested."

"I'd be fascinated. Everything about you fascinates me. For instance, what are you doing in this country?"

"Dancing."

"Where are your parents?"

"Dead."

"How did you get here?"

"Scholarship."

"Are you a citizen?"

"Laura, stop it! Why do you ask me such things? What has this to do with our vacation? I refuse to be quizzed like a criminal. We'll leave tomorrow at eight. Can you be packed by then? I've rented a car."

"I can't even get into my own apartment," Laura admitted. "You fixed me up just fine."

"Of course you can. Call the police." Her odd green eyes flashed.

"No. Maybe Jack could get my things. I'll call him."

"Who's Jack?"

"Jack? He's a—sort of—fiancé. A permanent fiancé." She smiled slightly.

Tris snorted. "Does he know you are gay?"

"Of course." She would tell her no more, If Tris were going to seal her private life behind a wall of secrets, Laura could play it that way, too. "Can I use your phone?" she asked.

"Yes. In the kitchen." Tris followed her across the empty studio into the sunny blue and yellow kitchen and while Laura was dialing she asked, "You will come, of course?"

"I'll tell you in a minute," Laura said. "...Jack?"

"Good morning, Mother."

"Jack, I wonder if you could—if you'd mind going over to the apartment and getting my clothes. Do you think you could? I hate to ask you, but I don't dare go near her."

"Sure," he said. "Did you pass your test?"

"My test? Oh." She glanced at Tris. "I—I flunked," she said and felt a tidal wave of pity and shame all at once. "Jack—I'm sorry. Oh, I'm so sorry. Let me come over—"

"Come get your clothes at five," he said. "I'll leave the door open." And he hung up.

Laura surprised Tris by dropping into a chair and sobbing.

Tris sat down opposite her and waited in silence till she caught her breath, expecting an explanation. But Laura only dried her eyes and asked for some coffee.

Jack wasn't home when she went to pick up her clothes. She had known he wouldn't be there, and still it made her want to weep. She was in a blue mood, and even the sight of Tris, waiting for her outside at the wheel of a rented convertible, didn't cheer her up. She made several trips with the clothes, leaving most of her other possessions behind, and on the last trip she wrote him a note. It said, in part:

You're the only man I would ever marry, Jack. Maybe it will still work out. Tris wants me to spend two weeks with her on Long Island. I'll call you the minute I get back. I'm crazy about her, but she's a sick girl and I've had enough of wild scenes with sick lovers. I don't know what to expect so am leaving most of my things here. Hope they won't be too much in the way. I quit my job, by the way. Will find something else when I get back. Thank you so much for everything, Jack darling. Hope Beebo didn't give you any trouble. Don't start drinking, I'm not worth it. I love you. Laura.

The cabin had two bedrooms, a kitchen and a living room, and a bathroom. It was furnished à la 1935, full of sand and ants, but comfortable. The walk to the beach was short and just enough to get you pleasantly warm before you soaked in the salt water.

There were a lot of other vacationers living all around them— young couples with dozens of hollering kids, mostly. Laura watched them romping on the sand, the little ones screaming and giggling and pouring water on each other. She wondered if she could ever want a child.

She lay on the beach with Tris, the day after they arrived, and luxuriated in the sun. Tris had lathered herself lovingly with rich sun cream and was sitting under a huge beach umbrella that she had erected with the help of a young man they discovered while they looked for a place to lie down. He was not very subtle about his admiration, which he confined to Tris. And Laura was not very pleased to see her prance for him. But she said nothing.

"You'll burn to a crisp, Laura," Tris warned her.

"I put some stuff on," Laura said lazily, wiggling a little and feeling the hot rays toast the backs of her legs.

"Not enough for one so fair," Tris maintained. "Such fair skin you have." And Laura heard the yearning in her voice. "If mine were that light I would never expose it like you do. I'd do everything to keep it as light as I could. Even bleach it. They say buttermilk works wonders."

Laura looked up at her through eyes squinted against the sun. "Your skin is beautiful, Tris."

"Oh, not like yours," Tris said, embarrassed.

"How can you say that? You're the prettiest color I ever saw."

"And you're a dirty hypocrite!" Tris snapped.

Laura stared at her, dumbfounded, for some seconds, before she answered softly, "No, I mean it." She was afraid to say more. "You think I only say it to flatter you, don't you?" she asked finally. "I won't say it, then. I'd rather you turned your temper on yourself than on me."

After an elaborately casual pause, full of much smoothing lotion and gazing around, Tris said, "Do you really like my color?" The little-girl pleading in her voice touched Laura.

"If I say yes, you call me a liar. If I say no you call me a bigot."

"Say yes."

"Yes." And Laura smiled at her and Tris smiled back and gave Laura the feeling of false but sweet security.

Tris said, "Did you ever notice, when we lie on the bed together, how we look?"

Laura finished, "Yes, I noticed." She looked at Tris in surprise. It wasn't like her to mention such things. "Me so white and you so brown. It looks like poetry, Tris. Like music, if you could see music. Your body looks so warm and mine looks so cool. And inside, we're just the other way around. Isn't it funny? I'm the one who's always on fire. And you're the iceberg." She laughed a little. "Maybe I can melt you," she said.

"Better not. The brown comes off," Tris said cynically, but her strange thought excited Laura.

"God, what a queer idea!" Laura said. "You'd have to touch me everywhere then, every corner of me, till we were both the same color. Then you'd be almost white and I'd be almost tan—and yet we'd be the same." She looked at Tris with her squinty eyes that sparkled in the glancing sun. And Tris, struck herself by the strangeness of it, murmured, "I never thought of it that way."

Laura hoped Tris would look at it that way for the rest of the vacation.

Chapter Seven

JACK WALKED into his apartment at five-thirty in the afternoon, tired and thirsty but dolefully sober. He was a stubborn man and he had dedicated all his resistance to fighting liquor. He meant to head for the kitchen and consume a pint of cider and fix himself some dinner. Since Laura had left five days ago he had not had much appetite. He did not admit that she would ever come back or that he had lost a battle. It was only a temporary setback. But it rocked him a little and it hurt him a lot.

He came wearily down the hall, stuck his key belligerently into the lock and kicked his front door open. He dumped a paper bag full of light bulbs, cigarettes, and Scotch tape on a chair, switched on a light and started toward his kitchen. It came as a distinct shock to find Laura sitting on his sofa.

He stared at her. She had her legs up, crossed, on the cocktail table, and her head back, gazing at the ceiling. She knew he was there, of course; she heard him come in. She turned and looked at him finally, and something in her face dispelled his melancholy. He felt elated. But he checked it carefully. He slipped his coat off without a word, dropped it on the chair with his package, and walked over to her, standing in front of her with his hands in his pockets.

"Run out of suntan lotion?" he said.

"No. But you're out of whiskey."

"I gave it to Beebo. Traded it for your clothes."

"Take the clothes back and get the whiskey."

"Later," he said, and smiled. Then he added, "Was it bad?"

"Very bad," Laura said and for a moment they both feared she would start crying. But she didn't.

"Want to tell me?"

"Jack," she said with an ironic little smile. "You'll have to write a book about me someday. I tell you everything."

He grinned. "I'll leave that to somebody else. But I'm saving my notes, just in case." He sat down beside her. "Well, it could only be one of three things, seeing that she's gay," he said. "She's a whore."

"No."

"A junkie."

"No."

"—or she's married."

"She's married."

He lighted a cigarette with a long sigh, his eyes bright on her.

"How did you know?" she asked.

"I didn't. But it had to be something that would shock you. And you seem pretty damn nervous about the idea of gay people being married." He paused and she had to drop her glance. "Does she hate him?" he asked returning to Tris.

"Most of the time. God, Jack, I need a drink."

"Steady, Mother. My neighbor always has a supply. I'll fix you up." He came back in less than three minutes with a bottle of sparkling burgundy.

"Ugh!" Laura said. But she took it gratefully.

"Now," he said, settling down on the cocktail table with a cup of instant coffee, "begin at the beginning."

Laura rubbed her forehead and then sipped the prickly drink. "It started...beautifully," she said. "Like a dream. It was all hot sand and cool water and kisses. We held hands in the movie, we sat up till all hours in front of the fireplace with a bottle of Riesling and sang, and danced. We traded secrets and we made plans. We made a boat trip to the point—"

"Did you make love?"

"You just can't wait, can you?" she said, half teasing, half irritated.

"My future may depend on it," he said and shrugged.

There was a long reflective pause and finally Laura said, sadly, "Yes. We made love. Only once."

"And that was the end?"

"It wasn't that simple. You see, she—well, she flirted. She flirted with men until I thought I couldn't stand it. Till I wanted to flirt myself to get even, if only I weren't so damn awkward with men. She's not. She's a genius with them. She didn't give a damn if they were married or not. She had them all proposing to her.

"After the first couple of days it got intolerable. She had been making me sleep on one bed and she took the other. And after she turned the lights out she made a rule—no bed hopping."

"And you obeyed her little rule?"

"I had to, Jack," she defended herself. "We had a sort of agreement before we left the Village…It was supposed to be up to her to choose the time and place."

"That's the lousiest agreement *you* ever made, Mother," he commented.

"No. She's sick, you see. Really. She thinks she's straight. And if you hint she's not, she gets terrified. Almost hysterical. She can't accept it."

"Why do you always fall for these well adjusted ladies?" he asked.

"Beth was well adjusted."

"Beth is dead. As far as you're concerned." Laura glared at him while he smiled slightly, lighting another cigarette from the one he was finishing. "So Tris is a queer queer," he said. "And she flirts with the opposite sex. Very subversive. So what came next?"

"Well, they followed us home—"

"Who?"

"Men!" she flashed peevishly. "They followed us at the beach, in the bars, in the stores. They followed *Tris,* I should say. I was cold as hell with them. I tried to keep quiet about it, but after three days of it I blew up. We had a miserable quarrel, and I was ready to pack up and leave right then. But she relented suddenly. I don't know why. I think she really likes me, Jack. Anyway, she got drunk. Just enough so that she wouldn't have to watch what I did to her...or hear what I said to her...or care too much..."

"That's pretty drunk," Jack said. He knew from the way she spoke that it had hurt her to make love like that, wanting so much herself, and herself so unwanted. "I know, Laura honey, I know the feeling," he said and the words comforted her.

"Jack, I hope I always love you this much," she said softly. He looked up from his coffee cup with a little smile. "So do I," he said. And they looked at each other without speaking for a minute before she went on.

"Well," she said, "it was torture. I didn't want it any more than she did if it had to be so cold and sad, and at the same time I *had* to have her. I was on fire for her. I have to give her credit, Jack, she tried. But it didn't mean anything to her."

"It's a lonesome job," Jack said. "And it's never worth it."

"I cried all night," Laura said. "Afterwards...I just got in my own bed and cried. And she was awake all night too, but she didn't come to me or try to comfort me. I think she was embarrassed. I think she just wished she'd never gotten mixed up with me.

"The next night—around dinner time—her husband arrived. I don't know whether she got sick of me or just scared and called him, or if they got their dates scrambled and he came too soon. You see, it turned out she had planned to meet him out there all along, after I left. But maybe I got to be too much for her and she told him to come and chase me out...I don't know. There wasn't time to go into the fine points. But I think myself she needed a man just then, to make herself feel normal. And protected."

"What was he like?"

"A nice guy. He really is. I know I sound—Tris would say—hypocritical. But I liked him. I understood right away, the minute I saw him, an awful lot of things about Tris."

"How?"

Laura paused, gazing seriously at Jack. At last she explained,

"He's a Negro. And so is she. Only he's much darker than Tris. Very handsome, but he'd never pass as an Indian. And right away he humiliated her, without meaning to." She smiled sadly. "She's from New York, Jack. She was born right here and her name is Patsy Robinson. She's only seventeen but they've been married two years. She makes him keep out of sight because she thinks he'd be a drag on her career. That's why she tells everybody she's Indian, too—because she wants to get ahead and she thinks it makes it easier."

Jack shook his head. "I feel for her," he said.

"And I weep for her," Laura said. "You should have seen her, Jack. She was wild when Milo talked about her fake Indian past. I think it made him pretty damn mad. That, and all the flirting, and having to live apart. And her gay and him straight! Lord, what a mess. He's in love with her; she's his wife. And she denies him, and hides him."

Laura stopped talking then for a little while, sipping the burgundy and staring at her feet. "I took the bus back," she said at last. "She screamed at me to leave. Milo apologized for her. That poor guy."

"Do you still think you love her?" Jack asked.

"I don't know." She sighed. "She fascinates me. I feel sick about it, about the way things happened. If I thought I could stand it I'd go back to her. But I know I couldn't. What is love, anyway, Jack?"

"If you have to ask you never get to know," he quoted. "More?" He reached for her glass and she relinquished it with an unsteady hand. She felt completely lost, completely frustrated.

"What's Beebo doing?" she asked.

He picked up the bottle and poured some more wine into her glass. "All kinds of things," he said. "She got fired, of course. Hadn't showed up for weeks."

"Of course," Laura repeated, bowing her head.

"She's shacking up with Lili at the moment."

"Ohhh," Laura groaned, and it made her feel dismal to think of it. She felt a spasm of possessiveness for Beebo. "Lili is a terrible influence on her," she said irritably.

"So are you." He handed her her drink. "The worst."

"Not *that* bad."

"Life with you," he reminded her, "damn near killed the girl."

"And me," Laura replied. "Did she leave the apartment?"

"No, she gets over there from time to time."

"I wonder how she pays the rent."

"It isn't due yet," he said. "Besides, I imagine Lili can help out."

Laura shut her eyes suddenly, overwhelmed with a maddening tenderness for Beebo. "I hate her!" she said emphatically to Jack. And he, with his uncanny ear for emotion, didn't like the emphasis.

After a slight pause he said, "I got her a dog. Another dachshund pup."

"That was nice of you," she said to him in the tone mothers use when someone has done a kindly favor for their children.

"Beebo didn't think so. She didn't know whether to kiss it or throw it at me," he said. "She finally kissed it. But the poor thing died two days later...yesterday, it was."

"It died?"

"Yes." He looked at her sharply. "I think she...shall we say—put it to sleep?"

"Oh, Jack!" she breathed, shocked. *"Why?* Did it remind her of Nix?"

"I don't know. It didn't cheer her up, that's for damn sure." Laura sat there for a while, letting him fill her glass a couple of times and listening to the FM radio and trying not to feel sorry for Beebo. "She doesn't really need me anymore, Jack," she told him.

"I do," he said, and she smiled.

"You didn't fall off the wagon," she said. "I'm so glad. I was afraid you might."

"I never get drunk over the women in my life," he said sardonically. "Only over the boys. And there are no more boys in my life. Now or ever."

Laura swirled the royal purple liquid in her long-stemmed glass and whispered into it, "Do you think I could make you happy, Jack?"

"Are you proposing, Mother?"

She swallowed and looked up at him with butterflies in her stomach. "Yes," she said.

He sat quite still and smiled slowly at her. And then he got up and came to her and kissed her cheeks, one after the other, holding her head tenderly in his hands.

"I accept," he said.

The day was hot and muggy, one of those insufferably humid August days in New York. Laura and Jack waited together outside the office of Judge Sterling Webster with half a dozen other sweating, hand-clasping couples.

Jack wasted no time when Laura said yes. As fast as arrangements could be made, they were made. Laura stayed with him in the Village apartment a few days while they hunted for another apartment, cooking for him and getting the feel of living with him. During the days, when he was out, she went uptown. This was Jack's idea. He had no intention of making his bride a sitting duck for Beebo. It was only for four days, anyway, and much to Laura's surprise, Beebo made no attempt to reach her.

They had found the apartment on the east side two days after Laura got back from the disillusioning sojourn with Tris. It was too expensive, but it was newly renovated, lustrous with new paint, elegant with a new elevator, and bursting with chic tenants.

"We can't afford it," was Laura's first comment, to which Jack replied, smiling, "You're beginning to sound like a wife already."

And now, here they were, waiting on yellow oak chairs in the hall, while one couple after another passed in and out of the judge's office with the classic stars in their eyes.

Laura, who was sitting quietly in her chair, said, "They all look so happy," and drew courage from the fact.

"They're scared witless," Jack said, pacing up and down in front of her.

"Jack!" Laura exclaimed, appalled. "They'll hear you."

"Ours will be a happier marriage than any of these," he said with a contemptuous wave of his hand. He sat down suddenly beside her. "Ours could be damn near perfect, Laura, if we work at it a little. You know that? We won't have to face the usual pitfalls. Ours will be different…better."

"I hope so, Jack," she said in a near whisper, and a little thrill of passionate hope went through her.

"Will you try, honey?" he asked.

"I will. With all my heart I will." She gave him a tremulous smile. "I want this to work, Jack, as much as you do. I'll give it all I've got. I want terribly for it to be right." And she meant it.

"Then it will," he said and his smile gave her a needed shot of confidence.

Laura had had some bad nights since she said yes to him. Awful hours of yearning for Tris had tormented her. Stray unwelcome thoughts of Beebo had hurt her even more.

There were the lonely times when she thought about herself and Jack, so different, so dear to each other, and wondered if marital intimacy might not ruin it all with its innocent vulgarity. She tried to imagine Jack shaving in the morning…the toilet flushing…his wrinkled pajamas, still warm from sleep, tossed on the floor…his naked loneliness mutely reproaching her. The idea of living with a man…a *man*…made her think of her father, her huge heavy domineering father, with his aggressive maleness stamped all over his body.

But for the most part, Laura tried not to think at all. She let Jack do her thinking. She let Jack make the plans. She let Jack take her by the hand and lead her where he deemed it best for her to go. And, trusting him, she went.

So here they were outside Judge Sterling Webster's door with its glass window and neatly stenciled name, and they were next in line. Their predecessors in the marriage mill were slower than the rest, or so it seemed. And by the time they came out Jack was very nervous.

He herded her in ahead of him, and Judge Webster, as dignified and antique as his name, stood to greet them with an extended hand.

In less than five minutes he pronounced them man and wife and they signed the certificate of marriage. Jack turned to Laura and kissed his tall and trembling young wife on her cheek. He gave the Judge ten dollars, and then he took Laura's arm and steered her out again to let the next impatient couple take over.

Laura had to sit down for a minute on one of the limed oak chairs and cover her face with her hands. Jack leaned over her and said, "You're setting a lousy example, Mother. Every female here is watching you and figuring me for a wife-beater. Come on, Mrs. Mann."

She looked up and saw him grinning at her, and it gave her a lift. She grasped his hand and let him pull her to her feet. He was beaming, and Laura had to smile at all the nervous cynicism of half an hour ago.

They went straight to the apartment to rest for a while before they went out to dinner. Jack had made reservations for them at the Stork Club.

"We'll have a proper honeymoon at Christmastime," he said, when they reached the house on East Fifty-third. "I'll take a month off then. I have it coming."

Ignoring Laura's protests, he insisted on carrying her across the threshold. He swung her up easily, to their mutual pleasure.

"Jack, I think you're the world's worst sentimentalist," she teased him when he set her down, but he denied it at once.

"God forbid!" he said. "I just don't want anything to go wrong. We're going to do it all right, right from the start."

"And you're superstitious."

He laughed with delight. "Laura," he said and came to take her hands. "I'm so happy. You've made me so happy."

"I haven't done a thing, yet," she said, wondering a little at him, at his uncontainable good spirits.

"You've married me. That's something," he said. "I'm a married man. God Almighty, think of it!"

"If you were any prouder you'd explode," she giggled.

"I just may," he said. And they gazed at each other with a huge, wordless approval and relief.

"This calls for a celebration," he said suddenly. "I got a little something—"

"Oh, Jack, no drinking," she said. "I don't have to have a drink, really. I don't want you to get started."

"No nagging on our wedding day," he said and produced a bottle of champagne from the refrigerator. He poured her a glassful and himself a swallow. "Medicinal," he explained, and they toasted each other. He made her drink all of hers and kept pace with her with ginger ale. "I feel so good, by God, I don't even need it," he said, and laughed.

Laura watched him affectionately. She had never seen him so animated, so happy. He glowed with it. He was almost handsome, with his brilliant eyes and his proud smile. It made her feel a little like crying, and she stopped him in the middle of a delirious tirade of compliments to say, "Jack, please. You embarrass me. I'm afraid I won't live up to it all."

"Oh, but you will. I'll beat you if you don't," he said, laughing, and kissed her cheek. And she caught his hands and kissed them.

"You'd think we were a couple of normal people," she said.

He sobered a little, sitting down on the floor in front of her. "They have no monopoly on happiness, Mother. We have a right to our share. We have a chance now. We can make something beautiful of it together." He stopped and chuckled at himself. "I sound like a bad poem," he said. "But I mean it. I have so many wonderful plans, so many hopes." And the thought of that bright-eyed little girl he had cherished for so long danced into his head.

Laura couldn't look at his face. She got up and went to lie on her bed.

They stayed up very late and Laura had too much champagne

and Jack had too much ginger ale, and they talked endlessly and held one another's hands tightly. And the next day they slept until four in the afternoon and got up smiling to treat Laura's hangover and make the beds and shop for groceries together. And Jack introduced her to the butcher with, "Meet my wife. She's a doll."

Laura blushed crimson and the butcher laughed at them and tried to sell them some oysters. "You want kids? Buy oysters," he advised. "Never fails. I know, I got eight."

It was smooth and sweet the first few months; smoother than either of them had dared to hope. Laura was naturally mild and yielding; Jack, efficient and good-humored and terribly proud of her. As soon as they had enough chairs and crates collected to seat a fair number of guests, they threw a party and Jack's office staff came to wish them well.

None of them knew he was a homosexual. Jack was a past master at deception. "You have to be if you're going to survive in the world," he said to her once. "It's either that or retire into a rotten little prison with the rest of the gay people and spend your life feeling sorry for yourself. No thanks, not for me. Sex rules my nights. But by God, as far as the world knows, I'm a normal man from dawn to dusk. And there isn't one guy in that office who'd question it."

She admired him for it. Her own vagrant sensuality had dominated her ever since the fatal day she first recognized it, and her efforts to hide it or deny it had always backfired sooner or later. Jack filled her with determination to make herself a part of what he called "the real world," the *straight* world. He made it seem very desirable to her for the first time.

Jack's office buddies brought their wives, except for two dauntless bachelors who spent the evening berating Jack for treason.

"Are they gay?" Laura asked him in a whisper. "The unmarried ones?"

"Not gay, just scared," he said. "Winslow is, though. That one over there with the gorgeous wife. Poor guy, I don't think he knows it. They aren't very happy." And he nodded at the suave young man in his early thirties with a stunning and rather bored young woman beside him. Laura looked at the girl without a trace of desire and felt a quiet little spark of triumph. The future looked bright if she could be around so lovely a woman without even a hungry glance.

The autumn months passed uneventfully, and they got used to each other, and most of their worst fears abated. Jack never wandered around the apartment naked, out of instinctive respect for Laura. He did drop his socks all over the floor and leave his dresser drawers open. But he never lost his temper. He took her out to dinner once or twice a week, and he brought her flowers and books and pretty things that caught his eye in the windows of the stores he passed.

And he loved her. It sustained Laura through her low hours of doubt and confusion. She was the weak one of the two, and they both knew it. There were times when Jack had to be strong enough for both of them; times when Laura would cling to him weeping and tell him it was all a horrible mistake and she couldn't live without Tris, no matter how godawful it would be.

And then he didn't argue with her. He only said, "If you have to go, go, but come back. I want you here tonight at dinner time. I want you here in the morning when I get up. There'll be women in your life, I'm prepared for that, honey. Tris won't be the last. But there's only one man, and there will only be one man and don't you ever forget it."

He sounded so sensible and firm to her that her unrest would disappear. Now and then, when she was not in a passion for Tris, they talked about it. And she would say, "I know it'll happen one of these days, but I won't let it hurt us, Jack. When I can think about it like this, rationally and without fear, I know I can handle it. I won't panic when the time comes. I'll just accept it as quietly as I can. I won't let it touch our marriage."

"Good girl," he said and squeezed her arm.

There was no sex between them. Neither of them wanted it,

and that was the way they planned it. Jack would make her take his arm when they went anywhere because he was proud of her. And he gave her a friendly peck when he left in the morning and when he came back at night. When she was frightened or depressed he held her and stroked her hair and talked to her the way she had always prayed her father would. And he liked to lie with his head in her lap and have her read to him before they went to bed.

But that was the limit of their physical contact. It was affectionate and gentle but utterly sexless. After the first few weeks, Laura began to like it. She had been shy at first and reluctant. But he didn't force her, and after a while she welcomed his little gestures of love. They spelled security and reassurance to her. Suddenly it occurred to her that Jack was a man who was taking care of his woman. And she relaxed. She felt her nerves ease and her tension relax. The apartment was quiet and pretty, and Laura, who was lazy as a cat for the first time in her life, felt like a princess.

They felt a mutual gratitude toward each other. Jack came home for the first time in his life to a warm kitchen and a charming young wife. And just the thought of Laura reminded him, with a deep fine thrill, that he was married; he was truly a man. It was worth a lifetime of homosexual adventures.

Laura went to pains to please him, to show him that she cared and that she was working to make things right as she had promised him. And they were, all things considered, happy.

It wasn't until Terry's letter came, forwarded from Jack's old address in the Village, that Laura felt even the slightest apprehension that anything was to go wrong. And the note was postmarked San Francisco and seemed so far away that she recovered promptly from the first shock and sat in the kitchen with the rest of the mail on the table in front of her, wondering what to do.

Laura and Jack had made a strict rule never to open each other's mail and never to ask prying questions. But Laura hated to think of the turn it would give Jack to have this ghost from his past rise up to haunt him.

She turned and looked out the window at the sparse snow, falling that first day of December, and played with Terry's letter, letting it slip from corner to corner through her fingers. She burned with curiosity.

I could just steam it open, she mused. *He'd never know the difference. Damn that Terry anyway! Who does he think he is! After the hell he put Jack through, he has a lot of nerve. I'll bet he wants some money.*

She could bear it no longer. She got up and went to the stove, where she had a kettle full of hot water left over from breakfast, and turned the heat on under it. The glued flap of the envelope surrendered to the steam in a quiet curl. Laura held the letter a moment longer before opening it, feeling very guilty. But she loved Jack and she felt a fierce desire to spare him more pain. Besides, her curiosity was smothering her. She rationalized that Jack had told her himself he had given up the gay life forever, and that included Terry. What if this set him to drinking again?

She sat down and pulled the letter out with nervous hands. It was rather a short note, folded twice, and she opened it and read it quickly. It was not dated.

> Dear Jack. Have been out here in S.F. since September. What a crazy town. You'd love it. Have a nice apartment on Telegraph Hill with a kid I met at a party a month ago. (Not the same one you beat up the night you kicked me out.)

God! He just has to rub it in. He's just the kind of guy to mention such a thing, Laura thought, hot with indignation.

> Don't know how long I'll be out here. I sort of miss the Village. And you. Why don't you come out for a visit? We've got lots of room.

He doesn't seem to realize it would damn near kill Jack, Laura thought. *He's hopeless. It never occurs to him that Jack would go crazy in a situation like that. Or does it?*

Laura was used to the idea of Terry as a good-natured scatter-brained boy who hurt people, mostly Jack, with monotonous regularity—largely because he didn't think about what he was doing. Usually, this was true enough. But the rest of his letter made her wonder if he weren't deliberately needling Jack, trying to get him to come out to the coast.

She continued to read the tidy blue ink script.

> I do miss you, lover. I was always so unsettled before we met.

Before, after, and during, Laura fumed.

> And now it's worse than before. I used to feel so safe and comfortable with you, like you'd always watch out for me, no matter what. I guess that's a selfish way to look at it, but I wish we were back together. If you by any chance want it that way too, write to me. Write to me anyway, I really want to hear from you. Love, Terry.

He signed his name with an elaborate flourish, like a fifth-grade child drunk on the possibilities of fancy penmanship.

Laura folded the letter and stuck it back in the envelope and wrote a brief sizzling note in answer. She said:

> Terry—Jack and I are married. You are not welcome here, now or ever. Jack asked me to write and tell you that he does not want to be bothered with any more letters from you and he will not answer any if you do write. Please leave us alone. Laura.

It sounded sharp and cold, and she had a momentary feeling of misgiving. Terry was a nice kid, in spite of it all. Everybody liked him, even Laura. But she couldn't risk having him torment Jack. It had to sound mean or he wouldn't believe it. She put the note in an envelope, sealed and stamped it, and copied his San Francisco address on it. Then she burned Terry's letter over the stove.

When Jack came home that evening Laura's note was in the mail and Terry's was in ashes in the wastebasket.

"Any mail?" he asked her.

"Just a bill from the laundry," she said.

But it bothered her. It came to her at odd moments and it seemed ominous and frightening to her, like the first sign of a break-up. She had broken her promise to him, and it didn't help much to tell herself she did it only to protect him. *I'm not going to let anybody hurt what we've got, least of all Terry Fleming,* she thought.

The thought of having it all end between her and Jack, suddenly and cruelly, in one big drunk on Jack's part or wild romance on hers, scared and depressed her. It mustn't end that way. They needed each other too much. Their marriage had helped them think of each other as normal. They felt as if they knew where they were going now and life was much better.

Laura missed women. She missed them desperately sometimes. But she was sure now, deep within herself, that the time would come when she and Jack would be secure with each other for the rest of their lives; when they would be able to trust each other without reservation and trust the strength of their union. When they reached that point, it would be safe to satisfy her desires.

As for Jack, he was through with men forever. He had said it and she believed him. The thought that he might take a lover himself some day never occurred to her. It just wouldn't happen. Nor had she asked him about Terry. Jack was so determinedly happy with her that she was afraid to mention Terry.

It seemed strange to Laura, however, that Beebo didn't try to find her. She might have found them, one way or another. But there was no word from her. Laura couldn't help wanting to know what she was doing. She didn't feel the old, urgent, painful need for Tris, but there was a persistent want that was strong enough to make her wince now and then.

Jack told her once, "If anything bothers you, tell me about it. Don't sit around letting it eat you up. Better to talk about it and get it out of your system."

And when he saw that she was pensive he made her talk. But when he didn't see it, she kept it to herself. There were times when Laura couldn't share her feelings, when she just hugged them to herself and brooded.

Several times she had nearly talked herself into going down to the Village to wander around. She wouldn't go near her old apartment. Or Tris's studio. Or even Lili's apartment. She wasn't a fool, she wouldn't risk being caught.

But she was tempted, sometimes almost hypnotized, by the idea.

Chapter Eight

IT WAS CHRISTMAS EVE. They had a fine big tree, freshly green in a sea of lights and tinsel. No honeymoon, as they had hoped; the office couldn't spare Jack. So they had a party instead.

"I hate those damn pink trees," Jack had said when they picked theirs out. "Or gold, or white, or whatever-the-hell color they're making them this year. Give me a nice healthy green."

They celebrated at the party and Jack drank eggnog without whiskey and Laura was very pleased with him. There was a lovely girl there—unmarried and probably gay. Laura flirted with her in spite of herself.

Jack teased her about it when they met briefly in the kitchen— he to make drinks and she to get more hors d'oeuvres from the refrigerator. "Looks like you got a live one," he said.

Laura blushed. "Was I too obvious?" she asked, scared.

"No," he said. "I just have X-ray eyes, remember?"

"I shouldn't—"

"Oh, hell," he said with a good-natured wave of his hand. "Flirt, it's good for you. Just don't elope with her." He gave her a grin and went out, holding five highballs precariously. She felt a flush of love for him, watching him.

It was three a.m. Christmas day before they got rid of every-body. Laura threw herself in their expensive new sofa and surveyed the wreckage with a sigh.

"I'm not even going to pick it up," she said. "I'm not going to touch a thing till morning."

"That's the spirit," Jack said. He fixed them both a cup of

coffee, settled down beside her in the rainbow glow of the Christmas tree and took her hand with a sigh of satisfaction.

"That's the first goddamn Christmas tree I ever had," he said. And when she laughed he protested solemnly, "Honest. And this is the first Christmas that ever meant anything to me." He turned his head, resting against the back of the sofa, and smiled at her....

"You shouldn't swear at Christmas," Laura told him.

He gazed at her for a while and then asked, "Are you in love with Kristi? Wasn't that her name?"

"Yes, it was her name. No, I'm not in love. With anybody."

"Me?"

"Oh, you. That's different."

She smiled a little and sipped her coffee, and then she leaned back on the sofa beside him, absorbed in the soft sparkle of the tree.

Jack was still watching her. "Laura?" he said in an exploratory voice.

"Hm?"

"What would you think of adopting a child?"

She stared at a golden pine cone, her face suddenly a cautious blank. "I don't know," she said.

"Have you ever thought about it?"

"A little."

"What did you think?"

"I told you. Kids scare me."

He bit his underlip, frowning. "I want one," he said at last. "Would you be willing to—*have* one?"

"You mean—" She swallowed. "—get pregnant?"

"Yes," he said, smiling at her outraged face. "Oh, don't worry, Mother. We'd do it the easy way."

"There is no easy way!" she fired at him. "What way?" He took a long drag on his cigarette and answered, "Artificial insemination." She gasped, but he went on quickly, "Now before you get your dander up let me explain. I've thought it all out. Either we could adopt one, or—and this would be much better—we could *have* one. Our own. We can tell the Doc we've had trouble and let him try the insemination. There's nothing to it, it doesn't take five minutes. It doesn't hurt. And if it worked...God! Our own kid. You wouldn't be afraid of your own, honey."

There was a long pause while Laura sweated in silent alarm. Why did he bring it up tonight? Why? When they were so contented and pleased with each other, and the world was such a place of glittering enchantment.

"Couldn't we wait and talk about it later?" she asked.

"Why not now?"

"Couldn't I have time to think about it?"

"Sure. Think," he said and she knew he meant, *I'll give you five minutes to make up your mind.*

"Jack, why do we have to do it right now? Why can't we wait? We've only been married five months."

"I can't wait very long, Mother," he said. "I'm forty-five. I don't want to be an old man on crutches when my kid is growing up."

"Maybe in the spring," she said. The idea of becoming a mother terrified her. She had visions of herself hurting the baby, doing everything wrong; visions of her old passion coming on her and shaming them all; selfish thoughts of her beautiful, new, leisurely laziness being ruined.

"What would I ever tell any child of mine if it caught me—with a woman?" she said awkwardly.

"Tell it for Chrissake to knock before entering a room," he said, and something in his voice and manner told her that he had set his heart on this long ago.

"Would you *insist* on having a baby, Jack?" she asked him defiantly.

He was looking at the ceiling and he expelled a cloud of blue smoke at it and answered softly, "I want you to be happy, Laura. This marriage is for both of us."

There was a long silence. "I think I would hate myself if I ever got pregnant," she said, ashamed of her vanity but clinging to it stubbornly. "God, how awful. All those aches and pains and months of looking like hell, and for what? What if the baby weren't normal? What if I couldn't be a good mother to it?"

He shrugged and then he said, "All right. We'll adopt one. That way at least we can be sure of getting a girl."

Laura wrung her hands together in a nervous frenzy. The last thing she wanted to do was hurt Jack. And yet she could feel the dogged one-mindedness in him, feel his enormous desire.

"A man needs a child," he said softly. "So does a woman. That's the whole reason for life. There is no other." And he glanced up at her and all the Christmas lights reflected on the lenses of his glasses. "We can't live our lives just for ourselves," he said. "Or we live them for nothing. We die, monuments to selfishness...I want a child, Laura."

"Is that why you married me?" she asked with sudden sharpness, feeling as if he had cornered her.

"I married you because I love you," he said.

"Then why do you keep badgering me about a child?" she demanded.

"This is the first time I've mentioned it since we got married," he reminded her gently.

"You act as if just because *you* want one it's all settled," she said, and surprised herself by bursting into tears. He took her in his arms, abandoning his cigarette, and said, "No, honey, nothing's settled. But think about it, Laura. Think hard."

They sat that way, hugging each other and watching the Christmas tree, letting the cigarette slowly burn itself out, and they didn't mention it again. But from that moment on it was very big between them, unspoken but felt.

Jack did not mention a child to her again for a while. But as the weeks slipped by Laura began to feel a growing dissatisfaction. She didn't know where it came from or what it meant. At home, in the apartment, it was shapeless. Outside it took the shape of girls. When she went out for groceries or to shop or to have dinner with

Jack, she found herself looking around hopefully, gazing a little too boldly, desiring. Jack saw it too before long, but he said nothing.

Laura felt selfish, and she didn't like the feeling. She blamed it on Jack. It made her want to get away from him for a bit. And soon the wish crystallized in her mind to a desire for the Village, and began to haunt her.

She knew she ought to tell Jack she wanted to go. He would never stand in her way, as long as she was there at night to cook his meals and be a fond companion to him. As long as she let him in on it and kept it clean.

But she was embarrassed. She didn't want to tell him and see his disappointment and know she was so much weaker than he. So she kept it secret and let it fester inside her until it had grown, by March, to a great, irritating problem.

Then, one fine, sunny morning in the first week of spring, the phone rang.

It'll be Ginny Winston, she thought. One of their neighbors. *She'll want to go shopping again. I guess we might as well, it'll keep me out of trouble.* Ginny was thirty-five, a widow, a nice girl but hopelessly man-happy.

Laura grabbed the receiver after the fourth ring. "Hello?" she said.

"Laura? How are you?"

"Fine, thanks. Who's this?"

"Terry."

"Terry who?" She gasped suddenly. "Terry! Terry Fleming?"

"Yes." He chuckled. "Guess how I found you?"

She hung up. She just slammed the phone down in place and stood there shaking. Then she sat down and cried; waiting for the thing to start ringing again. She had no doubt it would.

It did. She picked it up again, and before he could say anything she told him, "I don't care how you found us. I don't want you around here. Don't you come near this place Terry, or I'll—I don't know what I'll do. You can't, you mustn't. Do you hear me?"

"Yes," he said, astonished. "What's the matter?"

"Didn't you get my letter?" she asked him.

"Sure. You're married. Congratulations, I always thought It'd happen. You got a great guy there, Laura. I wish I had him." And he laughed pleasantly.

"Terry, you're incredible," she said. "I don't want you to come near Jack. That's final."

"Go on," he laughed. "I thought I'd come over this afternoon."

"You can't!" She felt as she did in nightmares when she tried to talk and no one could hear her. She felt as if all her words fell on deaf ears.

"Sure I can. I thought we'd—"

"Look, Terry, I'm not going to tell him you're in town," she said, fighting a nerve-rasping frustration with him. "I'm just going to let it go, and I'm telling you right now that if you show up over here it'll hurt him more than he can stand. You broke his heart and that should be enough for you. You won't get any more of him!" She felt fiercely protective and loving, now that their life together seemed threatened. She would fight Terry every way she knew. And yet she had to admit to herself that Terry had more to fight with than she if it ever came to a showdown. That was why it was so important to keep him away.

Jack was a very sensual man and he had been deeply in love with Terry. He still was, in spite of everything. His love for Laura was different; strong, she was sure, but could it stand up to a sudden white-hot blast of passion?

"You sound real bitter, Laura," Terry said reproachfully. "I thought you were sort of kidding in your letter."

"I've never been more serious, Terry. Stay away from us!" She hung up again. When she took her hand away there was a ring of wet on the black handle. She cried all day, feeling angry and helpless.

Jack got home at five, but she told him nothing. She was gentle and solicitous with him in a way he had missed for a couple of months. She read to him and she chatted with him, and underneath it all was a tremulous fear of disaster that made her feel a great tenderness for him. He seemed vulnerable to her. If she betrayed him she would embitter him more than she was able to imagine. The thought was terrifying.

"Mother, you need a change," he said when they had finished dinner.

"I do?"

"Leave the dishes and scram."

She felt a little spark of fear. "Are you kicking me out?' she asked.

"I sure as hell am, you doll," he said. "Get thee hence."

"Where?" His laughter relieved her.

'The Village. Where else?" And when she stared at him, wordless, he added, "You need it, honey. You're nervous as a cat. Go on, have a ball."

"You're kidding!"

"I'll give you three minutes to get out of here," he said with a glance at his watch.

Laura hesitated for a few seconds until he looked at her over the top of the paper again and then she ran, heels ringing staccato on the polished wood floor of the hall, and got her coat and purse. On the way out she stooped to kiss his cheek.

"Jack, I adore you," she whispered, to which he only smiled. At the door she turned and said, "I'll be home early."

"No curfew," he said solemnly.

Laura went first to the Cellar, a favorite hangout in Greenwich Village. The tourists had begun to stop there by this time, but the gay crowd outnumbered them still and it wasn't primarily a trap. The prices were reasonable and the decor smoky.

Laura settled at the bar with a sigh of sheer pleasure. All she wanted to do was sit there quietly and look at them...those lovely girls, dozens of them, with ripe lips and rounded hips in tight pants or smooth skirts. And the big ones, the butches, who acted like men and expected to be treated as such. They were the ones who excited Laura the most, when it came right down to it. Women, women...she loved them all, especially the big girls with the firm strides and the cigarettes in their mouths...She realized with chagrin that she was thinking of Beebo.

God, what if she's here? she thought with a wonderful scare running up her spine. She looked around, but Beebo was nowhere in sight.

I wonder if she has a job, poor darling. I wonder if Lili's still supporting her. I wonder if she's still drinking so much...if she thinks of me at all...Oh what's the matter with me? What do I care? She nearly drove me crazy!

She thought of Tris suddenly, of that marvelous fragrant tan skin. In fact she indulged in an orgy of suggestive thoughts that would have driven her crazy cooped up at home. But here, surrounded with people who felt and thought much as she did, it was all right. It was safe somehow. She could even spend the evening flirting with somebody, if anybody caught her eye, and it would come to no harm. Just a night's outing. Nothing more.

Tris...Tris...she would never show up in a place like this. She'd shun it like the plague. All the same it would be nice. So nice.

But the harder Laura concentrated on Tris the more insistently Beebo obsessed her. Laura shrugged her off and ordered another drink. She laughed a little to herself and said, *But I don't love her at all anymore.* And she turned to talk to the girl beside her.

The girl was very charming: small and curly-headed and pretty, and she laughed a lot. And soon Laura was laughing with her and learned that Inga was her name. But that face, that damned face of Beebo's, strong and handsome and hard with too much living, kept looking at her through the haze of Inga's cigarette.

"Did you ever have somebody plague your thoughts, Inga?" she asked her abruptly. "Somebody you'd nearly forgotten and weren't in love with anymore, and never really were in love with?"

"What's her name?" Inga asked sympathetically.

"Oh, nobody you'd know." She was fairly sure Inga *would* know, if she frequented the Cellar. If she'd hung around the Village long enough she'd know most of the characters by sight, if not personally. Beebo was one of the characters. And she had been around here for fourteen years. "How long have you lived down here?" Laura asked the girl.

"Two years next month."

Long enough, Laura thought.

"I'll bet I know her. She ever come in here? Come on, tell me," Inga said.

"I can't,"

"You're silly, then. I'll clue you in on something, Laura. If you can't get her off your mind it's because you can't get her out of your heart. That sounds corny but it's true. I found out the hard way. Believe me."

Laura shook her head. "I never loved her," she said positively.

"You're fooling yourself, sweetie."

Laura looked at her, bemused. "I'm in love with somebody else," she said, thinking of Tris.

"Me?" Inga grinned.

"No. No, an Indian girl."

"Indian? What's her name?"

"Tris."

"Tris! Gee, I *do* know her. She comes in here a lot."

Laura stared at her, too shocked to answer for a minute. Finally she said hoarsely, "Tris would never come in here. She hates gay bars. I know that for a fact."

"Well…" Inga looked as if she knew she had put her foot in her mouth and regretted it. "Maybe it's a different Tris."

"What's her last name?"

"Robischon, or something. Something Frenchy. I think she made it up myself. But she's a gorgeous girl. I was really smitten when I saw her."

Laura blanched a little and ordered another drink and drank it down fast, and Inga laid a hand on her arm. "Gee, I'm sorry, Laura," she said. "Me and my big mouth. I should learn to shut up. But I'm in here all the time. I come in after work and I see just about everybody—"

"I know, I know. It's okay, Inga." She ordered another drink. "I'd rather know than not," she said. "Besides, I haven't seen the girl for eight months. It'd be pretty strange if nobody found out about her in eight months. She's beautiful."

"That she is. Somebody's found out, all right. A lot of people, I hear."

"Does she come in here alone?" The whole thing seemed incredible to Laura. Tris! So aloof, so chilly, so much better than the rest of the gay crowd. Tris, who wouldn't go near Fire Island for a summer vacation because it was "crawling with queers." It just couldn't be. But Inga certainly wasn't describing anybody else.

"She comes with somebody else," Inga said reluctantly. "Look, sweetie, why don't you come over to my place and have a nightcap. We can't talk in here."

"I'd like to know, Inga. Tell me. Who does she come in with?" Laura turned and looked at her, swiveling slowly on her stool, a little tipsy and feeling suddenly as if the situation were something of a joke.

"Oh...a big gal. Been around the Village for years. You might know her. Beebo Brinker's her name."

Laura sat there frozen for nearly a minute. It *was* a joke—colossal, cruel, hilarious. She laughed uncertainly and ordered another drink.

"I knew you were going to say that," she told Inga. "Isn't that the damnedest thing? Isn't that the goddamnedest thing?" And she began to laugh again, repeating, when she could get her breath, "I knew you were going to say that." Inga had to slap her face to stop the shrieking, irrepressible giggles that were strangling her. Then Laura's laughter changed, in the space of a breath, to tears.

Inga talked to her quietly with that odd intimacy that springs up between homosexuals in trouble, and it helped. After five or six minutes Laura wiped her eyes and drank her drink and let Inga help her out of the Cellar. A few curious eyes followed them and Laura prayed again that nobody she knew had seen her.

The cold air braced her a little, and she stood on the corner weaving slightly and trying to get her bearings.

"Come on," Inga said. "Let's get some hot coffee into you. I live just a couple of blocks from here. Come on."

Laura let herself be led by the diminutive curly-head, but when she saw they were headed for Cordelia Street she began to get scared. "Beebo lives near here," she said, hanging back.

"I mean—she used to."

"She still does," Inga said. "I see her now and then. I live right over there." She pointed.

Laura brushed the girl's hand from her sleeve and turned to her. "Thanks, Inga," she said. "Thanks anyway, but I think I'll…" And her eyes wandered back into Cordelia Street

Inga followed her gaze, catching the idea. "I wouldn't if I were you," she said. "You'll be real sorry the minute you get there." When Laura didn't answer she asked, "Tell me, which one of them is it?"

"Which one?"

"That you just can't get off your mind?"

Laura looked back up the street where she used to live and said softly, "Beebo. It's crazy, isn't it? Beebo. And it's Tris I'm in love with."

"Yeah," said Inga with kindly skepticism. "Sure…Have some coffee with me?"

Laura leaned over on a whim and kissed her cheek. "That's for being a woman," she said. "You don't know what a help it's been."

Inga stood on the corner and watched Laura walk away from her. "Any time you want that coffee, Laura," she called. "I'm in the phone book."

Laura stood in front of the door into her old apartment building for a long while on trembling legs before she turned the knob and walked in.

What if they're together? she wondered. *They'll just grab me and wring my neck. God, all those questions Tris used to ask me about Beebo. And it never entered my love-sick head!*

She crossed the little inner court to the second door, opened it, and went to the row of mailboxes to press the buzzer. She found

Beebo's name, with her own crossed out beneath it but no other added. And a weird, wonderful panic grabbed her throat at the thought of Beebo.

She left the buzzer without pressing it and walked up the flight of stairs to stand in front of the door that had once been her own, with Beebo still swimming before her eyes.

She could picture her more and more clearly: wearing pants and going barefoot, tired at the end of the day and maybe a little high; a cigarette in her mouth and a towel tied around her middle while she did dishes or cleaned up the apartment; the smooth skin on her face and the handsome features that used to fire Laura's imagination and make her tingle; the tired eyes, blue and brilliant and somehow a little sick of it all...except when they focused on Laura.

Laura remembered how it had been and a sudden flash of physical longing caught her heart and squeezed until she felt her breath come short. She stared at the door, afraid to knock and still hypnotized with curiosity. Her hand was raised, quivering, only inches from the green painted wood.

Tris will open it, she thought, *and together they'll strangle me.* Oddly, she didn't care. She was too tight to care. She had a vision of herself falling into their arms and succumbing without a struggle. Just letting them have her life, her mixed-up, aimless, leftover life.

She knocked—a quick scared rap, sharp and dear. And then stood there on one foot and the other, half panicky like a grade-schooler nearly ready to wet her pants and flee.

Footsteps. High heels. From the kitchen, Beebo's voice. "Who the hell could that be? After ten, isn't it?" *Oh, that voice! That husky voice that used to whisper such things to me that I can never forget.*

The door swung open all at once, ushering a flood of light into the hall. Laura looked up slowly...at Lili! The two of them stared at each other in mutual amazement for a moment. And while they stared, mute, Beebo called again, "Who is it, Lili?"

Lili, her candy-box pretty face overlaid with too much makeup, as usual, broke into a big smile. "It's Laura!" she exclaimed. "I'll be goddamned. *Laura!*"

For a tense moment Laura could feel Beebo's shock across the rooms and through the walls like a physical touch. Then her courage melted—fizzled into nothing like water on a hot skillet, and she turned and ran.

She heard Beebo at the door, before she got out into the court, saying, "Let her go, Lili. If she thinks I'm going to chase her twice—" And that was all Laura got of it. It shot through her heart like a bullet.

Laura reached the door to the street, tore it open, and rushed out. But once there, with the door shut behind her and no sound of pursuing footsteps, she collapsed against the wall and wept. Between sobs, when she could get her breath, she listened...listened...for the running feet that would mean Beebo had changed her mind. Laura had to believe, at least for a minute, that Beebo would come after her. Because it was all tied up in her mind with Beebo loving her. If Beebo loved her she'd chase her. It was that simple. And it didn't matter a damn what Laura might have done to Beebo in the past, or how she might have hurt her.

Tris! she thought. *I've got to see her!* She said this to herself very urgently, but curiously, at the same time, she felt no desire to go and find the lovely tormented dancer. She told herself it would be all fight and misery. But in her heart of hearts she knew that real love would brave that misery now, being so close and so starved for passion.

She stood there for fully fifteen minutes before she was able to pull herself together and walk to Seventh Avenue. She went straight home in a cab.

Laura walked slowly up the stairs to her apartment. It was after eleven now, and Jack would be in bed. She had had too much to drink, but she was sober, a tired, bewildered sort of sobriety that made her want to lie down and weep and rest.

In the morning she would tell it all to Jack. Wonderful Jack. He would coax her back to living, coax her with his wit and his compassion and his incredible patience with her. And she would lie in a welter of dejection and let him work on her until she felt like lifting her head from the pillow and raising the shade from the window and going on with life. It was one of the things she loved him for and needed him for the most—this ability to revive her when she was so low that only death was lower.

Tonight was perhaps not quite that bad. But it was bad enough to have exhausted her. And Tris and Beebo! That had been the cruelest blow; the one she should have foreseen clear as a beacon in a black sea. She shoved a trembling key into the lock and walked into the apartment.

It was warm and well-lighted. It was pretty and it was comfortable. It was home. And Laura felt a sort of gratitude to Jack that needed words. She went to find him. But he wasn't in the living room, nor in the bedroom.

She stood on the threshold of the bedroom and said, "Jack? Hey, Jack! Where are you?"

"Here," he said from the kitchen.

"Oh. It's me. I thought you'd be in bed." She slipped her coat off while she walked through the living room to find him. "Hi," she said. He was sitting on a kitchen chair and he answered, "Hi."

Laura stood in the doorway and looked at him. And he stared back at her, and she knew something was wrong but she didn't know what. Her long fine hair had come loose when she ran from Beebo and she reached up and pulled it down in a shimmering cascade, watching Jack all the while through narrowed eyes.

"Have fun?" he asked.

"Beebo and Tris…are…shacking up." She threw it at him point-blank. She wanted his sympathy.

Jack put his head back and laughed, that awful bitter laugh she hadn't heard for months, and she knew with a sudden start of fear and pity that he was drunk. "That makes everything perfect," he said, still laughing, his eyes wicked and sharp behind the horn rims.

"Jack…," she said shakily, coming in to sit beside him and

seeing now the whiskey bottle on the table in front of him, two-thirds empty. "Jack, darling." She took his hands and her eyes were big with alarm.

Jack took his hands back. Not roughly, but as if he simply didn't want to be touched. Not by Laura, anyway.

"Mother, you are a living doll. If I had known you could keep secrets so well I'd have told you a few," he said. He spoke, as always when he was drunk, with a slow precision, as if each word were a stepping stone.

"Secrets?" Laura said.

"You are the living picture of guilt, my dear," he said. "It is written all over your beautiful face."

Laura put her hands over that face suddenly with a gasp.

"Terry!" she sobbed through clenched teeth. *"Terry!* If I hadn't gone out he wouldn't have come."

"He comes when the mood hits him," Jack said. "Which is most of the time, most anywhere. It had nothing to do with you going out, my little wifey."

Laura looked up, her delicate face mottled pink and white and wet from the eyes down. "He wrote—"

"Indeed he did. He told me the whole romantic story."

"Jack, darling, I only kept it secret because I was afraid you'd—you'd start drinking, or something—I—"

"You hit the nail on the head. I'm indebted to you. Your solicitude is exemplary." He waved the fast-emptying bottle at her.

"Oh, shut up! Shut up! I *love* you. I did it because I love you."

"You opened my mail because you love me?" He continued to drink while he talked…slowly, but steadily.

"I knew it was from him, Jack. I just had a feeling. The hand-writing and everything."

He laughed ruefully. "Just think what you've spared me!" he said. "I can drink in peace now. My wife loves me. Thanks, wife." He saluted her.

Laura slid off her chair to her knees and put her arms around him, still crying. "Jack, Jack, please forgive me. I'll do anything, I couldn't bear to hurt you, I'd die first. Oh, please—"

"You're forgiven," he interrupted her. "Why not?" And he kept on laughing. But his pardon was so light, so biting, that she cringed from it. She lifted her face to him, streaming with tears, and he said, smiling at her, "You make a lovely picture, Mother. Sort of Madonna-like. If I could paint you, I'd paint you. Black, I think. From head to toe."

She put her head down on his knees and said softly, "You'll never forgive me, will you?"

"I already have."

"Never," she whispered, stricken.

"Oh, let's not get maudlin," he said. "I admit I would have been grateful for a little forewarning. But after all, it's a simple question of sex. Maybe I should get rid of mine. That would solve everything." And his soft, insane chuckling underlined everything he said.

Laura felt terror then. It rose and fell inside her like nausea. Whenever she looked at Jack it surged in her throat. It wasn't the sweet guilty thrill of coming near Beebo that had cost her such sensual pain earlier in the evening.

"Jack, darling," she said.

"Yes, Laura darling." And the sarcasm burned her. But she went on, determined, raising herself back into her chair again with effort.

"Tell me what happened. Tell me everything."

"Oh, it was dandy," he said. "You should have been here. Incidentally, he asked about your health." Laura couldn't watch him while he talked. She looked at her hands. And all the while he told her about it she kept thinking, *If only I hadn't gone out tonight. Every time I do something completely selfish I suffer for it. And so does he. Damn Terry! Damn him to hell! He won't ruin Jack, I won't let him. This is once he won't have his way.*

It had been so completely unexpected, so startling, that Jack would never forget it or recover from it. Terry was as far removed from his life as if he were dead. And his life, Jack felt, had become a good thing at last. He had Laura to live for, not a wild, irresistible, good-for-nothing boy who wore him out and broke his heart and his bankroll. He had a new stature in the world as a married man, a new security. And the sweet hope of a child someday....

When he heard the bell ring, almost an hour after Laura had gone out, he took it for a neighbor and stood with the front door open while the elevator ascended. But when Terry stepped out, Jack was speechless. He couldn't believe it, and he would have slammed the door and passed it off as a nightmare if he could have moved a little faster.

But Terry caught him and from then on it was as degrading and overwhelming as it had ever been. Jack put up the best fight he could, but it was little more than a gesture of protest. He was helplessly angry, helplessly infatuated. And all the while Terry prated to him of San Francisco and the Beats and the fog and the styles in clothes and the styles in lovemaking, Jack kept wondering, *How did he find me?* And the answer was, had to be, *Laura.* Laura had failed him. Betrayed him. It almost tore him apart.

Terry didn't leave until nearly eleven, and Jack saw him out, still with the feeling that it hadn't happened, that it was all an incredible dream. It wasn't until he got the bottle and began to drink that he believed in it at all. By the time Laura got home he wished the whole damned world to hell, with himself first in line.

"And that's all," Jack said. "Naturally, the only thing to do after he left was get drunk." He had nearly finished the bottle and it was all he could do to get the words out. They left his mouth slowly, discreetly, each one a pearl of over-articulation.

Laura took away what was left—a shot or two at the most—and he didn't even try to protest. She helped him up and half dragged, half carried him to the bedroom, where she dumped him on his bed. He was unconscious the minute she pushed his head down on the pillow. Laura undressed him, tears running down her face.

"Sleep," she said. "Sleep and forget it for a while. I'll make it up to you, darling. All I wanted tonight was to cry on your shoulder. And you can't even hold yourself up."

She dragged and shoved and pulled until she got him under the covers. "He won't get you, Jack," she whispered. "You'd fight for me if I were in trouble. And I'll fight for you."

In the morning, Laura got up, moving softly as a bird on the sand, and left him to himself in the bedroom, still noisily and miserably asleep with a full-blown, brutal hangover brewing under his closed eyes.

She had to make it up to him, redeem herself. And she could only think of one thing. So before noon she called Terry and asked him to dinner.

"Sounds great," he said in innocent surprise and pleasure.

"I was counting on mooching from you," he admitted, laughing.

When Jack woke up she told him what she had done. She waited until he had had four cups of coffee and eight aspirins and some forced warm milk and raw egg. He said nothing but "No. No! *No!*" to whatever she was trying to get into him. He sat in the kitchen with his head in his hands, and Laura began to fear he was still a little drunk. She had thrown out the rest of the whiskey.

"Where's the bottle?" he asked her finally, around the middle of the afternoon.

"Gone. I tossed it."

He nodded painfully, resigned.

"Jack," she said softly. "Terry's coming to dinner."

He lifted his throbbing head to gape at her. "Are you trying to kill me, Mother? Or just drive me nuts?" he said.

"I'm going to save you. Save *us,*" she said passionately. "We're at the crossroads, Jack. This is the first real crisis we've had. We can't just fall apart. We have too much to save, too much worth saving. We have love, too, and I'm not going to let him hurt you any more." Somehow in the strength she found to fight Jack's battle was the strength to fight her own. The downright shock and humiliation of finding that her two ex-lovers were romancing might have thrown her into a full-blown depression. But now she hadn't time. It was Jack's turn. She loved him, she was absolutely sure of that. She was not absolutely sure she loved Tris any more. Nor was she sure now that she *didn't* love Beebo. Jack was her security, her chosen life; he deserved her loyalty.

But to her chagrin, her noble speech had very little effect on him. He got out of his chair with much agonized effort, making a face, and headed for the coat closet.

"Where are you going?" she asked anxiously, running after him.

"For a bottle."

"Oh, Jack, no!"

He turned to face her, sliding awkwardly into his coat sleeves. "Do you want me to go through this sober?"

"Darling, you don't even have to *look* at him! You can lock yourself in the john and sing hymns if you want to. I just want to talk to him."

"About the weather?"

"I'll get him out of here, I swear I will!"

"How? With a can opener? TNT?" He was moving toward the door as he spoke with Laura clinging to his arm and trying to hold him back.

"Darling, trust me!" she begged. She was not at all sure that she could get Terry out again, once he got in, but she had to make Jack calm down. She was frantic to stop him.

"Trust you?" He turned and looked at her uncertainly, his hand on the front door knob, and gave a little snort "That doesn't work. I tried it."

"Oh, you damn, fatuous idiot!" she cried in exasperation, dropping his arm to stamp to the middle of the room and face him from there as if from a podium. "I open *one* goddamn letter—out of love and anxiety—to spare you pain. And the thing backfires. Do you have to crucify yourself? I said I was sorry and I am. I'm sorry. I'm sorry, I'm sorry, I'm sorry!" she yelled.

"Were you born that way?" he snapped.

"Shut up and listen!" she cried. "Jack, let me make it up to you, let me *try*. You have no right to call yourself my husband if you won't give me a chance, and I'm telling you right now, Jack Mann, if you won't I'll walk out of this house and your life forever." She paused, flushed and trembling, for breath, while Jack stared at her, surprised, half convinced, and himself trembling slightly from the hangover. Finally he went to the arm of the nearest chair and sat down and said, "All right, Wife. Read him the riot act while I sing hymns in the bathroom, if you think it'll do any good."

"Oh, Jack." She ran to him, all pity and tenderness, and kissed his frowning face. He put his head back and ignored her.

Terry arrived at seven, half an hour late, with a huge bouquet of roses for Laura. "For Mrs. Mann," he said, bowing, and then gave her a quick embrace. "You look great, honey."

"Thanks," she said with reserve. "I'll put them in water."

"Where's Jack? Oh, there you are." Terry made a running jump to the couch where Jack was lying in state, wearing his hangover like a royal robe.

Jack let out all his breath in a wail of anguish when Terry hit him.

"Where did you get the flowers?" Laura asked, coming back in with them arranged in a tall vase.

"Nick's. On the corner. I had to charge 'em to you, Laura. I hope you don't mind." He smiled charmingly. "Your credit's much better than mine around here."

Jack laughed softly. "You haven't changed a bit, have you?" he said to Terry.

Laura sat down and looked at Terry's bright young face, smiling happily around a mouthful of salted pecans, and wondered if her little trick would work. It had to. But it might not. She felt a little sick, seeing Jack so miserable.

"No drinks?" Terry said, suddenly conscious of the lack of alcohol.

"Milk," Laura offered.

"Milk punch?" he asked.

"Just bare milk," Jack drawled.

"What's the matter with you?" Terry said and laughed at him. "Have a nut." And he popped one in Jack's half open mouth. "You aren't on the wagon, are you?"

"I was," Jack said. "Till last night"

"No kidding. God. Amazing. Since when?"

"Since we got married last August. A little before."

"Laura, how'd you do it?" He grinned at her.

"I didn't have to," she said. "The day you walked out of his life all the good things walked in."

"Including you?" Terry asked.

"Including me," she shot back.

"Oh." He smiled ruefully. "I wasn't *that* bad, was I?" he asked Jack. He seemed to think it was comfortably funny, like everything else connected with Jack. "Did I drive you to drink, honey?" he said.

"Only on the bad days," Jack said. "Unfortunately, there weren't any good days."

Terry laughed and stuck another nut in Jack's mouth.

"That's all," Jack told him, wincing. "The damn pecans sound like depth charges when I chew." He stroked his head carefully.

There was a silence while Terry ate, Laura stared at him nervously, and Jack concentrated on his pains. Laura wanted to make Terry uncomfortable, self-conscious. But it was nearly a lost cause.

"What's for dinner?" he asked suddenly, unaware that he was supposed to notice the silence.

She told him.

"Great," he said. More silence. Laura was determined to embarrass him, and Jack was too ill to care about conversation. Slowly, Terry began to realize something was amiss. Rather than take the hint he tried to lighten the atmosphere with chatter.

"How do you like the married life, old man?" he asked.

"He liked it fine the day before yesterday," Laura said crisply. Jack groaned. Terry understood.

He sat up and leaned toward his hostess. "Laura, honey, I don't want to mess things up for you," he said. "I just love Jack, too, that's all. You know that. You always knew it, even before you got married."

"I know you nearly killed him," she said quietly.

"No fair exaggerating."

"No fair, hell. It's true!" she exclaimed.

"It's not either!" he said with good-humored indignation, as if they were playing parlor games. "Is it, Jack?"

But Jack, his eyes on Laura now, kept silent.

"Well," Terry admitted, "I was pretty bitchy sometimes. But so was he. And no matter what, we loved each other. Even at the end, when he kicked me out."

"If he hadn't kicked you out that night he might have killed himself with liquor."

"I don't believe it."

Laura threw her hands up, exasperated. "What more do you *want* from Jack, Terry?" she said. "What do you want from *me*?"

Terry grinned. "Equal time," he said, nodding at the bedroom.

Jack laughed weakly and Laura got up and stamped her foot. "Terry, Jack loves you. I know that and I'll have to live with it. But that love is destructive, and I'm asking you now to get out of our lives forever and never come back to hurt us again." She said it with quiet intensity.

"Before dinner?" he asked.

"Oh, God!" Laura spluttered at the ceiling.

Terry lighted a cigarette for Jack, who had fumbled one from the box on the cocktail table, and told Laura, "I can't go away forever. Any more than you could desert Beebo forever. I love him. I'm stuck with him."

"I've *left* Beebo," she said.

"You'll go back," he told her serenely. "It was that kind of affair."

Laura held on to her self control as her last and dearest possession. She didn't dare to lose it. "Take me seriously, Terry," she begged, almost in a whisper. "Please let us live together in peace."

Terry shrugged. He didn't like to get serious. "What are you going to do the rest of your lives?" he asked them. "Live like a couple of old maids in your fancy little apartment? Pretend you're both straight? What a kick!" He said it sarcastically but without malice. "A kick like that won't last long, you know."

"It's not a kick. It's something we both need and want," Laura said earnestly.

"Nuts," Terry said amiably. "What you both need and want is a few parties. Get out and camp. Do you good."

"Sure," Laura said sharply. "So you make love to Jack and he goes out and drinks a fifth of whiskey, after *eight months* on the wagon. Was that what you had in mind?"

Terry made a little grimace of perplexity. "That was pretty silly," he told Jack. "Now she won't let me see you at all."

"He needs me more than he needs you, Terry," Laura said.

"Yeah? But he wants me more." He grinned at her. "You've got to admit that counts for something," he told her. "I can give him something you can't give him." He looked so smug, so sure of himself, that Laura, with her heart in her throat, decided to pull her rabbit out of the hat. If it didn't work, she would have to give up.

"And I can give him something *you* can't give him," she said, her voice low and tense. "A child."

There was a long stunned silence. Jack and Terry both stared at her—Jack with a slight smile of amazement and Terry with open-mouthed dismay.

"A child!" Terry blurted finally. "Don't tell *me!* I wasn't born yesterday."

"It's true," Laura spat at him. "And I'm not going to have any empty-headed, pretty-faced queers hanging around my baby! Not even *you,* Terry Fleming."

Terry turned to gape at Jack, his mouth still ajar. "She's kidding!" he exclaimed. "Isn't she?"

Jack paused slightly and then shook his head, and the strange little smile on his face widened. It was brilliant, he thought. Cruel, to himself even more than to Terry, because it wasn't true. But clever.

Terry stood up, bewildered, and walked around the living room. Laura watched him, her face flushed, sweating with expectation. Finally Terry turned to look at them. Jack, raising himself on one elbow, watched him.

"Do you still want me to have dinner with you?" he asked wryly, and Laura saw hesitation in his look and felt a first small hope.

She didn't know what to say. But she was thinking, *I've made Jack a man in his eyes now. He's thinking Jack can do what he could never do himself. He's thinking at least, if I was wrong about him ruining Jack's life, I'm right about ruining a baby's. He knows damn well he could do that. Or does he?*

But at least he *was* thinking. His lovely young face was screwed up with the effort.

Suddenly he said to Laura, as if expecting to trip her up, "When's it due? The kid?"

"November," she said. She had anticipated him.

"Well!" His face brightened. "If it isn't due till November, we've got a long time to play around." And it was Jack he looked at now.

But Laura jumped at him, bristling. "I don't want an alcoholic for a husband!" she said. "I don't want my baby to have an alcoholic for a father. A drunken, miserable, tormented man who doesn't know which sex he is, who has to chase around after a thoughtless character like you all night. I don't want to lose my husband, Terry. Not to you or any other gay boy in the world. You'd ruin his health and make him wild inside of a month."

She was crying, though she didn't realize it, and her cheeks were flaming. Terry stared at her for some moments in surprised silence. And then he looked at Jack, who was still propped on one arm, taking it all in with an inscrutable smile.

"Well...," Terry said again, almost diffidently. Apparently he believed they were having a child. He looked to Jack for moral support. "Is that the way you feel too, honey?" he asked.

"Why certainly," Jack said cheerfully, incongruously.

"Can't you tell? Whatever she says, goes." A soft note of hysteria sounded in his voice.

"I guess you don't want me to stay for dinner now," Terry said, glancing at Laura. For answer she only turned away and began to cry. Terry walked over to Jack and knelt before him on the floor, putting his hands on Jack's shoulders. "I do love you, Jack. I never lied about that. I didn't know it was so bad. For you, I mean. I still don't see how it could have been. But I don't want to mess things up for the kid. Shall I go? *You* tell me." He waited, watching Jack's face.

"I told you to leave me once, Terry. I haven't the strength to say it again. It's up to you."

Terry leaned forward and kissed him on the lips. "If you haven't the strength to say it, I haven't the strength to do it. No matter what she says," he said.

Laura came at him suddenly from across the room. "Go!" she flashed. "Go, damn you, and never come back!"

Terry looked uncertainly from Laura to Jack, and Jack covered his face abruptly with a noise rather like a sob.

Terry stood up. "All right," he said in a husky voice. "I'll go. I'll go for the baby's sake. But not forever, Laura. Not forever."

At the front door he turned to her. "You say you love him," he said. "Then you must understand why I *can't* leave him forever. I love him too." He said it sadly but matter-of-factly. And Laura, staring at him through tear-blurred eyes, realized that he never would understand what he had done to Jack or how. He thought it was a simple matter of giving a kid a break. And because he loved Jack enough he was able to do it.

"Enjoy your flowers," he said with a rueful grin, and then Terry went out the front door and shut it carefully behind him. Neither Jack nor Laura stirred nor made a sound until they heard the elevator arrive, the doors open, shut again, and the elevator leave.

"He's gone," she whispered. "Dear God, don't let him ever come back."

Jack rolled over, his back to her, and wept briefly and painfully with desperate longing. There was a moment of silence while she watched him fearfully. And then he stood up and headed for the door. Laura threw herself against it.

"No! Don't follow him, Jack!" she implored, her voice rising.

"I won't," he said, trying to reach past her to open the door, but she threw her arms around him and begged him to stay with her.

"I got him to leave, Jack. He won't dare come back for a long time. Maybe he'll find somebody new. Maybe we'll be lucky and he'll never come back."

"I should be so lucky," he said acidly.

She looked at him, dismayed. "Isn't that what you wanted?" she asked.

He stopped trying to grab the doorknob for a minute to look at her. "Yes," he said, with effort. And after a pause, "You were masterful, Mother. You really played your scene."

She looked at the floor confusedly, hearing all the sarcasm and the hurt and the grudging admiration in his voice. "Do you hate me for it?" she asked.

"No. I'm grateful."

"Do you still love me?" she whispered.

"Yes. But don't ask me to prove it now." He got the door open in a sudden deft gesture, but Laura was still clutching him.

"Where are you going?" she asked fearfully.

"For a bottle."

"Oh, God!" she gasped. "Then it's all been for nothing," she said despairingly.

"No," he said. "I'm not drinking this for Terry. I'm drinking it for the baby."

"The baby?" she said tremulously.

"The little kid who wasn't there."

He turned to go and she followed him into the hall.

"But Jack—" she protested as he rang for the elevator. "Jack, I—I—" She looked up and saw the long bronze needle moving swiftly toward "three" as the elevator ascended, having barely emptied Terry into the first floor. It seemed to be measuring off the last seconds of their marriage. She had to do something. Trembling and scared, she caught his lapels and said, with great difficulty, "I meant it, Jack."

"Meant what?"

"About the baby."

He stared at her, one hand holding back the door of the just-arrived elevator.

"I'll have a baby," she said. "If you still want one."

For a while they stood in the dim little hall and gazed at each other. And then Jack let his hand slip from the elevator door and, circling her waist with his arm, led her back into the apartment.

"He'll be back, you know," he said, stopping to look at her.

"I know. But by that time he'll know we aren't kidding," she said, looking dubiously at her tight, flat stomach. "By that time you'll be strong again. And ready for him. You'll know he's coming and you'll be able to take it. It won't be like now."

He kissed her. "Goddamn it," he whispered, grateful and amazed. "I *do* love you."

Chapter Nine

THE DOCTOR'S WAITING ROOM was crowded, heavy with the eager boredom of people waiting to talk about themselves. It was the fourth doctor they had been to see within a week. Jack, as Laura might have expected, was in a hurry. But he had to find the right man, too—a man he genuinely liked. Not just any bone-picker was going to perform the wizardry to bring *his* child into being.

Laura had simply sat in red-faced silence through Jack's expositions of their supposed marital troubles, both unwilling and unable to contribute a word. And the whole thing had been lengthy and bewildering and not a little tiring.

But when they finally got into Dr. Belden's plush, paneled office, it went well. And she knew, suddenly paying attention to the words of the men, that it was going to be settled. And it was.

She answered the standard questions, her voice low with embarrassment. They always bothered her excessively, like so many spiders crawling over her tender shame. Other girls might not mind, or even liked to yammer to doctors about their intimate selves, but not Laura.

Jack bolstered her up as they were leaving. "You were heroic, Mother," he assured her. "I know you hate it—yes you do, don't lie," he added impatiently when she tried to protest. "It's all right, honey, it's all in a good cause."

"Don't call me honey."

"Why?"

"Terry calls everybody honey." She was in a grumpy mood; he

saw it and let her be for a while. "When do I have to go back?" she asked as they rode home in a taxi.

"A week from Thursday." He looked at her somewhat anxiously as if wishing that Thursday had already come. "You won't change your mind, of course," he said to comfort himself. His voice was calm but his eyes were worried.

"No," she sighed. She looked at her gloved hands until his anxious gaze moved her to give him one and make him smile.

He looked strangely different, almost young. Jack had the kind of a face that must have made him look forty when he was twenty. In a sense it was an ageless face because it had hardly changed at all. Laura supposed that when he was sixty, he would still look forty. But for the few weeks after Terry disappeared it looked young. And Laura thought with an ache of how much of that was due to her. How much she had forced him to depend on her. She was deeply committed now. There was no retreating.

Laura saw Doctor Belden three days in a row, and it was unspeakably humiliating for her. But she endured it. By the time her appointment came due, she was too afraid for Jack not to go. But she prayed when she was alone, with big wild angry sobs, that the artificial insemination wouldn't work; that she was barren or Jack was sterile or the timing was off; anything. And she felt a huge, breathtaking need for a woman that absolutely tortured her at night.

After her first examination with Belden she went out of the office to meet Jack and told him she was going to the Village.

"I don't know why I need to. I just do," she said.

"Sure, sweetheart," he said at last, standing facing her on the pavement outside the doctor's office. "Go. Only, come back."

"I will," she said, near tears, and turned and almost ran from him. She couldn't bear to touch him, and it was painful even to look at him.

It was mid-day in the Village and mothers walked their babies in the park. Laura hurried past them. Old ladies strolled about in the unusually warm weather, dogs barked, and a few hardy would-be artists had set up shop in the empty pool at the center of Washington Square. A small crowd of students had gathered to offer encouragement and argue.

Laura walked quickly through the park to Fourth Street, and then she turned and walked west, not sure why. On the other side of Sixth Avenue she stopped and found a drugstore and went in for coffee.

I can't see Tris, she told herself, playing nervously with her hands. *I won't see Beebo. Or rather, Beebo won't see me. That's for sure.* She tried to think of anything but what she had just been through, but it didn't work. It never does.

Just so it's normal, she thought angrily. *I won't hate it but I couldn't stand an abnormal child. God, I've got to talk to somebody, somebody who doesn't know, who'll put it out of my mind.* She thought of Inga then, but she couldn't remember her last name and she wasn't too sure where the girl lived. She had been too drunk that night.

And then, for no apparent reason, she thought of Lili. Beautiful, brazen Lili. At least Lili would talk. Laura wouldn't have to open her mouth. Maybe it would be better that way. She wouldn't betray any secrets to Beebo's old lover about her marriage. But Lili would be only too happy to tell Laura what had gone on between Beebo and Tris if only to see her squirm, and Laura was burning to know.

She went to the phone booth at the back of the store and looked up Lili. She was still listed, still in the same apartment on Greenwich Avenue. It was late afternoon by the time Laura got there. Lili would just be getting out of bed, if she followed the same habits she used to have.

Laura felt very tired and reluctant when she finally found the right building and the right button to press; afraid and a little ashamed. But she rang anyway, as if she had no will to stop herself. And when the answering ring came she went inside and walked up the stairs.

Lili, hanging over the banister to see who was waking her up so early, saw her coming. Laura stopped on the first landing at her amazed, "Laura! Again! Are you a ghost?"

Laura gazed up, her long pale hair hanging defiantly free and her eyes blue-shadowed the way they were when she was tired or scared. Now she was a little of both.

"No, no ghost," she said.

"I don't believe you. But come in anyway. I have the most divine friend who's a Medium. Where the hell have you been? I thought sure you'd come back, after you saw Beebo a couple of weeks ago." She watched Laura mount the stairs as she spoke and took her by the arm when Laura reached her.

"You look worn out, poor lamb," she said. "I'll give you a drink. What do you want?"

"Nothing."

"Nothing!" It was an explosion, not a question. "God. Next you'll be telling me you've gone straight."

"I came to ask about Beebo," Laura said.

"Oh," said Lili knowledgeably. "I thought so." She went about fixing Laura and herself a drink in spite of Laura's objections. "Well, lamb, what about her?"

"Are she and Tris living together?"

"Mercy, who told you *that?*" Lili turned to stare at her.

"A friend of mine."

"Your friend lies. They aren't living together and they never did. Oh, Tris spent the night with her a few times. You know how it is." She laughed sociably, coming toward Laura with two filled glasses. "Here, lamb, I insist. It'll revive you. My doctor says—"

"Tell me about Tris and Beebo."

"Well," Lili said, confidentially. "It was just an affair."

"What does that mean?" she said.

"It means when you can't get what you want you take what you can get," Lili said archly.

"They saw each other all the time. Beebo even had Tris going into the gay bars. I know this, Lili, don't hide it," Laura said.

"All right, all right," Lili said soothingly. "Tris had to go to the gay bars to find Beebo, that's all. Beebo's never home. You know how she is. And she didn't chase Tris so Tris had to chase her."

Laura felt an ineffable lightening of the heart. Somehow, if it had to happen, that was the best way.

"Tris was nuts about her," Lili said juicily. "She came over when she got back from Long Island last summer...without *you,* if you recall."

"I recall."

"Yes. Well! Beebo was pretty low. You may remember that, too." She looked at Laura sharply, and Laura looked at the floor and refused to answer. "Anyway, Tris fell into her arms and Beebo just caught her. I wish I could say that Beebo fell for her. I think it would have spared her some of the agony you inflicted on her." So now it was out in the open. Lili spoke dramatically, but it wasn't all play-acting. She had loved Beebo once, and she didn't like to see her hurt as Laura had hurt her.

The two females eyed each other, wary but curious, each eager to know what the other could tell her. Lili was ready to hurt Laura to find out. She had seen what happened to Beebo when Laura left her, and it was shocking. Laura didn't know about it, and to Lili it seemed as if she was nothing but a spoiled, headstrong little bitch who didn't care whom she hurt...a little like Lili herself ten years before, and that made Lili even more critical.

If Laura were told how hard Beebo had taken it—how intensely she had suffered and torched for her—maybe it would touch her and make her sorry. Lili enjoyed the idea of Laura on her knees to Beebo, and Beebo kicking her out. For she knew what Laura did not—that Beebo was a different girl now. And to Lili's way of thinking it meant that Beebo would never take Laura back.

So they were agreed, without having said a word about it, that Lili would talk and Laura would listen to her; Lili because she had to hurt and Laura because she had to know.

Lili lighted a cigarette and stuck it carefully into an ebony holder with a water filter, a rather bulky conversation piece. Everything she did was staged.

"I'm going to talk turkey to you, lamb," she informed her guest. "Now that I have you in my clutches." She smiled slightly, a warning smile.

"Talk," Laura said. "But I'd appreciate it if you'd spare me the sermon."

"I'm sure you would." Lili gazed at her. "But, unfortunately, you need a sermon. Oh, just a little one, of course. I won't be crude about it."

Laura ignored her, picking up the drink she didn't think she wanted and sipping at it.

"Well," Lili began. "You almost killed her. I suppose you could have guessed that."

"I knew it would be hard for her," Laura said, "but not that bad." Her voice said she thought Lili was exaggerating, but in her heart she was afraid...afraid it was true.

"It was bad enough to send her to the hospital with a stomachful of sleeping pills. I know. I took her over." She said this with her green eyes flaring and her voice low enough to make Laura strain a little to hear her.

"Oh, damn it, Lili, don't make up a melodrama for me!" Laura cried.

"I thought I was stating it rather plainly. But I'll try again."

"Beebo wouldn't take sleeping pills!" Laura said contemptuously, and this she really believed. "It's not like her. It's too—I don't know—phony. It's more like something *you'd* do than Beebo."

"Luckily I'm not in love with you, pet," Lili countered.

They glared at each other. "You don't know her at all, do you?" Lili went on. "You lived with her for more than two years, and you just don't know her at all."

"I know her better than anybody! What do you mean?"

"All right, lamb, we won't argue the point. Anyway, when she got back from the hospital she was terribly despondent. I kept telling her you'd come back. Everybody did. I didn't believe it, of course, but I was afraid if I told her you were gone for good she'd try something worse than sleeping pills."

"Did she drink awfully hard?"

"Are you kidding? She drank like a fish, naturally," Lili said. "As if you had to ask. Then she got a job. But I'm getting ahead of myself. You wanted to hear about Tris."

Again she smiled, and Laura hated her smile. "Just tell me, Lili," she said. "Without the dramatics."

"Certainly, darling…Well, Tris came back and the first thing she did was come looking for you to tell you she was sorry. I don't know for what. But I was there when she arrived. I couldn't leave Beebo alone for five minutes, it was that bad. So anyway, we were having dinner when Tris came and she looked very surprised not to see you, but if you ask me, she was thrilled to death. She's been on the make for Beebo ever since you met at the dress shop. She strung you along for a contact with Beebo."

"I don't believe you," Laura lied bravely. "Go on."

"Well, darling, that makes it slightly awkward. It's essential to the narrative that you believe it." But Laura's cold white face discouraged her sarcasm and she went on. "Well, Tris was nuts for her. That time she burst in on you and Beebo got so mad—yes, she told me about it—she came to see Beebo, not you. She didn't care a damn if it got you in trouble. The only thing she cared about was seeing Beebo. She wasn't very happy about the way Beebo treated her then, but she's had better luck since.

"Well, Beebo didn't even try to fight her off. She just let her in and they spent a couple of weeks together. And the whole time that awful Milo—Tris's husband—I think you've met?—yes. That must have been jolly." She grinned maliciously. "Well, Milo was over there all the time, just mad as hell. It's a wonder he didn't kill Beebo, the way Tris carried on about her. It took him four whole months to drag her away, and Tris still comes over whenever she can sneak out. But Beebo and Milo get along better now. Since he realized Beebo's not in love with his wife.

"For some strange reason she can't seem to fall in love with anybody. I think she's crazy myself. I mean, after all, you're not *that* irresistible." She paused and Laura took advantage of it to switch the subject, fast.

"What about the job? You said she had a job."

"Oh, yes, I did, didn't I? Well, she's waiting on tables at the Colophon. Oh, don't look so disappointed, lamb, she *likes* it. Besides, she can wear pants." Lili knew how Laura hated Beebo's elevator uniform, and it pleased her to point out that Beebo hadn't reformed. "She works from five to eleven," Lili went on. "Really very good hours. And then of course she's free to get soused till dawn."

"Does she?"

"Sometimes."

"Is it very bad?" Laura asked, her voice a little shaky with fatigue.

"Sometimes."

"God, Lili, is that all you can say? Sometimes? *Tell* me about her, I haven't heard anything for eight months!"

"That's the way you wanted it, darling."

"No. No, it isn't," she whispered. "That's the way it had to be."

"I would say—judging strictly from your very interesting diary—that you were glad to get rid of Beebo. Maybe you're just here to ease your conscience, hm? Be sure she hasn't done anything messy you'd have to blame yourself for?"

Laura had to look away for a minute. The shame was too plain on her face. "That was a stupid thing, that diary," she mumbled. She started crying softly, helplessly. "Lili, cut out the sarcasm," she pleaded, knowing it would do no good.

"Why, don't be silly!" Lili exclaimed, enjoying the scene. "I haven't an ounce of sarcasm in me. I'm just a reporter giving you the facts."

"You're a lousy gossip columnist!" Laura said. "You're all dirty digs and snide cracks, and about a tenth of what you say is true. Tris Robischon was shy and neurotic. She hated gay bars. She wouldn't have gone in if she hadn't been forced. She hated gay people so much that she wouldn't associate with them."

"Like hell," Lili said elegantly. "She lived In the Village, didn't she? Who do you think her ballet pupils were, anyway?"

"Children! Men! Little girls!"

"And big girls, darling."

"She never had affairs with them. She might have slept with one or two of the men, but not with the girls. I'm sure of it."

"Have you talked to Milo about that?"

"No…not about that. But I *know* Tris!"

"Must be wonderful to be so sure of yourself, pet," Lili drawled. "The fact is, your little pseudo-Indian slept with dozens of her pupils. She went to the Lezzie bars because Beebo did, and Beebo's not the first girl she's done it with. You can check it. Go ask the bartender at the Cellar. Ask the lovelies at the Colophon. At Julian's. Go on. Scared?"

Laura stood up suddenly and headed for the door. "I've had enough, Lili. Thanks. Thanks a lot." She spoke briefly, afraid of more tears, and grabbed her coat as she went. But Lili got up and ran after her.

"But darling, I want to know where you've been all this time!"

"It's no business of yours."

"Oh, tell me, Laura. Don't be difficult," she said. "Beebo would be interested," she wheedled.

"Oh, I doubt it. After what you've told me. But just for the record, I've been living uptown."

"Where uptown?"

But Laura shook her head.

"Alone?" Lili said.

"No." Laura didn't know why she said it. It just seemed easier than arguing. Besides, she didn't want Lili to think she was friendless and despised everywhere.

"You know, Jack Mann disappeared from the Village the same time you did," Lili said, her voice vibrant with curiosity.

"Yes."

"Do you know where he is?"

"I see him now and then." She slipped her coat on and opened the front door, not bothering to look back at Lili. Her face was streaked with tears and torment and she wanted to go, to get out, to hide somewhere.

"Where are you going, pet? Why in such a hurry?"

"I'm a little sick, Lili, thanks to you. You have that effect on me," Laura said.

Lili laughed charmingly. "Imagine!" she said. "It's an even trade, then. Well, just so you don't go near Beebo, I guess it's safe to let you loose."

"I have no intention of going near Beebo," Laura said coldly, turning to look at her.

"Good," Lili said. "She'd kill you for sure."

Laura felt a red fury come up in her and she stepped back into the living room, her face so strange and tense that Lili, for the first time since Laura had come, became rather alarmed.

"Lili, goddamn you to hell, quit telling lies! Quit exaggerating!" Laura cried. "I hurt Beebo, but not that much. I didn't ruin her life, for God's sake! Or cripple her or kill her or drive her crazy! And I won't stand here and be accused of something I didn't do. Beebo's no angel, you know. Beebo damn near drove *me* out of my mind when we lived together. She hurt me more than once—I mean *really* hurt, and I've got scars to prove it. I know she loved me, but that doesn't make her perfect and me a double-damned bitch. Love affairs have broken up before. The world keeps on spinning!" She spoke fiercely to bolster up her words. For the truth was that Laura remembered only too well the night Beebo had told her she might kill her someday, and then herself.

But she couldn't let Lili see that, or suspect it, or think that Laura feared it. She hated Lili with all the force of her own fear and uncertainty and resentment at that moment, and her wild hair and hot face actually did scare Lili.

"All right," Lili said finally, putting her drink down on a dainty Empire drawer table near the door. "All right, Laura Landon, I'll tell you something." And Laura saw now that Lili had to defend the things she had said with a good serving of bitter anger: the *pièce de résistance*. "You think Beebo would welcome you back with loving arms? You think she'd forgive you?"

"I didn't say that!"

"You think I've been kidding about how hard she took it when you broke up? When you left her? Sure you do. You make yourself think it because you don't want to feel guilty about it. But you listen to this. Listen!" she cried suddenly as Laura made a sudden move to leave.

Lili threw herself against the door, panting with the exaltation of mingled fear and pleasure at hurting Laura. "Remember Nix? Remember that nice little dog you hated so much? Oh, you hated him all right. Beebo didn't have to tell me, I saw it with my own eyes. Everybody did. You did everything but kick him. And I wouldn't be surprised if you did even that when nobody was looking. Well, what happened to poor Nix?"

"You know damn well!" Laura flashed, feeling trapped and desperate. "You know as well as I do. Let me out of here, Lili!"

"He died, didn't he? Rather messily. Let's say, horribly. Such a nice little dog. You know how he died, Laura?"

"If you're trying to say *I* did it—"

"Beebo killed him. Sliced him in half with that big chef's knife you had in the kitchen table drawer."

For a horrified second, Laura was silent, paralyzed. She almost fainted. She actually staggered backwards and lost her balance. Lili grabbed her to break the fall and left her lying on the floor, her face buried in the plush carpet, sobbing, wailing with shock and horror. Even Lili, finally, was worried about her. She tried to snap her out of it with sarcasm.

"You could have shown a little concern when it happened," she said, "instead of saving it all for now. It's a little late now. Those are crocodile tears, Laura." But they weren't, and Lili couldn't get much conviction into her voice. She bent over Laura and said,

"Stop it! *Really,* Laura! Don't make a scene. Oh!" she exclaimed in exasperation and alarm. "And she accuses *me* of theatrics!" she cried to the ceiling, her hands to her temples.

After a long while Laura rolled over, her breath tumbling uncontrollably in and out of her, her face blotched and stricken.

"It isn't true, is it?" she whispered. "You just wanted to hurt me. Lili?"

Lili, sitting on the edge of her velvet couch, with her elbows on her knees and her chin in her hands, said, "It's true." She gazed at Laura and there was no pose, no elegance in her. It wasn't worth the effort now. Laura was beyond noticing or caring. With her face relaxed, the lines of thirty-seven years showed around Lili's mouth and eyes. She was wondering if the startling effect her words had had was worth it.

Laura looked sick. What a bother to have to call a doctor! She shouldn't have told her. She had had a good time roasting her. She should have let her go. But there was Laura, her bosom heaving, her face a strange color, her eyes enormous. *Odd, I never noticed how big they are,* Lili thought idly.

"Did anyone...really...beat her up?" Laura said, her breath betraying her and making her gasp. "Or did she make up the hoodlums, too—like Nix?" And she covered her face to cry while Lili answered her.

"She did that to herself. After she killed Nix. I don't know why she did it. I hate to admit it, but I guess she did it out of frustrated love. I tried to make her explain it when she told me about it—and believe me, she wouldn't have if she hadn't been fried—and she just said, 'Laura hated him. I thought she might stay with me longer if he was gone.' After she did it she beat herself. I don't know how. I don't know with what. She didn't say. Maybe she just whacked at herself with her fists. Maybe she used something heavy. Anyway, she did it while she was hysterical. At least, that's what I think. I don't see how she could have hurt herself that much if she hadn't been half crazy. She was mourning for Nix and she was afraid of losing you."

Lili stopped talking, and Laura realized dimly that there had been no cutting edge in her voice for the past few minutes.

After a little while of silence Laura got up dizzily from the floor and dried her eyes. Her face had gone very white and she sat down for a minute in a chair.

"Did you ever love her?" Lili asked. "Really?"

Laura turned to look at her, and her eyes seemed remarkably deep and different, as if she had seen something for the first time. She didn't seem to have heard Lili.

"Did you ever love her, Laura?" Lili asked again.

"Not until now," Laura said, and Lili stared at her.

When Laura got home, all she wanted was to go in the bedroom, turn out all the lights, and crawl half dressed into her bed. And try to make sense of her awful knowledge, try to live with it. She couldn't think of Beebo without pain.

Jack followed her into the bedroom where she sprawled on the bed sobbing. He went to her and said worriedly, "Jesus, honey. Tell me about it." He sat down beside her, his hands on her shoulders trying to ease her. "Did the stock market crash?"

She wept on as If he weren't there.

"You got a bad pickle in your hamburger?"

No response.

"Your girdle split?"

She rolled over and looked at him with mournful eyes. "Jack, this is no time to be stupid."

"I can't say anything very bright till you tell me what's the matter," he said.

Laura blew her nose hard. He made her feel ludicrous and she resented it "Beebo," she said finally. "Beebo. Oh, Jack." She looked at him with red eyes. "She *must* have killed your little dog. The one you gave her after Nix died."

"Must have?"

"She killed Nix. Nobody beat her up. She did it to herself."

They stared at each other, Jack beginning to share her feelings.

He heaped his scorn on Beebo. "Damn!" he said. "Damn silly hysterical female. I thought Beebo had more sense than most women."

"Just because she's not *like* most women?" Laura cried. "Jack, you make me furious! The more mannish a woman is, the more sense you think she's got! God! Beebo's *sick!* She's sick or she wouldn't have done it When I think what she must have gone through, I—oh…" And she wept again, silently and hard. "She's no damn silly female. You damn silly *man!*"

"What is she, then?" he asked, smiling a little.

Laura turned back to the bed and muttered, "I don't know. She's mixed up and unhappy and maybe she's still in love with me. She's miserable because she's still in love with me, anyway. I know that much."

"Isn't that touching," Jack commented acidly. "You have a desirable woman walloping herself and bisecting dachshunds out of love for you. It must do wonders for your ego."

Laura didn't even answer. She just flew at him, nails first, and took a wild swipe at his face. She missed; Jack was fast, and prepared. But she struggled desperately with him with her knees, her elbows, teeth and nails, until she was exhausted. She didn't last long. Lili had taken the fight out of her.

He laid her back down on the bed when she was gulping for air and went to get her some coffee.

"Now, tell me where you learned about Beebo," he said when he returned.

After a long, reluctant pause she answered him. Her basic trust in him persuaded her, but she promised herself that if he got sarcastic again she would stop speaking to him. Permanently.

"I saw Lili this afternoon," she whispered.

He gave a snort. "For old times' sake?" he asked.

"To ask about Beebo," she said haughtily.

"And she told you that romantic little tale? About carving up Nix?"

"Yes."

"And you believed her?"

"Yes. She wasn't kidding."

"Oh, she never does," he said with false agreement.

Laura flipped over to face him, her face red, but he interrupted her before she could get a word out. "Okay, she told the truth, we'll say." He moved her coffee gently toward her as he spoke. "And if she did it's pretty awful and it's pretty sad. And I wish like hell that it hadn't happened to Beebo, because she's a damn nice kid and I always liked her. I'm sorry about it, Laura—"

"Sorry!" she exploded. "What a stinking little word that is for what she must have gone through!"

"What's in a word, honey?" Jack shrugged, frowning. "You want a eulogy? I'm sorry, if Beebo really did it. That's not fancy but it's true. I can't put Nix back together. I can't order you to love Beebo the way she loves you."

There was a long silence then while Laura considered what he said. Her feelings for Beebo seemed to have undergone a transformation that afternoon. It was as if she saw clearly, and for the first time, into Beebo's secret heart, into her pain and frustration and passion. And Laura's own heart melted, touched, awed, a little exalted even to think that she could have inspired such a wonderful, terrible, mad, single-minded love in anybody. All of a sudden it seemed very valuable to her. She wanted it back, just the way it had been. She would know how to respect it now.

She lay there looking at Jack and felt a small fear licking at her heart like a flame. What if her love for Beebo became more precious to her than her love for Jack?

She said pensively, "I felt so bad about everything. I've been so selfish."

"Not with me, honey."

There was a long pause. At last she said, "You mean—going to the doctor, and everything?"

"That's only part of it." He got up and went to her.

Laura was standing in her bare feet, leaning against a wall and looking out at the East River. Her eyes were fastened on the night lights of the city. Jack touched her shoulder.

"Laura, darling, I've loved you for a long time…ever since we met, I think. I've never loved you less than I did at the start. And now I love you much much more. Just the fact that you were willing to try for a child means the whole world to me. Even if it never works out. I can't love you with my body. You wouldn't want it even if I could. But I don't think I've ever loved anyone as much as you, honey. Not even the lovely boys I could never resist. Not even Terry; and there never was a lovelier one. When all the sweat and passion are over with there's nothing but ashes and melancholy. Nothing's deader than a gay love that's burned out. But with you… I don't know, it just goes on and on. It's steady and comforting. It won't fail me, no matter what. It gives me a little faith—not much, but a little—in myself. In people. In you."

Laura turned her head away so he wouldn't see the tears. "Laura, you can say what you please but you'll never convince me that I did a cowardly thing marrying you. A selfish thing, yes. A hell of a selfish thing. I think I would have gone to pieces without you. But I wasn't running away from my old life as much as I was running to a new one."

Suddenly Laura felt a big ugly need to fight. Maybe it was just to let off steam after a nerve-wracking afternoon. Maybe it was to make her forget how guilty she felt about Beebo. Probably it was both.

Laura turned and walked away from him, feeling his hand slip from her shoulder, unwanted and unsure. "Well, I don't know why *you* left the Village but I think I know why *I* did. Finally," she said. Her voice was hard and she knew she was going to hurt him and she cringed from it almost as much as he did. And still she spoke, compulsively. "I left because it was the only way I could see out of my problems. You were my escape hatch, Jack. You were just too damn convenient."

"That's my charm," he said harshly. "Ask Terry."

"It isn't the first time I've run away from my problems. I ran away from Beth in college. I ran away from my father. From

Marcie—remember her? She was straight. I didn't find out till I tried to make love to her."

"I remember. You ran straight to me. And if you hadn't you'd be enjoying a protracted vacation in a mental institution at this moment."

"You helped, I admit it. I don't know what I would have done. But that's not the point. The point is, that here I am doing it again. Running away. Not *to* you this time, but *with* you."

"So?" he said. "So we run away. So what the hell? Let's run. Who gives a damn? What's *eating* you, Laura?"

"It's wrong, that's what! You told me when we left the Village I'd get over it and Beebo didn't matter...she'd survive. And I believed you. Until today."

"And now you think she won't survive?" he asked bitingly. "Because of something she did ten months ago while you were still living with her?"

Laura was swallowed up for a moment in a sob. "I want her!" she gasped finally. "Oh, God and Heaven, I want her!" And she stamped her foot like a furious child.

When she was quiet enough so he could talk without shouting, Jack said, "Sure. I want Terry. But we're poison together. So are you and Beebo. If you go to her you'll come running back to Uncle Jack before the month is out. Fed up all over again. Only this time there'll be a difference. This time Beebo really will commit mayhem. Or murder. Or both. And if you don't run fast enough, Mother, it may be you she murders. I wouldn't put it past her."

"I want her back!" Laura amazed herself with her own words, words she never meant to say. Jack stared at her, his face pale and determined.

"You can't have her."

"Jack," she said, suddenly pleading, "let me go to her. Just for a week or two. Please. Please let me." She walked toward him as she spoke, her arms extended.

"No," he said flatly. "Two weeks, hell." He was afraid she wouldn't ever come back.

"Jack, I wouldn't stay. I'd come back to you."

"No!" It was absolute. He couldn't take the chance. "We've had all this out. We agreed to it before we got married."

"Jack, darling—"

"I won't talk about it, Laura. You can't go back to her and that's final."

"But only for a week or two, just a few days..."

"You're my wife," he blazed so fiercely that she stopped in her tracks, startled. "You're my wife and you're not going to live with any Lesbian in any Village! Not while I live!"

She tried once more. "Jack, don't you understand? For the first time I'm beginning to realize how I feel about her, how I always felt. Tris made me realize it a little. And now Lili. And even living with you—"

"Living with me has made you lonesome for women, that's all. And Beebo's a handy woman. Goddamn it, Laura, I never denied you women. I've encouraged you. Admit it, go on! I've *asked* you to chase a few broads. It's not my fault if you've developed an itch. Go out and have yourself a fling; you should have done it long ago. I don't give a damn, only don't go to Beebo. And come back. Come back here, you understand? If you don't I'll come after you! And I'm capable of mayhem myself!"

She looked at his big burning eyes and trembled. "I just want to see her," she whispered.

"What makes you think she wants to see *you*?" he demanded. "What makes you think she won't greet you at the door with the same knife she used on Nix?"

"That's what Lili said."

"Well, for once Lili is right. I know Beebo; she's crazy. You catch her on a wrong day in a wrong mood and she won't even think about it. She'll just operate on you as she did on the dogs." He gazed unblinking at her. "That would kill me, Laura, as sure as it would you. Besides, I can't take any chances. You might be carrying my child."

This struck fury into Laura. She had nearly managed to forget the child, in the press of other things, but no longer. She picked up a pair of his shoes, sprawled near the closet, and flung them at him, one after the other. One flew through the window, splattering glass in its wake, and the other struck his arm.

"Why do you torment me?" she shouted. "Why do you talk about nothing but baby, baby, baby? I never wanted the damn thing! I hope I never have a baby! I hope I never have *your* baby! I hope it's born a boy! I hope it's born blind! I hope it's never born at all!" She was screaming at him, and he came to her carefully, coaxing her.

"You're all wrought up, Mother," he said. He could see that she was hysterical.

"Don't call me Mother!" she shrieked, her voice strained so that she could hardly articulate.

"Laura, for God's sake," he said, trying to brush it off, trying to keep calm, help her. "I call you 'Mother' in honor of my Oedipus complex. Purely a formality. It has nothing to do with babies. Come lie down, honey. Come on. I'll get you something to quiet you down. Come on," he wheedled gently, but she looked at him like he meant to murder her then and there, backing away from him. When he made a quick move to grab her, she sprang away, picking up the stool to her dressing table. She threw it at him with all her strength. While he dodged she grabbed her shoes and coat and ran from the room.

At the front door she paused briefly to stare at him with desperate eyes and then she heaved an ashtray at him and fled. It cut his hand, which he threw up to protect his face.

Laura ran down the stairs. There was no time to wait for the elevator. She could hear Jack behind her, running and calling her name. At the front door she turned swiftly toward the river and climbed a chain link fence, ripping the flesh here and there along her limbs and tearing her blouse. She dropped, torn and gasping, to the other side just as Jack burst from the door and looked wildly in all directions for her. She rolled soundlessly some feet down the long slope that ended in chill black water.

There she waited, sobbing quietly, clinging to handfuls of greasy mud and roots and embedded rocks. She heard his footsteps going toward First Avenue. He thought she would run for a taxi or hide in a doorway. Laura scrambled and stumbled south along the embankment, not waiting for him to come back looking for her. There was a suffocating panic in her. She didn't question it or wonder where it came from. She just did as it bid her, struggling through the dirt on the incline.

There was no looking back, no stopping for rest. She moved forward doggedly, tripping and sinking to her knees and clambering up again and going on, trying to stay near the fence in case she lost her footing. The going was slippery and rough and her breath rasped in and out with a fast whining sound. She had gone nearly three blocks when a jutting stone, invisible in the semi-dark, threw her, and she felt herself begin to skid and roll. She made a wild grab for the fence but it was already fifteen feet above her and receding fast. The wind was bumped out of her and she could not even scream. She had no idea how far she had fallen before she stopped.

Laura lay gasping and moaning for a few minutes, trying to get her breath back. She knew she was crying but she made no effort to stop. She moved herself gently to see if anything was broken, but the ground was not hard and she had missed the bad stones. She had no idea how long she had been there. It might have been minutes, it might have been hours. She thought vaguely it must have been hours when she finally stirred, chilled through, and opened her eyes. Beside her, on the ground, sat a man.

Laura screamed, a weak shuddering noise, and fell back, covering her face with her hands.

"Don't mind me," he said. "I won't hurt you."

Laura felt herself trembling with fear. She tried to pull her torn clothes straight, but it was so dark she could hardly see what she was doing. When he turned his face toward her she could see a little of it. It was very indeterminate; there was no way to guess his age or anything about him.

She stood up quickly and started to scramble up the hill, but he said, "There's an easier way."

She gave him one quick scared glance and then went on, but he stood up and said, "There's steps about a half block on."

Again she turned, very wary but willing to listen now. It looked a million miles to the top.

"I'll show you," he offered. His voice was not menacing and he stood facing her with his hands in his back pockets, a black statue with silver edges. "Come on, I'll walk ahead."

He turned then and went southward, agile and sure. After a moment Laura began to follow him, moving clumsily and with great effort, trying to copy his movements and praying that he wouldn't suddenly attack her. She stooped and grabbed a sharp stone glinting at her feet and held it tight in a sweating hand, just in case.

He heard her panting behind him and stopped, bringing Laura up sharp with a gasp. "You're tired," he said. "Want to sit down a minute?"

She shook her head at him.

"You can talk to me, I'm no devil," he said. And she had the idea he was grinning at her. But when she maintained her tense silence he shrugged and turned back. Now and then he glanced at her to see how she was doing. "Want some help?" he asked when she stumbled once, leaning toward her, but she drew back fast and he said, "Okay. Just trying to help."

They walked for a few moments and Laura was almost ready to bolt from him when she realized that the lights ahead she had taken for far distant were in reality small bulbs strung up to illuminate a row of steps.

"Maybe you're wondering who I am," he said almost hopefully as they neared the steps, as if he had a story to tell and was looking for a listener.

He turned, one hand on the iron rail that ran alongside the steps, and held out a hand to her. "Here y'are. Help you?"

She ignored him, turning her back to him to swing a leg over the low railing.

"Don't you wonder who I am?" he said. "I don't help just anybody, little girl." He spoke sharply. "Don't you want to know my name?"

"No!" she cried suddenly, angrily, startling herself. "You're just a man and all men are alike. No matter what their names are!" He gaped at her, astonished. "You don't really care about me, only about yourself. You don't want to know *my* name, you only want me to know *yours*." She spoke breathlessly at breakneck speed. "You can't suffer like a woman can. You aren't made to take it, you men. You're just made big enough and brute enough to hurt us. But we can't hurt you. We can't hurt you, do you hear?" And she stopped abruptly, putting her hand over her mouth in a storm of self-pity and shame and revulsion. It was Jack she was screaming at, not this stranger. She couldn't believe she had hurt Jack as she had hurt Beebo or it would destroy her. She screamed to make herself believe she couldn't really hurt him, no matter what she did.

The tears burst from her eyes when she saw it all for a lie. A lie shouted to spare her own tortured feelings. The man looked at her, patient now and unamazed. He was over his first surprise. And hers was not the first desperate speech he had heard on the shores of the East River.

Laura began to run up the steps.

"You won't get far, looking like that," he called after her. Momentarily Laura stopped and looked at herself in dismay. She turned and glanced back at her guide. He was standing on the steps some twenty feet below her, smiling at her consternation. He was a large man, big-boned, and she thought, *My God, he could break me in two. Like my father.*

"Cat got your tongue?" he said.

She started up again on shaky legs and he called, "Is that all the thanks I get?"

At this Laura began to run, but to her alarm he ran after her.

She felt her heart balloon in her chest, beating frantically, and when he caught her, only a few steps from the top, she yelled in fear. She would have screamed without stopping until somebody heard her if he had not wrapped a big hand around her mouth and forced her against the gate.

"I won't hurt you," he said. "I told you that. I never hurt anyone. I'm harmless." He grinned, and Laura, squirming under his big hand, was dizzy with panic.

He held her quietly for a few minutes as if to assure her that he spoke in good faith. Finally he asked her, "Where are you going?" and released her mouth. When she tried to holler at once he covered it again.

"I'll ask you again," he said. "But don't yell. Where are you going?"

When he freed her mouth this time she murmured, "Home. I'm going home. Let me go."

"How you getting home?"

"I—I'll walk. It's not far. Just a block."

"You know what block this is?" He smiled with superior knowledge.

"It can't be far," she said.

He shook his head quizzically. "I don't get it. You're not even drunk. You're tore up but you're no tramp neither. Mostly the ones I find down here are hitting the bottle. Or they wouldn't be down here. Or kids, exploring. Not pretty girls." He smiled and Laura's one intense hope was that she not faint and fall into his clutches.

"Let me go," she said, trying to sound controlled. But her big eyes and urgent breathing gave her away.

"Okay." He took his hands away from her altogether, and said, "Go. But I'll bet you need a dime to telephone with."

She turned, dragging on the gate behind her until he said, "Here. Let me." He opened it for her. And when she saw that he was really going to let her go, she allowed herself to turn and look at him. See him. He was holding out a dime.

"Take it," he said. "At least you can call somebody to come get you."

Laura stared at him. He was big and ugly, seamy-faced, and wearing dirty clothes with a worn cap tilted over his ear. But he had a nice honest grin. And he looked, for all his dirt and size, rather childish. Laura stood poised at the gate, wavering between flight and the dime. At last she took it, her face reddening. She had to drop her sharp stone to get it.

"Didn't need that, didya?" he said with a smile, watching it fall.

She shook her head and whispered, "Thanks."

"That's all I want to hear," he said and let her go. She ran halfway down the block, and then turned, overwhelmed with curiosity, to see what had happened to him. He was standing there behind the closed gate gazing after her, smiling. *He's nuts,* she thought. *An idiot. A damn man! That's probably all he does, save people from the river. But even that...even that pitiful life is worth more than mine. All I've ever done is hurt the people I love the most.*

At the end of the block she stopped running and looked once more. He was gone.

Chapter Ten

LAURA HID HERSELF for a minute in a shadowed doorway and tried to make sense of things. She was a mess, with mud on her torn clothes and on her face, tangled hair and dried blood.

She made an effort to smooth her hair down. There was some Kleenex in her pocket and she wiped her face off carefully, reaching every corner of it and rubbing till the skin turned pink. She brushed at her disheveled clothes rather hopelessly. Maybe it was late enough so nobody would notice her.

She began to walk, holding her arms together in front of her as if to keep herself warm, but in fact to keep the worst rips from showing. And she kept her head down. *If only the police don't stop me,* she thought. *I must look like a whore.*

Laura walked straight west on Forty-first Street, for it was Forty-first, past Lexington Avenue and Park and Fifth and Broadway and over to Seventh. No cops stopped her, although more than one passerby stared.

It was cold, a raw March night with the sting of coming storm in the air. Laura went south on Seventh Avenue, walking almost mechanically. When she thought of it she realized it was cold. But she hardly thought of it. There was too much else on her mind.

She was very surprised to reach Fourth Street so quickly. She had known, without thinking, that that was where she was going. In less than five minutes she had entered the little court in front of Beebo's apartment building and the old familiar trembling had begun.

She sat down on a bench in the court to gather her strength. At last she looked up the wall of dark windows behind her, twisting on the bench to see, and saw lights in Beebo's living room, and began to shiver.

Ten or a dozen times she looked up anxiously at the lights on the second floor. They were faint, as if only one small light were on. With a sudden rush of desire that eliminated the need to make a decision, she pulled open the inside door and raced up the stairs.

At the top she stood trying desperately to get her breath. But she knew after a moment that her whole body would shake and sweat and wear itself out with unbearable anticipation if she didn't get the door open. She reached for the knob, but it was locked.

She rattled the knob hard and then she knocked.

When the door swung open a moment later she gasped in amazement. It was Milo Robinson—Tris's husband.

"Milo!" she exclaimed.

He stared at her.

"Don't you remember me? I'm Laura. Laura Landon."

"I remember," he said quietly. "I just never saw you fresh out of the gutter before."

She looked down at herself and her cheeks went scarlet. "I look awful, don't I?"

"Somebody after you?" Milo asked.

"Yes. No. I don't know. Can I come in?"

"I guess you can," he said, stepping back. "You've got as much right to be here as me, that's for sure."

Laura walked into the living room and just the sight of it, warm and comfortable and a little raggy, made her want to weep. She sank down on the couch, exhausted.

"Want some coffee?" Milo said, staring at her.

"No, thanks. I've had too much tonight."

"Milk?"

"I guess so. Thanks."

"You look real bad, Laura. You'd better get to bed," he said frowning at her.

"Where's Beebo?"

"Tell me that and I'll tell you where my wife is," he said sharply.

"You coming back to Beebo?" he asked her.

"If she'll have me."

"From what I know of it, she won't. But I'm on your side, Laura. I'd do anything to pry Patsy loose."

It startled her to hear him call Tris by her real name. "Is Beebo in love with her?" she asked cautiously.

"Naw," he said with leisurely disgust. "She puts up with her but she's not in love with her." He ambled out to the kitchen to pour her some milk. "I should be so lucky," he called. "I'd dump her. Right now."

"How about Tris? How does she feel?"

He answered her while he poured the milk. "I don't know, Laura. I never could figure that kid. Living with her only makes it more confusing." He sounded very tired, like a man defeated. "I wish I could forget her, forget the whole thing."

He came back and handed her the milk and sat down in a chair near her.

They looked at each other. He was a tall young man in his early twenties, handsome and well educated. His skin was dark and satiny in the pink lamplight.

"Does she love you?" Laura asked gently.

He shrugged and gave a little laugh. "Who knows?" he said. "She says so now and then. But that's only when I lay down the law on the Lezzie stuff."

"What's the law?" Laura said.

"Well, goddamn it, enough's enough!" he exclaimed. "I like to see her once in a while myself. She's my wife."

Laura thought of Jack and felt the tears start quietly down again. "Excuse me," she sniffled. "I'm running like a sieve tonight. I don't know why. Did Jack Mann come over here tonight?"

"I wouldn't know," Milo said. "I've only been here since midnight."

"Did he call?"

"Nobody called."

"Nobody?" She had been so certain Jack would follow her here. "When does Beebo get in?"

"You tell me, then we'll both know." He sighed.

"What will you do with Tris, Milo?" She spoke softly, sympathetically, in a raspy tired voice.

"Take her home again."

"Do you understand her? What makes her so contrary?"

"No." He turned and gave her a doleful grin, lighting another cigarette from the first. "We've been married almost two years but I don't know her at all, to tell the truth. But I sure won't let her go."

"Does she want you too?"

"I don't think she does," he said. "Sound screwy? Well, not so very. She needs me. Because I'm a man." There was a pause and Laura mopped up the useless tears and tried to think of Milo's troubles, not her own.

"How long are you going to stay?" she asked him finally.

"I guess till they get back," he said.

"Are you sure they're together?"

"More or less. Patsy has a big thing about her."

"Milo? Would you stay here till they get back, then? I'm afraid—I'm afraid of Beebo. She might hurt me."

He looked at her thoughtfully. "Yeah. Okay," he said, studying her. "Say, haven't you been gone a while? Patsy doesn't tell me much, but I got the idea...I haven't seen you around or anything."

"Yes. I've been gone awhile," she said, getting up. "I'm going to take a shower and get cleaned up. Don't tell her I'm here if she comes."

"Patsy?"

"Beebo! Either of them."

"Who shall I say is in the shower?"

"Santa Claus," she said. She looked at him sitting glumly slumped in the chair. "Why do you put up with it?" she said. "She's too much. Tris is too much for anybody."

"Don't call her Tris. She's been Patsy ever since she was six years old and skinned her knees in front of my house. Tris. Christ! It's too affected."

"Did she...ever really love me, Milo?" Laura asked it with a catch in her throat.

"Did she ever love any of us? I don't know."

"Why do you keep coming back for more?"

He shrugged. "Same reason you do. You love Beebo. You know it's a mess and you're in for a lot of hell. It'll never be right. But you love her. So you take it." He gave another sad little chuckle. "I wish I knew what it is about you girls. What makes you love each other?" Laura stared at him. "If I knew there's one thing sure—I'd put a stop to it. What makes you queer, Laura? You tell me."

"What makes you normal, Milo?"

"I was born that way. Don't tell me you were *born* queer! Ha!" And he was sarcastic now.

"I was made that way," she said calmly.

"By who?" he asked skeptically.

"A lot of people. My father. A girl named Beth. Myself. Fate."

He snorted. "Why don't you give up women?"

"Why don't *you!*" she flashed.

He blinked at her, beginning to feel her stormy intensity. "Is it *that* bad?" he asked.

"Sure, it's that bad! Do you think I live this way because I like it? Would you live like you do if you could live like a white man?"

After a moment he shook his head, looking curiously at her.

"Neither would Tris. *Patsy.* So don't be too hard on her, Milo. You damn men, you're all lousy selfish bastards."

And to his astonishment, she threw the dirty dime at him. Laura was pulling on a pair of Beebo's big men's flannel pajamas when she heard the front door open, and her heart came to a sudden stop in her breast. It started again with a wild thump, and she stood with an ear to the door struggling to pull the roomy tops over her damp body and hear what was said.

"Where is she?" Milo demanded.

The front door shut and there was a pause. Laura heard the scrape of a match and the soft whistle of expelled breath.

"I sent her home," Beebo said. And her voice sent a sharp thrill of desire and recognition through Laura. She pressed her hands firmly over her breasts till the flesh nearly burst between her fingers, as if to still her own hard breathing.

"Where, the studio?" Milo said.

"Yeah. You entertaining, Milo?"

"What?"

"Who's the milk drinker?"

And Laura remembered suddenly the milk Milo had fixed her. She hadn't finished it; just left it sitting on the table.

"Santa Claus," Milo said.

"No kidding," Beebo said with a grin. "I used to leave Santa Claus a glass of milk. And cookies. When I was a little kid. But that was Christmas Eve. This isn't Christmas Eve, Milo."

"Check the shower," Milo said. "I didn't ask her over. You sure Patsy's home?"

"Hell, no," Beebo said and she was right by the bedroom door. Laura leaped backwards across the room, stumbling and catching herself on the bed. She straightened up, her heart in her throat, watching the door. Her long blond hair was still damp from the shower, and she had on only the long, striped tops of Beebo's pajamas. They reached to mid-thigh on her.

Beebo's hand twisted the knob. "Go home, friend," she said to Milo, pausing. "Your wife needs a man tonight."

Milo shrugged at her. "She asked me to stay."

"Who asked you to stay?"

He thumbed at the bedroom. "Says you might hurt her."

Beebo stared hard at him for only a second more before she threw the door open hard. It cracked like a shot against the wall and Laura opened her eyes slowly. Her arms were crossed at the wrists and clamped tight over her breasts, as if to ward off attack. She looked at Beebo and Beebo looked at her without a word for several amazed minutes. Laura felt such a flash of agonized desire for this big, handsome, passionate girl who had been her lover that she was unable to speak.

Finally Beebo walked slowly into the room, her hands shoved into the pockets of her pants, squinting through the smoke of the cigarette between her lips. "I thought Lili was kidding," she said softly. "Seeing things." And she gave a single short laugh. She walked to the bed and dropped her coat. "Relax, Laura, I'm not going to rape you," she said. She turned, with her weight on one foot and the other on the bed rung, and called to Milo, "You can go now, Sir Galahad."

"It's all right?" He came to the door and looked at Laura, who finally found the strength to nod at him. "Okay," he said. He looked her up and down, surprised to find how desirable she looked with a clean skin and no rags. "Lotsa luck, girls," he said with his rueful defeated smile, and he went out.

"Thank you, Milo," Laura called after him, but her voice was so low and husky with emotion that he did not hear her.

There followed a long strange silence while Beebo stared at her. Laura kept her eyes on her toes, afraid to meet that penetrating gaze.

At last Beebo crushed her cigarette and lay down on the bed, crossing her feet and stuffing her hands behind the pillow to raise her head.

"All right, Laura," she said calmly. "You're here. Tell me what you want."

Laura looked up then, slowly, still very afraid. She was prepared for any violence, any brutality. It no longer mattered if Beebo hurt her or not. She was ready to submit to anything if Beebo would only take her back.

"What do you want?" Beebo said.

"To stay," she whispered.

Beebo's eyes widened with surprise. "To stay? With me?" She looked away then at the wall. "You could have stayed last August."

"Last August I was miserably unhappy because of you. I had to get away. I found out I'm more unhappy without you than with you."

Beebo laughed outright then. "Doesn't give you much of a choice, does it?" she said and her voice was not kind. Her laughter made Laura realize that she was a little drunk. Laura walked over to the side of the bed and knelt beside it, with her heart working as if it had taken her up a stiff hill.

Beebo turned her head to watch her. "What's that for?" she said, catching a corner of her pajamas between thumb and forefinger. Her flesh was only inches away from Laura's for the first time in eight long months and there was a sudden current of feeling between them that leaped like a spark from Beebo's hand to Laura's breasts.

"I had to change. My clothes were filthy. I took a shower and borrowed your pajamas...I've been walking all night. All the way from midtown."

"What the hell did you do that for? Don't they still have taxis in this town?" She was cold. Her hand dropped away from Laura.

"I didn't have any money. And I had to see you."

"Why?"

Laura put her head down on the bed on her clasped hands and began to cry. "I love you," she wept. And it was the first time since they had met that Beebo had heard her say it that way.

She got up on one elbow and leaned toward Laura. Her face was impassive but shrewd. "Not Tris?" she said.

"Not Tris."

"Anybody else?"

"Nobody else." Laura lifted her tearful face. "Oh, Beebo, I've done you so wrong, darling. I didn't know how bad it was. Lili told me—"

"I know she did, the miserable bitch. Goddamn her soul. The only secret she can keep is her age."

"Beebo, I'll do anything for you—anything—if you'll have me back. Oh, darling, it took me months to figure out what was wrong with me. I've been so confused. And lately I've been thinking of you all the time. I don't think I ever stopped loving you, Beebo. I thought when you saw me here you'd beat the hell out of me. If you want to...do it...if it'll help." She looked at her out of large frightened eyes, half expecting Beebo to jump her.

But Beebo sat up then, grasping her ankles with her hands. "No, Laura, it's too late for that. What good would that do?" She made a face, frowning. "There was a time when I would have. If you had come back last fall instead of now. I would have loved you enough then to hate you. But I've changed, Laura...It doesn't seem to matter so much anymore."

There was a shocked silence from Laura. "You mean," she ventured finally, "you don't love me anymore? Oh, Beebo! Oh, Beebo! No!" She covered her mouth with both bands, pressed so tight they turned white.

Beebo looked at her curiously. "I love you, Laura," she said, but it was impersonal, detached, as if it were just another fact in her life like her job or her black hair. "I'll always love you. But I'll never love you again the way I did before you ran out on me last summer. That was too much. When it happened it was a question of either dying of it...or living with something else, changing myself. Becoming a different person. That's what happened."

Laura, in her desperation, found the courage to touch Beebo then. She reached out for her, and Beebo unexpectedly turned to help her. She dragged Laura up on the bed with her two strong arms, and Laura gave a long groan of need and fear and gratitude, all mixed up together. Beebo held her in both arms, her back pressed against the wall, watching Laura struggle to control her tears and trembling. She was kind, she was patient. And it scared Laura, who suddenly discovered that she missed the old stormy fury and passion. Beebe seemed odd to her, and it was true that she had changed.

"Laura," she said. "I've been doing some thinking. I want to tell you something. Maybe you won't want to come back to me so much anymore."

"Let me tell you something first," Laura begged. "If I don't tell you, Beebo, I haven't any right to touch you. I haven't any right to be here. Maybe I don't anyway. Darling, I—I'm married." Beebo gasped a little, and Laura said quickly, "To Jack."

Beebo simply gaped at her for a second and then she burst out laughing. "Good God! *That's* what happened!" she exclaimed. "You and Jack. Oh, God!"

"It wasn't exactly—ridiculous," Laura whispered, hurt. "We loved each other." But Beebo went on laughing.

"I'm sorry, baby, but it sounds so damn—goofy," she said.

And when she called her baby, Laura felt a small glow of warmth and hope. Maybe it wasn't hopeless; maybe things could work out. She clung to Beebo and found herself half laughing with her, and half weeping to hear Jack's name.

"Where is he now? Does he know you're here?" Beebo asked her.

"He knows," Laura said, for there could be no doubt that he did.

"Did he send you? Married life got him down?"

"No, I ran away. I—I hurt him. It meant so much to him to have a wife and all...." She couldn't say any more about it; it broke her up to think of it.

Beebo sobered a little. "You have a talent for that, Laura—hurting people. Sometimes I think that's your only real ability."

"I know," Laura murmured, shame-faced. "And the trouble is, I never want to. I never mean to. I'd give anything to undo it, once it's done. But I begin to feel like I'm smothering. Like I'd die of it if I can't get away."

"Is that the way *I* made you feel?" Beebo said.

Laura hung her head. "Yes," she whispered. "I won't lie about it."

"You can't very well. I read the damn diary—every word of it."

Laura flushed at the thought of the thing. "Beebo, I—I didn't understand before how you felt. Or how I felt myself. But I know now I love you." She said it quivering with hope.

But Beebo only answered, "Do you, Laura? How do you know?" There was a little smile on Beebo's face. She asked the question gently as if she were talking to a bewildered child, brushing Laura's hair from her forehead.

"Because I want so terribly to be with you," Laura said, shaking her head to emphasize her words. "I can't bear it like this, being apart from you."

"I've changed so much," Beebo said, wondering at it, "and you haven't changed at all. Have you? I think you're just tired of being a wife, honey."

"No. I love Jack. But it's different. I don't *need* him like I need you."

"How about Jack? Doesn't he need you?"

Laura covered her face again with her hands to stifle the sudden sobs. "A lot, I'm afraid. I'd be better off dead, Beebo, I swear I would. I've caused so much heartache. And most of all to myself. I'm no good to anybody. I wish to God you'd get that big knife and do to me what you did to Nix. I wish you'd beat me the way you beat yourself—"

"Laura! God, spare me!" And for a second the latent fire in her flared and gave Laura a curious thrill.

"I thought you would," Laura cried. "I was prepared for anything, even that, when I came here. I still can't believe you—I mean, you seem so funny. I thought you'd hurt me, and you're so calm, so quiet—"

Beebo shook her head, looking at Laura with her disillusioned eyes. "I won't hurt you, baby," she said.

"You said once you'd kill me," Laura said wildly, as if she were asking for it, as if it would be proof of Beebo's huge need for her.

"I know. I meant it then, too. I was nearly crazy. But things have changed, Laura. I don't throw my threats around so easily any more. There was a time when I could have done it, but no more. No more. Stop crying, baby. Stop, honey." She began to stroke Laura's long hair.

Laura looked up at her through pink eyes, her chest heaving in Beebo's warm embrace, and they gazed at each other for some time before Beebo told her, kindly, trying to ease it for her, "I said I loved you, Laura. But it's not the same for me, now. I don't love you the way I used to. I couldn't and go on living. You were my whole life for two years. I thought I couldn't exist without you. I thought it would be better to kill you and die with you than go on without you. So what did I do?" She smiled in contempt for herself. And pity. A bitter smile. "I chickened out. I slaughtered a poor innocent pup instead. In the fury I should have saved for you. And what did it prove? Nothing. How did it help? It didn't. It was a wasted gesture, Laura. A stupid, senseless thing.

"But you see, I was out of my mind in love with you at the time. Now all the madness has gone out of me, Laura. There's not much fire left." And she bent suddenly to touch Laura's brow with her lips. Laura felt the sweet touch flow through her to her toes and she nestled close against Beebo, weeping at her words. "It's not wild and wonderful and tormenting anymore."

"How did it happen?" Laura begged her, cruelly disappointed. "Maybe it'll change." She felt almost betrayed, as if she were in the arms of a stranger.

"No. I wouldn't want it to change, now. It happened because if it hadn't I would have died, Laura. I was so sick, so lost without you, that I would have gone to pieces. I'd have used the damn cleaver on myself."

"Oh!" Laura breathed, horrified.

"I changed to save my life...and my sanity. It took all my strength, but I did it. And strangely enough, it was a relief. I felt as if I'd laid down a killing burden." She looked down at Laura, pulling her so tight that they could feel one another's hearts beating, and Laura, her eyes shut, was saying to herself, "No, no, no..."

"I love you still, baby," Beebo told her. "I know I should be proud and angry with you. I should kick you out or beat you up or both. But if I did it wouldn't mean anything. It would only hurt, like I hurt Nix, for no purpose. I know Lili and the rest of them will bitch at me for taking you back—"

"Oh, will you, Beebo? Darling, darling, will you?"

"If you want it that way...." She stopped, looking into Laura's tear-bright eyes.

"I want it that way," Laura gasped.

But at the same time she had to realize that this was not her Beebo anymore; that things had changed irreparably and forever between them; that the love they had left now was only good and tender, not the exalted, shivering passions of the past. It had to be so, because Beebo could never have forgiven her, let alone taken her back, otherwise. *And it's my fault—all my fault. It's the price I have to pay to get her back,* Laura told herself.

"If you had been like this last summer...so calm, so casual," she whispered humbly, "I would have stayed."

"And now that I've calmed down, you want me wild again, don't you?" Beebo laughed a little, a sad, wise laugh. "Crazy, isn't it? Ironic and crazy. And there's not a goddamn thing we can do about it, Bo-peep. Either of us...baby...She lifted Laura's face and kissed it.

"I won't tell you how I missed you. I won't tell you what I went through. I wouldn't even know how. It took a lot out of me. Too much. But you're welcome to what's left. If you want it."

"I want it," Laura said passionately. "I want *you,* Beebo." She hung her head. "Unless...unless you still want Tris?"

"I never did. I never wanted anybody else. I've been trying to give Tris back to Milo since she walked in on me the first time," Beebo said. "She'll give up on me when she finds out you're home. She won't want to make it a threesome."

"Home," Laura repeated. "Oh, Beebo..."

And suddenly her arms were locked around Beebo's neck and they were lost in kisses and thrilling, half-forgotten caresses and the warm satin touch of each other's bodies. The pajama top Laura had pulled on so frantically slipped off with no trouble, and she stretched out on the white spread beneath the girl she had loved so much, in spite of so much, and surrendered with a groan of delight tempered with sorrow. And perhaps the beginning of understanding at last.

It was only a matter of hours the next day before Laura knew that the feeling of strangeness she felt would not wear off. It was another two days before she could bring herself to give up hope that Beebo might change, that being together again would reawaken their crazy, beautiful, love affair.

But it was two whole weeks, two very long weeks full of wondering and self-pity and struggle and doubt, before Laura could tell herself that she had made a mistake.

Beebo was drained of feeling. She was tired, tired of love and even tired of life. Perhaps time and innate toughness would revive her, but she had nothing to give Laura now. Laura realized with chagrin how little she had to give Beebo. She had never given much, always taking, taking, taking, from the older girl, who seemed to have so much to offer. It had been too easy to help herself to that wealth of love and she understood now, painfully, that she had come back to Beebo to be worshipped again.

She had turned tail and run at the moment when her problems with Jack seemed too much for her, and she had run to the one person who had adored her spectacularly in the past. She needed her ego bolstered, she needed flattery and passion and reassurance from a woman. So it had come to her as an eye-opening blow to find her tempestuous lover subdued, transformed, almost a different person.

It never was right, Laura thought, watching Beebo over the dinner table. *She had to give beyond her strength and I took it all with no return. At least she was generous with herself. I was the selfish one. I always have been the selfish one. I thought the world was giving me a bum deal, but I was too selfish to see the good side. Even with Jack...Oh my God, Jack. My poor darling. With him most of all.*

"What are you thinking about?" Beebo asked her, seeing her absorption.

"I—I have to go back, Beebo," Laura said and her own words startled her. "I have to see Jack once more." Once expressed, these feelings so long in the making made her feel like crying. She looked apprehensively at Beebo, expecting her sarcasm.

But Beebo only said, "I thought you would. Well, go on, baby. Go tell him you're sorry, it was all a nasty misunderstanding." She spoke mildly.

"Don't make it sound cheap, Beebo," Laura pleaded.

"It won't be anything *but* cheap unless you go back to stay," Beebo told her. "Otherwise there's no point in going back at all."

"But—but I'm going to live with you now," Laura faltered. "I just have to see him once more. Explain to him—"

"You're his wife. Either go home to him and grow up or don't go back. What do you think you'd accomplish with a quickie visit, Bo-peep? Just pep him up a little? Make it all bearable? You'd be lucky if he didn't run you out with a rifle. If you haven't learned anything else in all this time, you *must* have learned that you can't play around with love as if it were a bargain basement special. Real love isn't a production line thing, it isn't waiting for you in any old shop window. Haven't you learned that yet, baby?"

Laura nodded, putting her head back against the chair and letting the soothing tears flow quietly. "I've learned it. But it's so hard to live by what you learn. I needed you so much when I came back two weeks ago. But I needed you the way you used to be." It was a difficult admission, but Beebo understood it.

"Sure," she said gently. "Now you've seen me. Now you know what I couldn't find the words to tell you. It's over, Laura. I'll always be here, I guess we'll always need each other a little. Maybe we'll see each other now and then. But there's no point in our living together."

Shame colored Laura's cheeks pink and she said warmly, "I'm not a child, Beebo, and I didn't come back here just to run off and leave you again. I gave up too much to come back."

"Yes, baby, I think you did. You gave up too much. It wasn't worth the price, and you see that now. Admit it. Don't be a stubborn idiot."

Laura was appalled at the apathy in her voice. "What would you do if I insisted on staying with you?" she asked.

Beebo shrugged. "I'd let you stay, of course. I haven't the ambition to kick you out. Besides, I love you still, in my way. I meant it when I said it."

Laura stood up, unable to look at her anymore. "I'm going back to the apartment, and I'm going to talk to Jack," she said. "I'll be back in a couple of hours."

"I doubt it." Beebo did not even leave her chair. She lighted a cigarette slowly, watching Laura's back.

Finally Laura turned around and faced her. "Please, Beebo, don't talk to me as if nothing in the world mattered anymore. I can't stand it, I can't stand to think I did it to you."

"Jack still matters, baby. Don't do it to him, too."

Laura went and got her coat and purse from the bedroom, and then she looked into the kitchen. Beebo sat with her back to the door, still smoking thoughtfully. "I'm leaving," Laura told her. "I should be back around nine."

"Sure, sweetheart. Tell old Jack I said hello."

"I will." Laura looked at her dark curly head, not sure if the frosting on her curls came from the kitchen light above or from the first gray hairs. She walked over to Beebo and kissed her cheek, leaning over her chair from behind. Beebo smiled though she did not turn her head.

And then Laura walked out, knowing somehow, deep within herself, that it was for the last time.

Chapter Eleven

LAURA APPROACHED the apartment building with her legs trembling. It was all she could do to keep from turning around and running. It was hard to imagine what she might find. She left Jack a desperate man, and her absence for two weeks would not have made things any easier for him.

She stopped at the front door to marshal her strength, and the chain link fence at the end of the street caught her eye. She marveled that she had been able to climb it the night she ran away. It looked almost insurmountable now with the long shadows creeping along the ground beneath it. She touched one of the cuts on her arm, still healing, and wondered where her shabby guide with his friendly dime was now. All unaware, he had taught her a valuable lesson about herself and turned a spotlight on the lies until even Laura had been forced to see them and confess the truth. She loved Jack too much to hurt him, and she had come back now to heal him if she could.

That thought gave her the most strength as she pushed open the lacquer-red front door with its brass knocker. *If he didn't need me so desperately, I couldn't do this,* she told herself. *And if I didn't love him so much, I couldn't do it, either.* She pushed the button for the elevator and felt a thrill of shame and fear that almost made her sick. And then, out of habit, she glanced at her mailbox. It was so full that it could not be locked and the door hung open. Laura went to it and pulled the bundle of mail out with a sudden premonition.

The box had not been emptied for days, perhaps weeks; perhaps not since the night she ran away.

Is Jack—is he gone, then? she wondered. For a second her weakness and humiliation overwhelmed her and she hoped he was. She hoped she would never have to face him. For she dreaded what she had done to this man who loved her, in his own odd way, more than he loved, or ever had loved, anyone else on earth.

And then, suddenly, she whispered aloud, "No! Oh, no! He's got to be here!"

She took the elevator to the third floor in a frenzy of impatience and crossed the carpeted hall to her apartment door swiftly. Like the mailbox, the door was unlocked, and that gave her hope. He wouldn't go out and leave it open for any stranger to wander into. It wasn't like him.

Silent and tremulous, Laura entered the living room. "Jack?" she said softly, knowing already there would be no answer. "Jack? Be here. Darling, please be here," she murmured. Slowly and fearfully she entered each room, saying his name as she did so, and silently, each room revealed nothing but his absence. Never had a home seemed so empty.

Never had her own voice awed and saddened her so.

She had been through all the rooms a couple of times, half-heartedly picking up a thing or two and looking with frightened eyes into the dark corners, before she spotted the note. It was rolled into the top of a whisky bottle, one of several sitting on the kitchen table. She picked it up with trembling fingers and read:

> *Laura darling.* I'm with Terry. I guess you've
> gone back to Beebo. Maybe that's fate, but I still
> think we could have made a go of it. You're my wife,
> Laura—that's the difference between life and death
> to me, even now. If you ever read these words,
> remember, I love you, Mrs. Mann. And remember it
> too if you ever want to come home. Jack.

Laura wept silently, her throat and chest painfully tight with it, crushing the letter against her neck.

She walked dazedly into the living room, still holding the letter, and stared around through her tears. She thought of Beebo and the warm, slightly worn rooms she lived in and the worn-out love she had left. And she thought of Jack. There had been none of his usual piercing sarcasm in the note. Nothing but gentleness, nothing but love.

After a long moment Laura pulled herself together. She sank down on the sofa by the table and picked up the mail. She felt weak, and she shuffled listlessly through the pile of bills and ads and notes and papers. Near the end she almost passed up one with Dr. Belden's name in the return address spot. His name registered suddenly in her mind, and she tore his letter open with hands newly sprung to life.

She read only the first half of the first sentence:

> Dear Mrs. Mann. I am delighted to inform you
> that next November, if all goes well, you and Mr.
> Mann will be parents, and...

She fainted.

When Laura awoke she was lying on the couch with her head back and her mouth open and uncomfortably dry. Carefully she lifted her head on a stiff neck, turning it gingerly, and sat up straight. On the floor at her feet was the doctor's letter. She picked it up and found her hands shaking so that she had to grab at it three times before she caught it between her fingers.

For some moments she sat there, her cornflower eyes enormous with shock. Finally she whispered, "I'm going to have a child. *Me.*" A first hysterical thought of abortion flew through her mind, but she dismissed it almost before it formed.

"I'm going to be a woman. I have eight months to get ready and I've got to be ready when it comes. I've got to love it and take care of it."

Cautiously she stood up, and unsteadily walked toward the bedroom, one hand warm across her stomach. "Now that I know, it's not so bad," she said, speaking aloud as if to reassure herself. "I don't resent it so much anymore. Strange...I'm not afraid of it. I don't know why, exactly. Yes, I guess I do...It's Jack's. It's a part of him. It's a way to make it up to him for what I've done."

She reached her bed and raised her eyes to the windows, and the darkness and sparkle of the city outside. It looked very beautiful. Jack was out there somewhere. He had to be; he couldn't have gone away, not this soon. His note sounded too much as if he were going to look for her, as if he knew he and Terry couldn't last, and he would have to search her out and make her try again.

Laura swept some pajamas and shoes off her bed and sat down with a curious feeling of elation and exhaustion. She stretched out, still fully dressed, and gazed at the ceiling.

I'll find him, she thought. *Terry was staying at the Bell Towers. I heard him say so. Somebody'll know where they are.* She felt very tired and she was surprised to find that she was crying again. There seemed to be no reason for it, except that she was having a baby. And it belonged to Jack too, and that made her smile through the tears.

A little later, when she dimly realized she was falling asleep, she thought of Beebo, and the thought twisted in her heart like a pain and almost brought her awake again. But it was over for Beebo now. Her life lay in another direction. Laura had to save Jack, and somehow, in the saving of him, would come her own life and strength. She knew it now, and it gave her the first peace she had known in all the years since she had first realized that she was a Lesbian.

Only the lightest rustle of air awakened her. She opened her eyes. It was still deep night; the room was dark except for the small bedlamp she had switched on when she lay down. And yet she was wide awake, and she knew he was there.

Laura turned and saw him standing in the doorway to the bedroom, disheveled, his hands in his pockets, his round horn rims sliding down his nose. She came up suddenly on her elbow, so fast that her head swam a little.

They looked at each other in silence for a minute; first startled, then embarrassed.

"Jack?" Laura said timidly, the way she had whispered it to the empty rooms earlier in the evening. And again her own voice awed her into silence.

He straightened and walked slowly toward her bed. At the foot, he stopped, his hands still in his pockets, his tie loosened, his shirt a little gray. His face was serious and tense, as if he were quite ready to believe she was a mirage.

At last he spoke to her softly. "I've been coming back every night. I was hoping...I thought you might..." He stopped, shutting his eyes for a minute as if to search for composure.

Laura sprang up to her knees on the bed and put her arms around him. "I'm here," she cried. "I'm home, I love you, I won't leave again, Jack."

But he loosened her arms gently. "I don't believe you," he said. "I'm afraid to."

"Believe me," she exclaimed passionately. "Jack darling, please believe me."

"We were going to leave for San Francisco Thursday," he said, still slightly incredulous. "Terry and I. I promised him, if you didn't come back."

"When did he ever keep a promise to *you*?"

"I love him, Laura," he reminded her.

That stopped her for a minute. She bowed her head and cast about desperately for something to say, something to convince him forevermore, as she herself was now convinced, that it was their only hope to make this marriage work.

"Jack, I'd have gone anywhere in the world to find you," she said, unable to look at him while she talked for fear the sight of his face would make her cry again. "I've had to hurt so many people— too many—to learn my lessons. And I was hurt as badly as the others. I've made mistakes, ugly ones, and I've been selfish and silly. But I've been trying, I have, Jack! And I've been learning. I—I—love you." She looked up at him now and for the very first time, in all their long acquaintance, she felt a pleasant flush in her cheeks at the sight of him. Him...a man. She felt flustered suddenly, unable to go on speaking.

Jack saw it too after a moment, disbelieving it at first and then accepting it slowly, with wonderment. "Laura," he said. "Do you still believe we're just a couple of scared kids? Do you still believe we're running away from the world by marrying each other? Do you think we're going to spend our whole lives running after a love that doesn't exist?"

"No," she whispered.

"You're still my wife," he said softly, and put his arms around her now, at last, and made her tingle with awkward new feelings and unbearable tenderness. "Do you want to live with me again? As my wife?"

"Yes, Jack." It wasn't the passionate unreasoning yes she had flung at Beebo in desperation two weeks ago. It was quiet and intensely felt. It was a recognized necessity, but a beautiful one.

"For how long?" he asked skeptically.

"I'm your wife," she repeated gently to him. "I'll stay with you now." There was a new sound, a new tone in her voice that caught in his heart. As for Laura she was once more bewildered by an unexpected tide of emotion that made it impossible for her to look at him. "Say yes, Jack," she whispered. "Say it's all right. Please, before I start crying again."

He took her head in his hands and kissed her forehead and said, "It's all right. It's all right honey," and suddenly they clung hard to each other and Laura began to sob with relief and joy. She could hardly articulate, trying to spill her lovely secret to him. "Jack, Jack, it worked. We're going to have a baby! Darling, we're going to have a baby!"

She felt his arms tighten till she lost her breath and when she looked up at him this time, with her face blotched and her eyes red and her lips curved into a smile, he found himself crying happily with her.

When he could talk, he murmured into her neck, "I saw the letter in the box. It came two days after you left. The damn thing terrified me. I swear, Laura, I couldn't open it, I couldn't even touch it. I wouldn't even *look* at the damn mailbox. I was hoping so much it would be true—and so damn afraid if it was you wouldn't come back. That I'd lost you and you might have to have it alone and you wouldn't want it or love it—"

"Oh, stop," she begged. "Jack, darling, stop."

And they fell back on the bed together, crying and laughing and touching each other's faces.

"My God!" Jack exclaimed suddenly, aware of his weight on her. "Did I hurt you? You ought to take it easy, honey." But she chuckled at him.

"If you knew what this poor baby has been through already you wouldn't have a single qualm about it," she said, smiling.

He stroked her face with such an expression of love that she had to shut her eyes again. "I love you, Jack. I keep telling you that. I don't know why, it just seems like I have to. Like I really believe it myself now, for the first time. I love you."

And he kissed her mouth then. It had never happened before but it was right and wonderful.

They lay in each other's arms and talked and made plans. They talked about Beebo and Terry, about themselves, about their baby, about life and how good it was when you were brave enough to face it.

Laura was afraid of Terry still. "Where is he?" she asked.

"God only knows," Jack shrugged. "I left him in his room at the Towers. I've been doing this every night since you left. No drinking, no cruising, until I've checked the apartment to make sure you haven't come back. I just told him, 'If I don't make it back some night you'll know she came home. Don't wait for me.' I don't suppose he waited very long, either. He's not the type." He looked down at her, his face serious again and frowning. "What about Beebo?" he said.

"It's over. She knew it long ago. I finally realized it, too." She raised her eyes to his. "I'm not in love with her now. Maybe I never was. But I respect her and admire her. She's amazing. And much stronger than I ever gave her credit for. I wish to God I could change some things—"

"Don't play that game, darling," he said quickly. "That's the surest way to break your heart and lose your mind. Save yourself for now. And for later. Save yourself for me and the baby." He leaned down and kissed her again and, silent and amazed at herself, she returned his kiss with warmth.

"Besides," he added, whispering into her ear, "Somebody's got to clean up the apartment."

"I'll take the living room. You can have the kitchen," she offered.

"Thanks." He grinned and pulled her close in his arms, and she didn't resist him; just nestled against his warm body and relaxed in the circle of his strength, a real strength, a man's strength. It felt very good to her.

"After all, we aren't expecting any visitors today, are we?" he said sleepily into her long light hair.

"Not a soul," she murmured. She wondered, in that violet twilight before sleep, how long it would take her to get used to this closeness with him. She was so comfortable...more comfortable, it seemed, and more safe than she had ever been.

And they fell asleep together with the sigh of relief and hope that only the lost, who have found themselves, can feel.

Afterword

There are dark and bright times in every life. This book was written in what was, for me, one of the darker ones. It was a period when a measure of wisdom was setting in, both in terms of my personal life and in terms of what I had learned about the lives of gay men and lesbians. When my first book, *Odd Girl Out,* was written, I was full of optimism. I believed I could make a go of a challenging conventional marriage. And privately, in my dream life, I was convinced of nothing in the world so deeply as the beauty and passion of same-sex love. I thought I could access it through books, through fantasy, through imaginary friendships, without rocking the domestic boat. Indeed, I thought that was my only option, and it had damn well better work. If it did not, I knew I would self-destruct.

When I wrote *I Am a Woman,* my second book, I had learned a lot, almost all of it exciting and confirming, about lesbian and gay life. I had been to the mountain—Greenwich Village—and I had seen and touched and watched and absorbed and treasured so much about that life and that place. I could not live in it—there were children now—but I could feel it and possess it and give it back to my readers.

Ah, but time went by and now I came to the task of writing book number three in the series, *Women in the Shadows,* having learned a great deal about what it means to soldier on through a tough relationship and, as important, what a range of problems existed in the lesbian and gay community. I did not imagine, when I first visited New York, that the law was so particular nor so cruel as to criminalize private sexual activities between same-sex partners.

It was frightening to learn that police raids targeted the gay bars on a regular schedule, and that one could be arrested and publicly humiliated simply for being found in one having a glass of beer with friends. I was appalled to discover that there were gangs of adolescents roaming Greenwich Village at night terrorizing gay people, beating them up, threatening them, doing bad things to good people just to score points in their tribal hierarchies.

From the point of view of the miscreants, gay men and lesbians were both easy and socially sanctioned targets. Why? Because the legal system was intractably biased. For those who wished gay people ill, the Establishment had almost—not quite—provided a license for mayhem. Young boys, some uncertain of their own sexual drive, took advantage of the prevailing prejudice to do a lot of irreparable harm to people who could protest—at their peril—but almost never prevail. Such was the atmosphere of the time. It pushed some gay people over the edge. For a brief moment in her life, Beebo was one of them. I guess the fact that I let something calamitous happen to her in a sense deflected calamity from my own door. Better to dump misery on Beebo's stubborn back than risk a crack-up that would bring my own family down around my ears.

Most pointedly, I was saddened when I found bias within the community itself: confusion and shame over one's own sexuality, alcoholism, partner abuse, broken relationships. This was the community I had taken to my heart, that I had romanticized and loved, that I had clung to in imagination when my daily life threatened to overwhelm me. It was shattering to let go of my ideals; unfair though it was, I felt betrayed. Why couldn't the gays and lesbians in the Village realize how lucky they were? How much they had that the rest of us, outside looking in, could only yearn for?

And yet, as I was learning these disturbing things, I was trying to find my balance. My life and my discoveries about the gay community seemed to be developing in parallel. This book is dark—despite my dislike for the negative connotations, the title is probably apt—and there are things in it difficult to read, as you will know when you've finished it. Still, I feel affection for it, for the girl I was when I wrote it, for the gropings toward elusive happiness, even for Beebo and Laura painfully pulling their love asunder. This is a part of what lovers do; remember, they were young, too.

It would not be accurate to say that I became embittered. But I did feel the need to explore some of these newly discovered imperfections in a place and a population I had always admired without reservation. Perhaps it was analogous to reaching that point in a love affair where reality begins to overtake romance. You don't fall out of love, but you have to restructure the relationship and lift it to a new plane. And so, while acknowledging the problems, I looked for other things to keep hope alive, to ease the heart even while coping with the pain.

There were themes I wanted to develop. In this age before the Civil Rights Movement burst upon us and changed the world forever, it seemed to one naïve young writer that two lovely women, one black, one white, ought to be exploring the possibility of interracial romance with one another. It seemed logical that a lesbian and a gay man, both of whom wanted children, should get together and, based on respect and deep affection, possibly even marry. After all, they were "nice" people, and one didn't drag a baby into a world of illegitimacy in those days. These motifs may have been a bit clumsy in the handling, but they were rare in lesbian story-telling of the day. And they were constructive as well as unusual. It pleases me now to realize that I cared as much then as I do today about harmony between the races; that I saw and encouraged the affection, the cooperation, the whole sense of being family together, that can spring up between gay men and lesbians. It was out of this matrix of caring that the marriage of Jack and Laura came to my mind; that the cautious romantic minuet between Laura and Tris developed. But the obverse of that hopeful coin was the coin of disillusion. And there is plenty of it here.

The tentative romance between Laura and Tris, the ultimate decision of Jack and Laura to marry, were offered awkwardly, in the absence of rigorous insight, in the intellectual vacuum before the great enlightenment just ahead of us. I had yet to sort through my well-intentioned emotions and figure out why, objectively, it was more than just all right when two women of vastly different cultural and ethnic backgrounds fell in love. It just felt good to tiptoe up on the possibility. In my determination to marry off Jack and Laura, I tried to make more erotically of their feelings for one another than could realistically have been expected.

As for straight men, alas, I was never very kind to them; they represented the wardens of society, the stern, self-righteous "moralists," the reprovers, the naysayers, the judgment-passers, the anhedonic social cops one had to circumvent to make it to the ball. They were all Oliver Cromwells, puritanical, controlling, condescending, or outright contemptuous. But I was looking for Oliver's opposite number, that one-in-a-million man; I was looking for, say, Charles II, the Merry Monarch, who succeeded him. (Never mind that Charles was straight—very; he was nonetheless a man of illuminating tolerance, wit, generosity, and kindness. Anybody who brings back Christmas, the theaters, and maypoles to a country starved for joy is my kind of guy.) Sadly, there were too few Charles's and too many Olivers in the world.

Perhaps a part of the problem for me lay in the fact that, like most women of my generation, I inhabited all the "good girl" traditions, myths, and strictures of the years following World War II. I did not know they were a stone mirage beyond which other possibilities not only existed, but were survivable, even nourishing. It can be healthy to breach the wall. One of the ways in which I did that was to provide my characters with a sort of transcendent sexuality as an antidote to the constraints of their lives. In his enlightening book, *Foundlings: Lesbian and Gay Historical Emotion Before Stonewall* (Duke University Press, 2001), Christopher Nealon makes this point eloquently, referring to the tendency in lesbian pulp paperbacks to use "transporting sex as a solution to homophobia." This is astutely observed; we needed stalwart social networks, we needed confirming friendships, but most of all, we needed the fire and enchantment of wonderful sex to validate our lives. Nothing else was going to help. It had to come from within us, and no aspect of human emotion is more deeply within us than that most delicate and powerful of mysteries, our sexuality. It was the glory of that sexual transport that eased the desperation of one's queerness.

But when you light that fire, as humans have been observing in wry and regretful ways since they could first think about it at all, you can get scorched. That's what happens to Beebo and Laura in this story. Laura becomes stifled by Beebo's intensity; Beebo goes a little mad. But hang on—good things are coming further down the road. I could not stay angry at the characters I birthed and loved for very long.

Not long ago, I discovered an interesting analysis of *Women in the Shadows* from French writer and critic Hélène Cixous. She surprised and pleased me by observing, "This novel has important historical significance. Originally published in 1959, this novel broke from the formula of 1950s lesbian pulp fiction. It dealt with real issues in lesbian relationships like domestic violence, racism, and internalized homophobia. Other lesbian pulp fiction novels of the time were simply voyeuristic looks at lesbians and fostered the image that lesbians were predatory monsters. The women in this novel were tied to 1950s conventions, but they were still ahead of their time. The plot leaves much to be desired. However, this book should not be brushed aside because it is outdated. In its proper historical context, this novel is a masterpiece."

The commentary is quoted on the Queer Theory Web site. I am abashed to hear the book described in such strong, affirming terms, but gratified, too, to be taken seriously, after so many decades of dismissal as a producer of "sleaze."

There are those who have been kind enough to say that Ann Bannon offered a more positive portrait of lesbian life in the 50s and 60s than did many of her contemporaries. You would be tempted to doubt that reading this novel. But, while there are wrenching disagreements among the characters, and a small but telling tragedy, I remember thinking as I wrote that it was an uplifting story. There was violence, but it was intended to dramatize the toxic bias of the time and the inward turning anguish of the women who confronted and survived it. In their anger at the injustice of it all, they sometimes turned their frustration on themselves and those they loved. It was not because they were evil people; it was because they were wounded and there was no hospice for such wounds. There were only one's personal friendships, which thus bore a heavy strain at times. And there were the women's bars, those temples of danger-ous comfort where sorrows could be drowned, but at a cost. No gay and women's bookstores yet, soon to become the bricks and mortar of the community. And no World Wide Web, the new universal "bar" or meeting place. No forum for frank and open interchange. Back then, there was just unimaginable isolation and a lot of trouble. It was not a time and place for sissies.

One final thought: you don't always know the power of your own words, especially when you're not sure there's anyone out there reading them. I half convinced myself, while writing this book, that I was writing a letter to myself, that these words would not be read by anyone but their author, and therefore I could spill emotion all over the landscape. I have mixed emotions about the story that came out: some good, some not so. But on the whole, it was a valuable transition for me. I'm glad to have the validation from Cixous that I was anticipating important social developments and capturing a part of the truth of the times.

Here they are: my characters, warts and all, working through the pain toward better days. And here was I, working through it with them, trying always to remember this: that without the night, there would be no stars.

Ann Bannon
Sacramento, California
May 2002